# Bohemian Serenade

D. THOMAS GOCHENOUR

# Contents

# Chapter One



**Windows Chat Messaging**                    **April 22, 2009**

MaddyGirl: Coo, coo. Can you chat?

HautBois Cam: Yeah, I'm here. Just finished practicing for the morning.

MaddyGirl: For this weekend's concert? No?

HautBois Cam: Uh huh. I have a difficult solo part.

MaddyGirl: I just got back from my audition at Cincinnati. Want to tell you all about it. Have time to get together for lunch tomorrow?

HautBois Cam: No, not tomorrow. I already agreed to have lunch with Milos.

MaddyGirl: You mean you're still seeing him from time to time?

HautBois Cam: Yeah, quite regularly.

MaddyGirl: Dating?

HautBois Cam: Not exactly. I wouldn't call it that but getting together.

MaddyGirl: SMH. I thought he disappeared long ago. But he's still not your VBBF?

HautBois Cam: I like Milos a lot. But we're not BF and GF.

MaddyGirl: Too old for you?

HautBois Cam: AYS? It's not that.

HautBois Cam: Have you got time Maddi to come by my place TN8? We can hangout. There's so much to talk about. I mean besides your audition.

MaddyGirl: I guess I could. Tell me all the racy details?

HautBois Cam: No. I want to show you his letters.

MaddyGirl: He's not sexting you, is he? Sending you pictures of himself with no clothes on?

HautBois Cam: NO, he'd never do that. He's too old-fashioned. And shy. Besides, he's too technologically backwards. He only uses email. But I'll tell you more this evening.

MaddyGirl: Okay. Come around 7?

HautBois Cam: Yeah, that works for me.

MaddyGirl: CU then. Bring anything to eat?

HautBois Cam: Yeah, do. I have wine and some cheese. B4N.


At six, I picked up some boxed salads and some cream pastries at the local deli. I live in Allston on the south bank of the Charles River. Cammy's apartment is in Somerville, just off Washington Street, and I have to take the T to get there. It's kind of a roundabout way, but there are no buses to get to her house directly. And of course, the T at that hour is a crush, with all those rush hour commuters getting out of downtown Boston. Going inbound on the Green Line was no problem really, but I had to squeeze in the car to get onto the Red Line. Altogether it was a sweaty one-hour ride and even then, I had to get out at Central Square and hoof it up to Inman Square on foot. By the time I got to Cammy's place, I was exhausted and sweaty. It was a very warm spring evening.

I'm Maddie—that's my nickname from my real name which is Madonna. My mother named me after the artist Madonna when I was born, because she was her favorite singer at the time. But if people hear that my real name is Madonna, they get bent all out of shape and laugh at me. Or snicker. The boys especially get cruel. They say things like, "Could you sing for us in just your bra and panties?" or "How about if you sing something sexy while petting your pussy?" In short, obnoxious comments, so since high school I have chosen to be called Maddi. No one has to know. Of course, Cammy knows.

She's been a friend and rival since high school orchestra. Probably my best friend. She's not really Cammy either. Her real name is Camille. Camille Newman. Kids teased her all the time in high school and even earlier about the name Camille, so she started using Cammy, and there've been no problems since. I say rival, not really, except in a friendly sort of way we compete against each other. I play the flute, and she plays the oboe. In music, and life in general it seems, she's been more successful than I've been. She wins the auditions. She marries the superstar violinist. But I'm only a little jealous of that. Because I think I play the flute better than she plays oboe. Ha ha. But I confess she's playing first chair oboe in the Boston Symphony Orchestra, and I'm not yet won any seat in any top orchestra.

I really did not know what to expect from Cammy concerning Milos before I got to her apartment. Over the last few years, she's told me only select glimpses into her relationship with Milos. I don't think they are a couple. Far from it. And besides she's married. Granted, married to an absentee husband, but she's just not the type to carry on an affair behind the back of her husband. She wouldn't do that. Certainly not in Gus's house—he owns the apartment in Somerville. And as I went up on the porch of their three-decker, I could see the condition of disrepair of the house that indicates Gus's long absences and negligence.

Cammy eagerly greeted me at the porch door of the first floor. Their apartment was on the third floor, so she had to scramble down two flights to open that main door. She could have just rung me in by the door phone, but she's like that. Generous and very considerate. She was smiling broadly to see me but turned quickly to run back upstairs.

"Maddi, at last," she shouted back to me. "Come in. I have even more news." She saw the sacks of food I had brought. "We can have something to eat while I show you what I got."

When I entered Cammy's apartment, I noticed that she had set up a laptop on the butcher block table in the middle of the front room, sitting in the midst of a bottle of wine, two dinner plates, cutlery, and a plate of cheese and sliced cold cuts. "Here, put the salads here." Cammy pointed to an empty spot on the table.

"I wanted to tell you about Milos and our relationship just now but not over the phone or over a chat line," she said as she turned the computer screen toward me. "You see, over the past two and a half years, he has been writing me letters and sending them to me by email. And the latest one just came last night. I wanted to show you what I mean."

She pushed the computer screen toward me and focused on the first page of text. I sat down and began to read it.

19 April 2009

My dearest sweet Camille,

You must know by now the depth of my love for you. You have the soul and grace of an angel and, perhaps I have told you so often. you have awakened the passion and love in me which so long has lain dormant. You have stirred up again my love of music and since I first spoke to you almost three years ago, I have felt inspired to write again.

And now I can tell you that your beauty and sympathy for me have borne fruit. I have composed two pieces of music inspired by you. I have now completed one of them: a quartet that incorporates a theme that you wrote for your final exam composition in my composition class three years ago. I haven't told you up to now how deeply that theme moved me, then and ever since. Tears of love come to my eyes when I hear it, and I see that first moment when I truly saw you sitting in the café. The theme is the inspiration of both these pieces. The second piece being an oboe concerto that I want to dedicate to you. But it is not quite ready yet. The quartet is ready, and I attach an electronic score to this letter so you can see it.

By meeting you and coming to know you, you must know, has completely reawakened my compositional life. When we take our strolls together through the Back Bay you must know that I hang on every word you say. They sound like the ringing of fine crystal goblets. I crave your smile and your furtive glances at me, hoping that they might reveal your love for me.

I long to kiss your red lips, which would be like tasting the most exquisite berries. And now I can hardly wait for the day when I see you perform the oboe solo of the concerto I am now finishing for you.

Camille, you must know that you are the sparkling love of my life. And my heart is always bursting with the passion that I have for you, and have not adequately expressed for you yet. I write this letter knowing that we will get together for lunch in less than two days. What bliss it will be to hear your reaction to my quartet. I can hardly count the hours until then.

Your ever loving, Milosh.

"Wow!" I said as I nearly whistled. "Now that is a love letter!"

I paused to look at some of the key phrases again.

"He signs his name Milosh." I asked a little puzzled. "But I thought his name was Milos."

Cammy chuckled. "Yeah, that's his birth name. Milosh. It means 'dear'. He told me that when he came to America in 69, no one could understand or say that name—it's Milosh—so he changed it to a sound—like name, Milos, which people were more familiar with. Like Maddie for Madonna."

"Or you being Cammy." Cammy ignored this.

"You asked earlier today whether we still are seeing each other. Well, we are. We see each other about once a week at least, and he writes me a letter, a love letter almost as frequently. And he has been since that summer when I first started seeing him. Almost three years ago."

"And don't you love this guy? What girl could ever dream of getting such wonderful love letters? Have you, you know, slept together yet?"

"No, no sex, no love making up to now. I keep telling him that I am a married woman, even if Gus doesn't live with me. But his letters are quite intimate and passionate. He wants to make love to me, I can tell."

"I don't think I'll ever get such a wonderful love letter in my whole life. And you've gotten scores of them, it seems. You never told me."

"No, I didn't. At first, I didn't know how to react to him and to his letters. I was a little overwhelmed and very embarrassed by the heavy petting and passion in his letters. And I didn't know how to react. He wasn't a dirty old man like we all thought. He's a lonely old man who likes me—I mean really loves me—and writes me lots of love letters and wants me to love him in return. I cannot possibly answer them. Not the way he has written them, anyway."

"Yeah, I remember when you told me about the first approach he made to you, outside the Au Bon Pain. We both thought he was just another old professor looking to seduce a young co-ed. But we were wrong, it seems."

"We really were. He's really a sweet, very respectful man. And not an old fart trawling for some pretty young twat of a coed. And actually, he's shy. Even if he was quite forward at that café on the first day. You know, I think it was hard for him to write and send me these letters at first. And he'd be mortified if I shared them around. I think he'd die. I share this one with you in all confidence. You mustn't tell anyone about it."

"I won't."

"I'll kill you, if you distribute this around the internet."

"I won't, Cammy. I said so. Really I wouldn't dare."

"Okay. So, let's eat. I've printed out the score of the quartet he sent me. We can look at it while we eat."

While we were eating and reviewing the quartet's score, I wasn't really focused on the notes. I was thinking about how Milos first made an advance on Cammy. It was about three years earlier, almost the same time of the year in mid-spring as this meeting in Cammy's house. Cammy and I had been sitting on the sidewalk seats of the Au Bon Pain café/bakery across the intersection from the New England Conservatory, on Huntington Ave. We were having coffees and were just chatting about nothing special following a rehearsal we'd just finished for the Boston Phil. That's the Philharmonic Orchestra, kind of a minor league outfit for those not ready or talented enough to win a place in the Boston Symphony Orchestra, or any other major orchestra. A training ground for the inexperienced. We were both first seat players in the BPhil, but not then ready yet for the first-string big orchestras. I remember that it was a particularly hot afternoon, and the sunlight came slanting up Huntington Ave, bright and fierce, but with none of the usual wind.

We had been sitting there, our coffees finished, for almost an hour, when from another table at the café a tall slender man stood up and approached us. Cammy didn't notice him at first because she had been sitting with her side to him, showing her profile to him. But I had glimpsed him once or twice before he made his move, and it had seemed to me that he had been staring at Cammy, intently, but I had not thought much of it at the time.

"Excuse me, miss. My name is Milos Novak. Perhaps you know me? I teach at the Conservatory."

Well of course Cammy knew of him and knew his name.

"Oh yes, I know who you are," said Cammy calmly without even the slightest delay. "I'm taking your composition class this semester. You've probably seen me."

"Yes, I realized that just now, seeing you here, out of class. It has been like I have seen you before, twice a week for the past two months, but have never really looked at you or seen you until just this last hour. If I may, can I ask you your name?"

At that time Cammy seemed to blush a little. She told me later that she had assumed that he would know her name. But she had fallen for that fallacy that most of us do that we think we know the people we see all the time as newscasters on the TV screen, or lecturers, or actors, or conductors of the orchestra. And that they know us, by name. But, of course, while they might recognize our faces, they do not know us at all, and in truth we do not know them either. It had not occurred to Cammy that this professor in whose class she sat twice a week along with twenty-five other students for almost three months did not recognize her and connect her face with a name on his attendance list.

"My name is Cammy, Camille Newman."

"Yes, I remember that name on the class list." He said. "And frankly I've seen you before sitting in the back of the class but never knew who you were. It's just that for the past forty minutes or so while I have been sitting over there, I noticed you and for the first time I actually saw you, and I recognized that you were the young woman who sits by the rear windows in my class. But I did not know your name."

"Well, that's it, Professor Novak. I guess we've made our acquaintance now. You can call me Cammy."

"And it would be very nice, and entirely proper if you called me Milos. And excuse me, I didn't mean to ignore you." He offered his hand to shake me. "You can call me Milosh also. You're a friend of Cammy's"

"Yes. And you can call me Maddie, a friend of Cammy's." I remember his handshake was not firm and his hand was moist. It hadn't occurred to me at that time that he might have been nervous. He was really good looking, tall and lean, his hair was just beginning to have white splotches. An attractive older guy.

"Well, I'm sorry. I did not mean to interrupt. But I just had to know your name Cammy. Because really you have the most beautiful face, especially in profile. And I was really curious and a bit dumbfounded that in class I had never really noticed before just how beautiful your face is. I just had to tell you that. And perhaps understand better how I could have missed seeing that before."

So that explained why he had been staring at her from the other table. Not merely because he was a rude, dirty old man. Or that he needed glasses and he was trying to match the vision of Cammy at a sidewalk coffee table gossiping with her less than beautiful friend with the occasional glance he no doubt gave her in the classroom. Don't get me wrong: Cammy is much prettier than I am, and her skin is clearer than mine, and her hair is nicer, and her smiles are glowing and her teeth are beautiful shining ivories, and her facial features are more symmetrical. But he hadn't come over to the table to get my name. He came over because he, for the first time, recognized what a beauty Cammy is— especially outside the classroom. And it was obvious even then that he was completely taken and enamored of her.

It was also clear that he spoke like an old timer, kind of old fashioned and stilted and formal. Like old people speak. And he had the slightest of foreign accents. I couldn't place it. But it was clearly not a Baahsten accent, or from anywhere around the Massachusetts Bay. Nor a Jewish accent, nor a New York accent—which we hear so much in the Conservatory. A mysterious and faintly quaint foreign accent.

Now when strangers come up to you and commend your pretty looks for no particular reason it is a bit off-putting. Cammy blushed now and was right away without words. Of course, boys had often awkwardly tried to tell her she was pretty. But she had known that since high school. She was the prettiest of the bunch—and did I tell you that she has a knockout figure too? The boys in high school and college only really notice a girl's breasts and when they say that a girl is pretty, they mean to say, 'Nice boobs, babe.' but are too ashamed to openly say that.

"I also wanted to ask you," Milosh continued, "of course, only if you're finished with your coffee and your conversation, if you might be willing to take a stroll with me so that we might talk."

Cammy again was caught off guard, this request took her breath away it was clear; but she recovered pretty nicely. "That would be very nice." I remember her saying and thinking at the time, 'how could she possibly know that that would be nice?' "But my husband is coming home this evening—one of the rare times when he's here—and I do need to see him in about an hour. So maybe another time, Professor Novak?"

"Yes, I see. Well perhaps we can get together and talk over a coffee? Maybe after our next class? On Monday?" he said with aplomb.

I was amazed at his self-assurance. He had just been brushed off by a young co-ed who had telegraphed that she was a taken, married woman, and he had an immediate come back.

"Maybe."

"Well, Cammy, I would like that a lot. Perhaps you could give me your email address, and I could write you a reminder on Monday before class? I wouldn't want to embarrass you in front of the others in the class—we can even come our separate ways and meet at the table. Or maybe at the Quickie Qoffee on Mass Ave if that keeps us out of prying, curious eyes?"

He was insistent, and very self-assured. It was not as if he were asking Cammy out for a date, so much as he was politely requesting that she meet with him, just as he would request that his students do an assignment. Like I said, he had enormous aplomb on this first acquaintance.

Cammy took a scrap of paper out of her backpack—the one she carried her oboe in—and wrote down her email address and gave it to him. He was still hovering over our table like a waiter waiting on cash payment. I remember at the time that he looked of indefinite age. Late middle aged, 45 to 55, still color in his hair, clean shaven and not at all chubby like so many of the male profs at the Conservatory. He looked lean and masculine, not soft and effeminate. I thought from the very first that he was a very good-looking man.

He excused himself for interrupting us and then said to Cammy, "Until Thursday then." And then he turned to look at me, and said, quite sincerely although it was totally false. "So nice to meet you, Maddi." And he walked away calmly up towards Mass Ave.

When he was suitably far away, I remember, Cammy and I as if by a common signal started to giggle and splutter. "Can you imagine the nerve that guy has?" she said. "Pretty good, eh?" I said. "Bold and forward. How is he in the classroom?"

"Normal, I think." said Cammy. "I would not put him in that class of predators who are always chatting up the coeds to get them in bed with them. You know who I mean? The gossip always knows which ones are the dirty old men on the faculty—sleeping with the students, the ones who make passes at the pretty girls. You know the friendly pat on the rump with a hearty smile, pretending that it was accidental? That type. Usually not as well dressed, nor as fit and polite as this fellow, Milosh. We'll see. Maybe I'll have coffee with him."

And actually, I didn't think he was like any of the dirty old men that Cammy was talking about. I thought he seemed very sincere, and that he was really, really attracted to Cammy. We left and I forgot about the incident almost at once. But Thursday evening I got a text message that reminded me of it again.

**Windows Chat Messaging**                                    **April 17, 2006**

HautBois Cam: You remember, Professor Milosh?

MaddyGirl: Yes, how could I forget?

HautBois Cam: He wrote me an email as he said he would, and we met at the Quickie Qoffee.

MaddyGirl: And so?

HautBois Cam: It was something. We talked for more than two and a half hours. Like we were long lost best friends. The nicest conversation I've had with a man, maybe ever.

MaddyGirl: Wow. And did you take a walk too?

HautBois Cam: Yeah, after coffee we took a stroll around the Back Bay. He lives in the South End. Not far from the NEC.

MaddyGirl: Did he invite you to his house?

HautBois Cam: No. But he offered to walk with me to my house.

MaddyGirl: Did he?

HautBois Cam: No, I met Gus for an early dinner. Here downtown. And then went with him to his concert. He played the Sibelius.

MaddyGirl: You should've told me about that. I would have liked to hear it.

HautBois Cam: Sorry. It was good. But it seems he's really not a virtuoso soloist anymore.

MaddyGirl: Oh, too bad. So, are you going to see the Prof again?

HautBois Cam: Yeah, next week we agreed to meet after rehearsal and again go for a walk.

HautBois Cam: He says all kinds of nice things about me.

MaddyGirl: Flattery? He thinks he'll get you through flattery?

HautBois Cam: No. I don't think so. He's so sincere. We talked about our life stories. You know he's a conductor, too? And he really composes lots of things. And he's married. But has been separated for more than 35 years? Can you imagine? And that he's originally from Czechoslovakia.

MaddyGirl: You learned a lot about him. What did you tell him about yourself?

HautBois Cam: I told him again that I was married. Showed him the ring. But not happily. Then he asked me all about Gustav. And he listened very closely. He had a lot of good insights about Gus. I told him I was an oboist. In the B Phil. He asked if I would like to play in the BSO? And he asked me if I was interested in composing my own music?

MaddyGirl: And what did you tell him?

HautBois Cam: Well, no not really, I told him, about composing. But maybe conducting. He offered me conducting lessons. You know he is one of the principal guest conductors of the BSO? And he sometimes guest conducts at the B Phil too? GtoG.

MaddyGirl: Bye, can we talk after rehearsal next week?

HautBois Cam: Sure. TTFN

I don't remember when it was, we next spoke at length, maybe it was a week later after our rehearsal at the BPhil, maybe it was two weeks later. No, it was probably three weeks later. We had had a concert weekend in between. I remember it was a sloppy rainy day, when Cammy asked if we could have dinner together before she hiked back to her apartment in Somerville. She had something she wanted to tell me. We went to the pan-Asian food restaurant up on Mass Ave behind the Symphony Hall. Our umbrellas were blown apart and didn't keep us much dry, but I remember we were laughing about this when he finally got into the restaurant. She wanted to talk to me more about Gus than about Milosh.

She told me how in the three or so weeks that Gus had been back things were just not working out between them. He had not wanted sex with her, even when she tried to seduce him, and in general he showed her no affection. He was cold to her most of the time. He expected her to fix his dinners, but she couldn't because of her rehearsals and course schedules. That annoyed him. But she was working really hard that month. He got angry with her over that. And the weekend before he did not even want to attend our concert where Cammy had a major important excerpt to play. The oboe part in the Tombeau de Couperin really stands out and is a real showcase for Cammy's talent and great oboe sound. I remember she played it brilliantly. And I might add, since I was playing that evening also, that the other piece we played, Mendelssohn's Third Symphony, pitted her solo against mine on flute. Gus missed that also. But Gus simply had refused to attend, for reasons that escaped Camille. She told me that he had said he was tired and not interested in hearing the program of a junior orchestra. That really hurt. It was clear as she was telling me about this that Cammy was still very upset. It was all she could do to keep from crying. And then he told her really offhand, like, that he wouldn't be staying at home all summer. He told her that he had been accepted into the very prestigious Lucerne Festival Orchestra and so he would be leaving in late July and would be there through September. And when Cammy asked him if she could join him—it's a residential orchestra for the festival—he had told her that it was better if she didn't. That it would cost too much. Ouch. That had to hurt. I sat there at the table and couldn't say anything. They had been married less than three years, and it sounded to me—I didn't say it at the time of course, there was no need—as if their marriage was all over. This sad tale certainly made my meal taste insipid and flat.

After a long silent pause Camille then tried to compose herself and she said. "But you know what? Milosh was at that concert. And maybe you didn't notice him." I hadn't, but I wasn't looking either.

She told me that he had gone to that concert after he learned that both Cammy and Maddie were going to be playing in it. And he met Cammy afterwards and offered to escort her back home. I hadn't even noticed that they left Jordan Hall together. She told me that they stopped in at a lounge in Inman Square, quite close to her house and talked for another hour. He told her all about his flight from Czechoslovakia after the Soviet invasion at the end of the Prague

Spring. How he and his wife at the time felt that their careers would be crushed by the Soviets because they had so actively participated in the Prague Spring, so they had driven to the unmanned border with Austria and left the country seeking asylum in America. She said that he had told her he was twenty-four at the time, the end of 1968, so that would make him sixty-two then. I was amazed. He didn't look like he was in his sixties. She said the same. "He's so attractive and in such good shape for a man of sixty-two." were her words. But he suffered in leaving. He had fled with his wife and his best friend who was also a composer and conductor. A guy named Jiri Beloslovacheck, or something like that. And they stopped in Germany for several months while waiting for asylum to be granted. It was very hard on them because they had lost all the structures of their lives in Prague. They couldn't get work, because of course they did not know German well enough and what they had done before was unknown outside of Czechoslovakia. Milosh wrote to the famous Czech composer, Karel Husa, who had fled to the US much earlier and this Husa wrote him back saying he had heard some of Milosh's music and that he would apply on this end to get the process speeded up. That he'd act as a sponsor for them. You see at the age of twenty-four he had already published some significant music. So into 1969, they—Milosh, Martina, and Jiri—were lonely, often hungry, and penniless in Germany. Hard times. And that was when Milos discovered that his wife—they had married young while still in the university—actually didn't love him at all (other than the sex, and for that too she had started having sex with Jiri)—and Jiri, she actually did love him. So, when he finally got his application and asylum visa given to him, she told him that she and Jiri were going to go back to Prague and make their careers there. And so, he and his wife Martina separated and afterwards she and Jiri got married and had children, but although Jiri kept in touch with Milosh, he had not heard nor seen her since. And technically they were still married, they had never actually divorced, or at least he had never seen divorce notifications coming out of Czechoslovakia, not even after the Iron Curtain came down. Cammy said it was a sad story, but Milosh—Milosh—was telling her that in the lounge in Inman Square, over beers, as a way of saying that Martina and Milosh had just not been right for each other—that they had married far too young—and that perhaps it was the same for Gus and Cammy. "I have found myself in an empty marriage for most of thirty-seven years," she remembered he said as he chuckled, "with an empty house and empty bed. But now I have met you."

But Cammy told me that he had also said that Jiri remained a friend and that in those early years when he became a big conductor in Prague, he championed Milosh's compositions and played them whenever the authorities didn't forbid them. So that Milosh's music, including music he subsequently composed in America, was better known in the Czech Republic, as it is known now, than it was in America.

And she told me that when he dropped her at her door, he told her that she needed to start work rehearsing the excerpt materials because there was going to be an audition for the coprincipal oboe seat in the BSO at the end of the summer, and that he wanted her to participate, because after what he had heard that evening in the concert he thought she could win the position. And he would push to support her candidacy in every way he could.

In telling me this story about Milosh, Cammy became quite a bit cheered up. "I'm going for the BSO and this man, my professor, and Guest Conductor, is going to support my bid." she had said.

I recalled all this while trying to review the score of Milosh's latest work, a quartet which used a theme that Cammy had composed in April 2006 as the final exam for Milosh's course on composition. I didn't see much that I could recognize as Cammy's theme, but then I was not paying very close attention to the score. I was thinking about Cammy's stories of three years earlier while trying to eat some ham and cheese canapes and salad.

Cammy said, "Sure, look, the theme starts here in the viola part in the sixth bar of the first movement. And then it is restated, in a variation and in a minor key in the final section of the fourth movement, by the first violin and cello."

I guess so. I couldn't hear it, but it seemed like a romantic tune, so I couldn't really see it. But when it was pointed out to me, I did recognize it.

"I said that I thought Milosh was a little technologically old-fashioned," said Camille. "But you know, it seems he composed this on a musical notation program, and he sent this score to me as a print document. Not bad. He does all his composing on the computer. He even uses a piano projection program to be able to play what he is doing right below his computer keyboard. Impressive don't you think so?"

I did think so. I'm not very good at solfeggio so I can't so readily hear in my mind what a string of notes sounds like. I can sight read a line of music on my flute, but I can't hear the same line and then write down in notation what I just heard. So, we finished reviewing his score—Cammy had printed out two copies—and then she put both copies into a notebook. And then we cleared away the dishes. But she just threw them in the sink. She came right back to the table and invited me to move to the living room right next to the open dining area/kitchen. She offered me another glass of white wine. But because of the late hour I declined. She poured herself some more.

"Is this really a theme that you composed for Milosh's composition class three years ago?" I asked Cammy.

"Yes, it is. He told me outside of class that he really adored the melody and that it stirred something in his heart. He also laughed and said that it sounded to him like the voice of the oboe. In the forest, like a lark. He gave me an A on the final. And he said I should consider writing music."

"That must've been really high for you."

"He's been very supportive of my music career right from the start. It was he who pulled levers to get me into the BSO. And he arranged everything so that we both went to Tanglewood in the summer of 2007 and will again this summer."

Her face was really shining. It seemed obvious to me that she's really fond of Milos. Or maybe the wine was working its magic. It was late for me and the T doesn't work so regularly after 9. So, I had to go. And I had a morning rehearsal that next day. It was a shame. I had wanted to tell Cammy all about my audition in Chicago. But there was no time. I could write to her on the chat line. But it is always better to talk person to person, and since Cammy has gotten into the BSO, I don't see her nearly as often. We now have to make special arrangements to get together. She reminded me that she was meeting Milosh for lunch in the Back Bay the next day. She said that she always looked forward to their lunch get-togethers. The talk was always so interesting, and he always made her feel so good inside after their conversations.

As I was getting my raincoat on to leave, Cammy told me as a by the way that Milosh had offered his quartet to the Kronos Quartet to premier the piece. And he thought they had accepted it.

# Chapter Two

I met with Cammy that Wednesday evening on short notice because we couldn't meet for lunch in Boston the next day because she had already agreed to lunch with Milos on one of their regular "dates". So, I was kind of waiting to hear from Cammy, even that same night. But I didn't hear a peep from her on Thursday evening, nor through the weekend. She did have concerts that weekend, as did I. Of course, mine are in Jordan Hall, while hers are in Boston Symphony Hall. And on big concert weekends, neither of us have much free time. And I don't mean to meet—although it is possible if we make special efforts. I mean even communicating on chat lines. But Monday finally I couldn't wait any longer. I had to know what happened on Cammy's lunch date with Milos the previous Thursday.

We usually texted each other whenever we had something to say. Texting is useful for brief chats, but if there is something really important or complicated to explain, only a face to face get together works. And by this time in our lives, we no longer saw each other face to face very often. We had started to drift apart, we met maybe once a month, sometimes less often. And it all started in the summer of 2006. That was when Cammy auditioned for the BSO co-principal position. In the six weeks before that audition—through the middle of the summer— she was working so hard, learning the audition materials. She didn't answer her phone, she didn't reply to text messages, and she didn't get out of her house very often. Of course, at the end of that summer Gus abandoned her to go to the Lucerne Festival. No support from him.

I always thought that he was way too self-centered to offer anyone support or encouragement, even if that someone was his wife, as she was at the time.

So Gus flew off to Switzerland and Cammy had her audition, and just as Milos had told her she would, she won the position as co-principal oboe in the BSO. She sent me a text as soon as she had learned the results.

**Windows Chat Messaging**      **August 24, 2006**

HautBois Cam: Hey Maddie, Great news. I did it. I WON!!!! They picked me in the final and have told me that I start in September!

MaddyGirl: Hurray! So proud of you, Cammy. Of course you won. You're the best! You're the boss of oboists.

HautBois Cam: The final was in two sessions. After the first session—which lasted two hours—they declared that the two of us were both winners. So today we had a run-off trial where we played with the orchestra the same pieces we'd prepared for yesterday's final. And you know what? Milos was conducting. He said he voted for me, and he also said that I won the orchestra's favor hands down.

MaddyGirl: Was your competitor good?

HautBois Cam: Yeah, he was technically very good, but I didn't think much of his sound or his tonguing technique. He sounded sharp to me. He's oboist with the Atlanta Symphony. Went to Julliard. I played better than him.

MaddyGirl: Of course you did. So, we'll have to get together and drink to your triumph. I knew you could do it.

HautBois Cam: Milos has suggested that too—drinks. Can you come downtown this evening at about 7?

MaddyGirl: Yeah. Would love to. Where to meet?

HautBois Cam: Milos proposes the W near the Boston Commons. They've got a classy restaurant.

MaddyGirl: I know it. But it is a bit rich for me.

HautBois Cam: Milos is paying.

MaddyGirl: Too bad Gus won't be there.

HautBois Cam: Yeah, I wrote him, but it's already late there in Lucerne, so he hasn't answered. Maybe they're playing a concert just now. But no matter. Champaign tonight. CU

We had a great time that evening. I drank maybe too much champagne. Milosh couldn't take his eyes off Cammy even for one second. Cammy also was glowing and she smiled and laughed with Milosh without stop, in a way I had never seen before. Not even at her wedding party to Gus had she looked so happy. Or maybe it was love.

Anyway, in the following year after she won that position and joined the BSO, not long after she had gotten tenure with the orchestra, she became simply principal oboe when the other co-principal fell ill and had to retire. And that is when we began to drift apart. Our schedules changed, we had both left the Conservatory, and I no longer saw her at the BPhil. We kept in touch of course with my text messages and emails. We remained best of friends but were no longer spending much time together. We would share photos and videos electronically, but just like my girlfriends who got married and had children, we no longer had the time to visit with each other very much. The opportunities for long face to face conversations fell off. And she did not want to put any of her closest feelings into words on the internet. Naturally. And that of course is why we didn't often talk about her relationship with Milosh, or with Gus, for that matter.

But I did learn of course at the time that Cammy had attended Tanglewood that next summer, in 2007. But I didn't know until quite recently when we had a long talk together and she told me that she had attended at the same time as Milosh had been attending as composer-in-residence. She only casually told me this, like it was no big deal. But she did not tell me until this year - 2009—that they had spent as much of their free time together as possible while they were at Tanglewood. It's like a summer camp for musicians, especially top musicians and the members of the BSO. They took their meals together, they took long walks together or stretched out on the lawns in the sun, and they would sit talking in the evenings when there were no concerts. Apparently, they even went swimming together several times at the Stockbridge Bowl. It's a lake, not a bowl. I was really impressed to learn that. Not only did they get good views of their mostly undressed bodies, but most surprising to me was that Cammy went swimming with Milosh even though she is very allergic to water that is the least bit cold. She told me she enjoyed it. That surprised me the most. Cammy in cold water, saying she enjoyed it. But she enjoyed even more boating with Milosh on the lake. Milosh rowing her around—said the oars were not good for her delicate hands so he would do the rowing—like some scene from an English romance novel. She did not need to get wet in cold water if she was in a rowboat. She mentioned at the time that he had an attractive body—that she had been surprised at how fit he was—he looked much younger than his sixty-three years. At the same time, she mentioned how she felt a bit embarrassed by her figure which she felt was still not so attractive, at least not in the swimsuit she wore that summer. It didn't fill out the swimsuit; her breasts were too small; she thought she's since thrown it out and bought a better fitting one. But she's always thinking nonsense like that about her looks, when she is in fact the very model of feminine beauty. Makes all the other girls jealous.

So, I learned these things about Cammy and Milosh long after they occurred, because we were meeting and talking much less since 2007. She would no longer automatically answer my chat inquiries, "Cammy, want to hang out?" with an emphatic, "Yes! That was why I was surprised to learn that she and Milosh in 2009 were still regularly meeting and taking walks together. And why I was really bowled over by the fact that he continued to write her such wonderful love letters, even though they were not lovers. Or at least that is what she told me.

But she was definitely attracted to Milosh from the start. And she liked him, and it seems she liked him more and more in the years after he first came up to her and asked for her name and email address. I think she was naturally attracted to older men, much more than to men her own age. I had thought that when she first fell for Gus—he was after all only eighteen years older than she was when they married. She became Mrs. Camille Tichon, the wife of an established, even well-known violinist, even a recorded violinist, who performed with orchestras throughout Europe and America. And that made her appear also more accomplished in music. But I noticed her reaction to Gus, and then to Milosh, and to other older, good-looking men at the Conservatory for instance— oh and they had to be tall, she had to look up to them literally—was more open and affectionate than her reaction to our male peers. I told Cammy that once; that she had a 'daddy complex', that she preferred older men. She loved older men more than boys and her reaction was to shrug and say, "Maybe." But I'm sure of it. Her own father—who was a musician and according to Cammy a tall one at that—had left her family when she was only 13. She was still seeking the approval, affection and love of a father figure, one that had been missing in her life for a long time—throughout her teen years when she developed the most as a musician. An older man who paid attention to Cammy received shows of her affection. You could always see it. But Cammy never wanted to talk about that, or the pain she may have still had at her absent father. And those few times when I was with Cammy and Milos together, I noticed that she fairly beamed at him. It certainly looked to me that she adored him. Just the way she had initially looked at Gus. But unlike Gus, Milos gave Cammy lots of support, approval and encouragement. I've never had a father fixation myself. I got more than enough attention from my pa when I was growing up, not all of it the right sort of attention either. I despised him by the time I left high school—I was certainly ready to leave home and be rid of him. And I like boys—my own age thank you—and they like me, I think.

So, I always wondered how Cammy put up with the frequent and prolonged absences of Gus from her life. They started only shortly after they got married. He was constantly touring, giving concerts both as a soloist and as a member of a quartet, in the U.S. and from 2006 in Europe. He became a member of the Lucerne Festival Orchestra that summer and continued in the next two years, and I understood that he was going to again play there, his fourth year, this summer. His absences really bothered Cammy, but she never wanted to talk with me about them or how she felt about Gus. Cammy had once said in an indirect swipe at Gus, that love was about always wanting to be close to a person, or something like that: if you always wanted to be with a person then that indicated that you loved him. In the past few years, Gus would come home and stay for two or three weeks and then leave again for several months. I don't know what they did together while he was in town. I know that Cammy almost ceased to communicate with me or her other friends while he was around. I learned later that they frequently went out to eat at restaurants, especially at Legal's in Kendall Square. Occasionally—when Cammy was free—they would go together to hear a concert or recital downtown. But Cammy suggested often that for the most part they did not spend much time together when he was at home. Mainly because she was so busy with practicing new programs, rehearsals, and her own concert schedule, but also because he just did not seem to care. He was always out of the house during the day. And then, after she started at the BSO, she spent her summers at Tanglewood, which was alright with Gus because he would leave for Europe again to go to Lucerne from July to the middle of September. And then in the summer of 2007 Gus informed her that he was going to move full time to Germany that Fall. It seemed that the Frankfurt Symphony had appointed Paavo Jarvii as their new music director, and that he recalled how excellent Gus had been when they were together at the Cincinnati Orchestra. So Jarvii had arranged for Gus to get the appointment as the concertmaster. This, Gus wrote Cammy by email, was an opportunity too good to pass up and he had accepted and would start later than September. He might be back to visit her at the end of December. So since then, the summer of 2007, Cammy saw even less of Gus than she had in the previous three years

**Windows Chat Messaging**                                    **April 27, 2009**

HautBois Cam: Maddie, can you meet me for lunch tomorrow? Around 1? Maybe that Pan Asian restaurant on Mass Ave? So much to talk about.

MaddyGirl: About Milosh?

HautBois Cam: Yeah.

MaddyGirl: Sure. See you then.

So that Tuesday I hauled down to the Saigon—Hong Kong Express and got in there just minutes before Cammy did. She must've seen me ducking in front of her, as she was coming up from Symphony Hall and I was jogging down from Boyleston Street. I hadn't even sat down at the empty table in the corner window before she came in, all smiles and waving. She looked really happy. And as usual, when she is all smiles, she looks so pretty. I can understand Milosh's attraction, but I don't understand why dozens of other guys aren't chasing after her for her fabulous, good looks.

We cheek kissed and sat down.

"Maddie, I'm so glad to see you and that we have time to talk. So much has happened since last week when we met!" She veritably chirped.

"I'm all ears, Cammy. I've been dying to hear what Milosh told you."

"You know, he always has loads of surprising things to tell me. And that is regardless of the two letters he sends me every month. This time he told me a bit about the background of that quartet that he sent me. The one we reviewed together last week."

So even before we put in our orders—I ordered shrimp and she ordered noodles in curry sauce she started to tell me what Milosh had told her.

Milosh had been initially a composer using the most modernist and avant-garde techniques that were circulating in the early Sixties. When he first started at the conservatory he was absolutely blown away when he heard the premier performance of Fluorescences of Penderecki. He had to compose music like that. While still at the conservatory in Prague he composed several pieces following the teachings of Schoenberg. He tried to follow the tenets of serialism and dodecaphony. He admitted that he did that as much as to seem modern and progressive as he was trying to defy the Communist authorities at the time, as well the conservative, timid professors at the conservatory. And he wrote a rhapsody and a concerto for piano and a small symphony in mimicry of Bartok. He said that maybe it was his rebellious attitude that first attracted Martina to him. He said that she jumped into bed with him on their very first meeting as much for the sex as for the status she got being linked to a rebel and a cool innovative composer of modern music. My professors didn't like what I composed. It wasn't their taste just as they didn't approve of Bartok's or Penderecki's music. But they accepted his graduation piece anyway and awarded him top prize in his graduating class. He felt he was on top of the world—he had written a number of major pieces of music, he was tops of his class at the conservatory, and he had married the prettiest girl at the conservatory.

He had all kinds of ambitions for new compositions. And in the next four years he was able to start several works, another symphony, a quartet, and a couple piano sonatas. He even laid out the bare bones of an opera he thought of. He wanted to emulate Janacek but he looked to Schoenberg and Webern as models. He found it easy to compose. But in those years, he discovered that he had been somewhat sheltered in the conservatory, that his professors had been discouraging because they were merely trying to protect him. After he graduated, he found that none of his works were accepted for performance or publication. His friend Jiri, who had gotten a conducting job with the Czech Philharmonic, told him that the orchestra had gotten word that my works were banned and not to be performed. And try as he might, Jiri was unable to get any of them scheduled. It was difficult to get work.

"And he said he was so thankful that the Prague Spring started, because immediately the bans and restrictions on modern music, on his music, fell away. His symphonies were publicly performed for the first time, and he was able to perform his piano sonatas—on the stages of Prague, Ostrava, Brno and Bratislava—and get paid for them. It was a very exhilarating time, in the seven months until the Soviets invaded. He had already told me about his escape."

"He said he was lucky in his asylum case that he was sponsored by Karl Husa. And when he first came here to America he went to Cornell and did graduate studies with Husa. It helped that the very same year that he arrived, in 1969, Husa won the Pulitzer Prize for one of his compositions, a modernist work. That meant that afterwards when Husa recommended Milosh's works to orchestras around America, they often heeded his advice and performed them. Milosh said that he would not have survived as a composer if it hadn't been the many recommendations of Karl Husa. His studies at Cornell were really useful because he was able to listen to recordings of the music of all the latest contemporary composers and study their scores—something that had been impossible in Czechoslovakia. But also, Milosh spent his time in graduate studies learning conducting and was able to find work immediately upon completing his studies in 1972. His income from conducting around the U.S. supported his composing. And in the next twenty-five years he composed a lot, three more symphonies, a number of orchestra pieces without the classical structures, a symphonic poem, two operas, more sonatas. And three quartets and two piano concertos, and one flute concerto."

"Maddie, he told me all this hurriedly and excitedly." said Cammy, interrupting the narrative. "You can't believe it, but he was not being boastful. He had a fascinating story to tell."

"Excuse me, but has he ever shown you any pictures of him when he was at Cornell?"

"No, I haven't seen early photos of him. I have looked up on the internet some photos of him conducting. But they have been from recent years.

"Anyway, Milosh was really getting to a point that he wanted to tell me. It was important to him, especially in light of that quartet he completed just recently."

"He told me that in those years he began to ponder about the career of Jan Sibelius, and especially why, at the height of his powers and success, Sibelius just completely quit composing, and never composed again till the end of his life. It was a case that mystified him and aroused his curiosity. But then when he turned fifty Milosh said the same thing happened to him. That one day he woke, looked at his piano and suddenly felt that there was no more for him to write. The taps had turned off. He knew at once that he was finished as a composer. He didn't have anything more to say or write. Just like had happened to Sibelius—although he added he didn't have near the success nor fame that Sibelius had achieved. He continued to work as a conductor and teacher of composition, but he said he did not try to compose anything. The well had gone dry; he had no inspiration or interest in writing modernist music at all."

"And he said that for twelve years he didn't even try to write any music. And this was the point of the story he was telling me. He took my hand and looked me in the eyes and very earnestly told me, I remember his exact words, "Cammy, my musical wellspring had become sterile and dried up, until I saw you sitting at that café three years ago. I saw you, and you were sparkling and joyful as you spoke to Maddie, just ebullient with love. And when I spoke to you that first time, I heard a voice that confirmed that vision, beautiful and happy as birdsong, as divine as the bubbling waters of springs."

"And he continued, I remember his words, so well, 'So that when I went home, with your phone number and email address, all I could think of was what a wonderful inspirational woman you were. And still are. I realized in the days following that first real meeting that I met my first muse. And I was convinced of that even more, a few weeks later, when I saw and listened to the little piece you composed for my class final exam. I suddenly realized that I had been through my entire early career composing music for contrived and artificial reasons, for mechanical, mathematical, rational, and theoretical reasons that had nothing to do with music. Research into sound, maybe, but not music. I was composing music for the approval and favorable judgment of other composers and music theorists. And not for people who would listen to it, not for the essential reasons for music. Music is above all about love, about emotion, it is a language of those feelings and emotions. You, Camille, had reawakened music in me, by reintroducing me to love. The love that is at the heart of music. And that is why your little melody is at the heart of the quartet I composed for you. I have so much I want to write and get performed. And I have been frantically composing little bits ever since I met you. And all of it will be a complete repudiation of all that I had composed before. All that I had composed before was barren and lifeless, and it had died. You, Camille, resurrected my original feelings for music, back when I was still a boy at my mother's piano, or when I heard marches in my head when I walked to school. Or heard love songs when I saw movie romances. I have found in you a true Muse; you are my Euterpe, the muse of song, and giver of pleasure."

"He then went on to say, that since that date three years ago, he has composed this quartet, and he has finished two long pieces for voice and orchestra, and that he is almost finished orchestrating an oboe concerto, which he said reproduces my voice, and captures my joie de vivre."

"He then asked me if I liked the quartet. Of course, I said I liked it, but I had only sight-read it in my mind the night before. It would be better if I could hear it."

"He said that critics would not like it. It was too tonal, or neoromantic in the terms of their dismissals of all music which is not avant-garde or modernist enough for them."

"I liked what I could understand of it from sight reading," I said to Cammy, not admitting that I wasn't able to hear it in my mind from just sight reading. As I said, my solfeggio is not really my strong point in music.

She continued. "He said that I might soon be able to hear it too. He had sent the draft score to the Kronos Quartet, who he said had always invited him to compose pieces for them. They had already performed two of his earlier quartets. And they like his work. They hadn't answered yet, but he felt confident that they would accept it soon enough. I said that I couldn't wait to hear them perform it. And he said that maybe when they were ready to give its premier, we could travel together to hear it played. That took me by surprise."

"What could I say to Milosh? He was saying that I was responsible for his return to composing. That he loved music making again. I said that of course I was flattered that he thought I had inspired him. But I felt that he probably had it in him all along, that it just took longer to gestate."

"He said, no, no. In the past two years he had heard me perform at many concerts and he adored my 'voice' on the oboe. And he recognized that the theme that I had worked on for his composition class, came from the voice of the oboe, not the voice of a piano, that the two instruments sang entirely differently. And he had never realized before that he was stuck in music that came out of the piano's voice, even if he had tried to write a flute concerto. His oboe concerto would sound entirely different from anything he had written before."

It was then I remembered the chat flow from the spring before:

**Windows Chat Messaging**                    **March 28, 2008**

HautBois Cam: Hey Maddie, last night's concert went super. I knocked out the Rossini. And Milosh was in the audience. He said he loved my playing!

MaddyGirl: Great news! Does Milosh attend many of your concerts?

HautBois Cam: No. Not so many. Only the ones where the oboe features prominently.

MaddyGirl: I would think that would be most concerts.

HautBois Cam: lol. I guess you're right. He has attended a dozen or so this season. And of course, he's conducted four concerts in place of Levine this past season.

HautBois Cam: He says with Levine's poor health he might be conducting a lot more in 2008-2009.

MaddyGirl: Is it the Scala di Seta overture?

HautBois Cam: Need you ask? Of course it is.

MaddyGirl: A good part for flute also. Are you performing it Sunday?

HautBois Cam: Yes, matinee.

MaddyGirl: Good. I'll be there. At two or three?

HautBois Cam: 2. Come backstage after the concert.

MaddyGirl: OK CU

I had not realized up to then that Milos was conducting regularly at the BSO. It seems he had been only two or three times a season guest conducting there, but things changed after James Levine came in. Almost from the start he had health problems which forced him to withdraw from conducting. He turned to Milos Novak to be the principal backup because he did not feel threatened by him—he was after all older and about the same age as Levine at the time so he would not be considered as someone who could succeed Levine. Cammy told me she really enjoyed his conducting style. And he never showed her any favoritism or revealed that he was head over heels in love with her. And even more important he never once in rehearsals, at concerts, before or after going onstage, did he make a pass at her. He respected her and Cammy said once that he was probably too shy to bring himself to publicly grope her or give her an undeserved kiss. I went to that concert and was blown away by Cammy's performance in the Scala di Sete. I had never noticed at the BPhil just how good she sounds.

Anyway, I have not attended a concert where Milos conducted, and Cammy had a big role. So, I can't really say how the perform together.

"Maddie, are you listening to me?"

I guess I wasn't really. Thinking about Cammy's playing in the BSO. "Yeah, I heard you say something about a big surprise Milos sprung on you."

"Well, yes. He's been invited by his friend Jiri to conduct a premier of his newest work at the Prague Spring Festival in early June."

"What work is that?"

"He said it was a piece commemorating the twentieth anniversary of the Velvet Revolution. He calls it Liberty, a short nationalistic piece celebrating both the false liberties won in the Prague Spring and the final liberation from the Soviets in 1989. Built on Czech tunes, mainly from Smetana and Dvorak, and variations on the national anthem. And he gets to conduct it."

"That's great. But I'm not all that familiar with Czech music, except maybe for Dvorak's ninth."

"But that's not all. He's invited me to come with him and to attend both that concert and a few others that week—if of course I have time off from BSO concerts. And as it turns out, the first week in June is empty. I can take the time to go. And he's offered to pay for my ticket and hotel."

"Super. Cammy, that's great news. Maybe he will make that first pass at you, a passionate kiss, or an invitation for more while you're in Prague."

"We kiss all the time, Maddie. After every long get together, lunch or stroll."

"Have you told Gus about this?"

"The trip to Prague? Or the kissing? Yes, that very same day. He said he didn't mind. But he wouldn't pay for it. Of course I didn't tell him Milos's role in all this. Or that I was going with him. I simply told him, I've been invited to play. And then Gus said he also would be leaving for three weeks about that time, on the 5th of June. And would only come back briefly before going again to Lucerne. It'll be his third season there. But anyway, I can afford to pay for it myself. Milosh doesn't have to pay anything. I have such a big salary now I don't need charity. But of course, I appreciate his generosity. And I will insist on separate rooms. You can imagine, I accepted Milos' offer almost at once. I checked my schedule right there in front of him. He was so pleased. He smiled and clapped his hands together, like a little boy who's just gotten his favorite toy, or a birthday cake."

"Gus is still working as concertmaster at the Frankfurt Orchestra?"

"Yeah. And that's where I think he is going in early June."

"Do you ever talk to Milosh about Gus?"

"Not much anymore. I did when we first started lunching together. I told him that Gus is always absent. I told him that he got an appointment at the Lucerne Festival. He said that was a super honor. Abbado was probably the best conductor of the past forty years. And I told Milosh when Gus got the appointment as concertmaster at Frankfurt."

"And what did he tell you?"

"Well, he asked me if Gus wanted me to live with him in Frankfurt. Of course I don't. And he had never asked that I move. His appointment there came after my appointment here with the BSO. Anyway, I don't think there was anything Gus could have said the other day to change my mind and desire to go with Milosh to Prague. I really want to travel and see more. And I've heard that Prague is so beautiful."

"Yeah, I've heard that too. And I'd also like to travel to some place romantic like Prague. But I won't go by myself. It'd be better to go with a boyfriend."

"Yes, and Milosh said he'd show me all around the city, where he grew up, the conservatory, the castle. Our strolls around the Back Bay will have been good preparation for walking all around Prague. It will be so exciting."

"Sounds to me like you love this man, Milosh."

"What? Me? Yeah, I guess so. He is so adorable; I like his company. And he always says the nicest, sweetest things to me."

"Will you share a bedroom"

"I don't think so. He continues to point out that I am a married woman and he won't take advantage of that. He says he's not looking for an affair."

"And you, couldn't you see yourself in a relationship with him?"

"Well, he is old. I think that is one reason why he doesn't want marriage. He says he loves that doesn't mean he wants to make love to me."

"Did he say that to you?"

"Not in so many words."

"Well, it still sounds like the trip of a lifetime. I'm jealous."

"Come to think of it, I need to start planning for it. What to take to wear. What's the weather like in early June? I have to get a passport—right away. I wonder if I will need a visa?"

"And when you get back, we have to get together again, and you'll tell me all about it. I want more than a postcard's worth of news. And of course, you can still send me emails or sms or messages on the iPhone."

"Okay."

Needless to say, Cammy did send me some messages—short-on-detail text messages—and some photos she took on her camera but sent by her computer all while she was in Prague. I reproduce them here. Better than getting postcards through the mail, four weeks later.


**Windows Chat Messaging**                          **June 3, 2009**

HautBois Cam: We arrived early this morning. I am so exhausted. Overnight flights are hard. I slept half the flight to London head on Milos's shoulder. The entire flight to Prague, head in his lap. He didn't complain.

HautBois Cam: Now I know what jet lag is. Our hotel is really fancy. We have separate rooms. Milos said he wanted to keep things proper between us. Even if I slept with him in the same bed, I'm so tired I wouldn't notice him.

HautBois Cam: Milos is forcing me to go out and walk around to get adjusted. No events for tonight. Pilsner beer is too bitter for my taste. Tomorrow, he has rehearsal after lunch and then we go to a concert, not his, at seven.

HautBois Cam: Milos has a younger sister, named Martina. We met her and she took us to her house for a light supper. She's a super woman. She's just remarried. Her first husband was 25 years older than her and he died. She is all white haired and looks like a granny but only has one grandchild. Very friendly woman. She calls Milos Milosh. She hasn't seen him in 18 yrs.

**Windows Chat Messaging**          **June 4, 2009**

HautBois Cam: Milos is such a wonderful man. He really looks after me. He found a chamber group I can play in for a concert in four days. He introduced me to Jiri. He says everyone loves Milos's music here. Husa's concert is tonight.

HautBois Cam: Milos took me to the Conservatory. Showed me where he used to practice piano and compose.

HautBois Cam: Milos took me to a really nice Czech restaurant after the concert. Delicious food, violin music in the background. But I could barely keep my head from falling on the table. AAK

**Windows Chat Messaging**          **Jube 5, 2009**

HautBois Cam: Everyone we meet here calls Milos Milosh. He actually prefers that. So, I will be calling him Milosh from now on. He introduces me as his muse and inspiration. In Czech of course. I heard him say Euterpe. Jiri said I was a beautiful inspiration. They're all so nice here.

HautBois Cam: Milosh went to a registry office today and got a copy of his divorce certificate. Says they had a hard time finding it, it was so long ago. He also said now he is free to marry me! Kind of a joke. But he hasn't asked me yet.

HautBois Cam: Last night's concert was super. Husa conducted his piece, Prague Spring 1968. He got four encores; people were so happy to hear it. We all met after the concert—Jiri came without Milosh's ex—and we had lots of Czech champagne.

HautBois Cam: Milosh took me today to Old Town Prague, the Charles Bridge, and we walked up a long hill to the Castle. Everything's so beautiful. Flowers blooming everywhere.

HautBois Cam: Tonight, there's a concert conducted by Jiri, including another orchestral piece by Milosh. Milosh's concert is tomorrow.


**Windows Chat Messaging**                                 **June 6, 2009**

HautBois Cam: Day on my own today. Milosh is going to hold rehearsals in the morning and afternoon. Last night's concert had a very interesting oboe concerto by Martinu. Would love to play it in the future. The festival schedule is so full I've never seen anything like it. And it lasts over nearly a month. This year they're also observing the 20th anniversary of the Velvet Revolution, even though that was in November.

HautBois Cam: I went for part of the morning rehearsal to watch Milosh. He spoke only in Czech. He sounds like an entirely different person when he speaks Czech. I am surprised he remembers it so well after so many years. He says he could teach me Czech and that it is not hard at all. I wandered around the city. I sat at an outdoor café and read an informative guidebook about Czech history and culture.

HautBois Cam: We met for a light dinner next to the concert hall. It's a super place—blond wood paneling everywhere and crystal chandeliers—feels like Dvorak and Smetana everywhere. And lots of artwork by an art nouveau artist named Mucha.

HautBois Cam: Milosh bought me a really pretty garnet necklace set in silver. Art nouveau style. Says it is a Czech specialty. I wore it to the concert and will wear it for the rest of the visit.


**Windows Chat Messaging**                    **June 7, 2009**


HautBois Cam: What a wonderful concert last night. Milosh conducted a concert comprising his music and Husa's music. First half ended with his new piece Liberty the Velvet Revolution. The whole audience stood and sang along at the end. It was so moving, I cried along with the audience.

HautBois Cam: In the second part there was Sinfonietta by Janacek. And Milosh led one of his piano concertos with a local pianist. It was very good, very emotional. Milosh got five encores at the end. I felt so proud of him.

HautBois Cam: The people here are really pleased to see him back in Prague. You wouldn't believe how many bouquets of flowers people brought up for him. Jiri says he is a cultural hero, like Husa. We got roaring drunk again afterwards. More sweet Czech champagne. They call it sekt.

HautBois Cam: I have such a hangover from all that sweet wine. I don't know how I will perform this afternoon with the quartet. I'm overeating here too. Today between concert and opera Milosh took me on a long walk around the city, and up the river, the Ltava.

HautBois Cam: Tonight, we're going to the opera to see Janacek's Katya Kabanova. One of his last and greatest. And very popular too. I hope they have subtitles in English so I can follow the storyline.

MaddyGirl: It's really a shame that we no longer have an opera company here in Boston. We were less than 10 years old when the old Boston

Opera closed—the Caldwell Opera. Remember we went to see Tales of Hoffman together on a school trip? First opera I ever saw.

MaddyGirl: Great info you're sending. Better than getting dull old postcards. Sounds like you're having heaps of fun. And Milos is your man. Love the photos you've sent. Milos is always hugging your shoulder. Keep sending the messages. And photos.


**Windows Chat Messaging**                         **June 8, 2009**

HautBois Cam: It was a really great opera. Enjoyed it more because of English subtitles so I could follow the story. Milosh also sat close to me and helped explain some things. He told me it is loosely based on the love story of Leos Janacek himself. But it seems all turned around compared to what happened between Leos and Kamille from what I understand.

HautBois Cam: I played three pieces with the New Dvorak String Quartet. What a fabulous bunch of artists. One of the pieces I played was Milosh's which he wrote dedicated to me on my graduation theme. Without telling me he had re-written the viola part for oboe. We gave the concert in the chamber music hall of the Rudolfinum. The place was packed. I enjoyed myself despite a hangover.

HautBois Cam: Tomorrow, we fly out of here early in the morning. To London and dash for a change of plane and on to Boston. Be home in the mid-afternoon. We really have to get together again before I go off to Tanglewood. Will you be able to come over to my place on Thursday or Friday?

MaddyGirl: Yeah. I'd love to see you. How about Thursday? Friday, I have a rehearsal and evening concert with the BPhil.

HautBois Cam: Oh yeah. I forgot. I have a concert series too this coming weekend. Thursday afternoon, say for early lunch down at our Pan Asian restaurant? I will then go on to rehearsal. I will have to remind the administrator to email me the scores of our program so I can start to practice them. I will be so jet-lagged.

MaddyGirl: CU lunch, 12 noon, Thursday.


As I wrote, Cammy sent a bunch of photos by email with her messages coming on the chat line. She sent about a dozen. Most were taken with her new Apple phone. Not the same quality of photos as you usually get with postcards, but then unlike postcards all of them were focused on Cammy and Milos together. Usually in front of some architectural wonder of the city—none of which I recognized except for the general pointy spires and fairy tale looks of many of the older towers. Very often Milos's arms are around Cammy, either her shoulders or around her waist. But they are not shown hugging or kissing. She didn't identify anything in the background or the date either. One or two were pictures of them in a restaurant, different restaurants, laughing or toasting. Big smiles. Again, she did not identify the other people in the photos at the table with them. Cammy wrote that she was jet-lagged or hungover during most of her visit. But strangely enough it was Milos—or should I say Milosh now?—who looked especially tired. Big dark bags under his eyes, and—I hadn't seen him in a while—his hair has begun to go white in splotches, or gray—it's hard to tell in the photos. iPhone photos are not always the best quality or sharp focus. It is clear that someone else was taking the photos for Cammy. So now the age difference between Cammy and Milos looks more extreme than it did in the past couple of years. If I understand from what Cammy reports, Milos is working very hard on new compositions. So maybe that is taking a toll on him. He's over retirement age now, after all. But despite how tired they looked, and the low quality of the photos, I could see clearly in all of them that Cammy looked really happy, and often she was broadly smiling at Milos. She definitely likes him.

We met up as planned at the Pan-Asian restaurant and I ordered my usual stir-fried rice with shrimp. It turned out that we didn't have much time to visit. She had to leave only an hour and a half after we met. And I had a rehearsal later that afternoon as well. Cammy, despite being tired, was bubbly, and between bites she told me a bit about this or about that about her trip to Prague.

"You can't believe how beautiful the city is. And so much of its old buildings survived the war, and also Soviet occupation. It's magical in places. I especially liked the Baroque churches."

"Yeah? I had no idea." I said. "I didn't have any images of the city until you started sending your photos."

"And it is much more musical than I had thought. I didn't realize that Mozart went and performed there because his music was so popular. Everyone knows about Dvorak, but the real musical giant of Czechia is Smetana. And to a lesser extent Janacek."

"How does Milos fit into the Czech music constellation?" I asked, trying not to sound sarcastic.

"I guess he does. His music was well received. It was Jiri who said that he thought Milosh's music was great and he schedules it often for concerts in the Prague Philharmonic. But Milosh is not as beloved as much as his mentor, Carl Husa. I met him by the way at the festival. He is a real fan of Milosh's music. But then Milosh admires his works also. They form a kind of mutual admiration society you could say."

"You wrote that you met with Milos's younger sister. Did you like her?"

"Yeah, she's super. Most people we met there assumed that I was Milosh's daughter. But I think she assumed that we were lovers, boyfriend and girlfriend. Milosh apparently has written to her a number of glowing e-letters about me. So, she was forewarned about me and expected me. She even said that I was prettier than how Milosh described me. And she knew right off that I played the oboe, in the BSO. She treated me like a member of their family. She looks a lot like Milosh, except that she doesn't dye her hair, so she was completely white, and her face shows wrinkles. But she smiles all the time."

"Why do you think she assumed you were lovers?"

"You know, at her house, over dinner, she told me—without prompting—that when she was very young, she married her first husband who was much older than her. And that her son at the table with us was from that first marriage. He's about our age. She very much loved her husband, and he loved her, but he died of old age about ten years ago, she said. That comes as a condition of having an older man as a husband. She had no regrets. You know, as if she was telling me about my relationship with Milosh. But she wouldn't have it any other way. She loved her first husband very much. And only remarried two years ago. Her second was there with us. And he looked younger."

"You know, you wrote that you felt really proud of Milos."

"Yes, I felt that way especially when he conducted his own piece and the audience went crazy."

"So isn't that a sign that you love the man?" I asked, having saved up that question for a week. "Pride in someone usually indicates a kind of personal and deep familiarity and possession."

"I hadn't thought about it that way. I really like Milosh. He's very special to me, and it's pretty clear that he is crazy in love with me."

"But you're not yet ready to be lovers? In some of your photos, it certainly looks like you are."

"No, we are just dear friends. I like being in his presence, all the time."

"That sounds to me like you love him, if you always want to be close to him."

"I suppose I do, and I find the longer I know him the more I want to be in his company. I hadn't thought about it in that way. But he makes me happy and pleased to be with him."

"You don't feel that way about Gus, then?"

"I did, initially. But as you know he's never around anymore. And distance definitely makes the heart grow cold. I never hear from him either when he's in Europe. I don't want to talk about Gus."

"Okay." I said, remembering a time several years ago, before Cammy got into the BSO, when she told me that her plan in life was to get a man (that is to get married), to get into a top class orchestra (and by that it was clear that the Boston Philharmonic was not top class—but we both knew that), and to have a baby or two. I wondered there at that little restaurant if she felt she had checked off two of her life goals from her plan. Because it seemed to me right then at that moment that it was unlikely that she would ever achieve her third goal in her plan. But I didn't want to say that at that moment. It was clear that Cammy was tired. And it would crush her for me to say it. And I also felt like trying to correct her life plan. It should be one: to get the love of a man (and get married to him), followed by two: career success, and then three: having a family. In that corrected version, she had only achieved one of her life goals. That's still something, of course. And you don't have to have a husband to be able to have a baby or two. But it helps to have love. But as it was, I kept my mouth shut at this moment. I don't actually have such a conscious plan for my life. If I meet the right man, I'll go with that, and everything else can just follow. Although I still would like to get into a more professional orchestra.

"On the flight back from London, Milosh confided to me that he has trouble speaking his feelings, especially his feelings for me. But he wanted to tell me how immensely happy he was that I was with him in Prague. Most everyone assumed that I was his lover. And he said that he didn't correct anyone. And then he thanked me for coming and accompanying him—and he said that even if he was an old, washed-up composer. He chunked his glass of champagne at me."

"And you didn't kiss him?"

"Yes, actually, I did. After he put his glass down." Cammy said jokingly as she signaled the waitress to bring the check.

"He's busy this next month or so. Going to some little college in Kentucky to teach. So, he's only getting to Tanglewood in July. I'll kind of miss him."

As we got ready to leave, she ended her recital about her Prague trip by saying that she had probably gained weight there during the week. "The food is so heavy, dumplings with everything. And they eat so late in Czechia. And then again I drank so much wine."

"You'll have to work it off at Tanglewood then, I guess. But Milosh won't be able to help you." Then just to give her a hard time, I pointedly said, "Everyone always says sex is a great way to take off the excess pounds."

She threw me a harsh look and walked off in front of me.

"Hey, Cammy. You don't want to forget your oboe bag, do you?"

She had and she turned sharply around, came back and picked it up and stormed off in a huff, pretending she was angry with me. I guess she does feel irked that Milosh has not made a pass at her or taken her to bed yet. Or even tried to, it seems.

I wish I had a boyfriend to take me on a lover's trip to a romantic place like Prague for great music and too much good food and wine. Even an old man would do for me just about now. I followed Cammy out, but she was not waiting for me, even though we were both walking in the same direction. I wouldn't need much of an invitation to get into bed with such a man. Maybe I'll find love yet.

# Chapter Three

After that brief conversation in the Pan Asian in mid-June, I did not see Cammy again for almost five months. We exchanged text messages through that summer while she was away at Tanglewood and by emails for longer messages or photo or video attachments. But she wasn't the only one who was busy that summer. I had arranged three auditions in July and August, as unlikely as that seems, and was busy practicing the set pieces each orchestra assigned to applicants. You can't win an audition with scores or even hundreds of other flutists vying against you without working really hard on perfecting the musical excerpts that you will be judged by. And once you start that cycle of intensive practice and repetition, you shut out the world, turn off the iPhone and stop looking at the computer screen where social media constantly tries to force their way into your house, demanding your attention. I try to compensate by connecting with my friends, including Cammy, in the evening but that summer she was busy evenings with something or other, usually a performance. That's a roundabout way of saying I didn't call her (or get through to her) and she didn't call me in return either. At least not very often.

But throughout that summer I kept thinking about how a younger woman comes to love a much older man and falls into that famous May-December relationship or marriage. In the pop psychology press—which I read from time to time and which the internet search engines always refer you to if you ask about such relationships—they always give the most superficial of reasons for how such relationships get going.

And one thing is clear in all of their speculations; they never examine the man's motivations for wanting a sexual relationship with a much younger woman. The articles always are questioning the young woman's motivations and reasons. And of course, what you can find in the social media is only pop psychology—giving shallow explanations and speculations but never actually examining the feelings and emotions of real women who have lived in such relationships. But does a young woman actually fall in love with a much older man? I mean full sexual love, where the couple come to passionately and actively have sex full of ardor and lust. The love that actually alters both partners hormonal balance and makes them go crazy for an indefinite period of time.

My own first reactions to such questions were skeptical. How does a twenties-something girl—still maybe less sexually experienced—fall madly, passionately, heart-racing, and head-over-heels in love with an experienced man who is much older, could even be old enough to be her father? Well, if it happens in real life, I think it is rare. I myself have never felt even the slightest sexual tingle when encountering late middle- aged men, even when they are making moves at men. I have to admit that such occurrences have not happened to me very often. And the pop psychology press just doesn't go there—never addresses the possibility that a young woman just gets so sexually turned on, hot and hungry, for a man who is as old or older than their father, that she finds him sexy and attractive. That, I guess in our society, today, is understandable, as the vast majority of men in their late middle age or silver age are most of the time anything but sexy and manly attractive. Most are at best candidates for body shaming—plump and dumpy figures, looking a little drawn and wan and bored with life, out of shape and lacking both sexual electricity and general energy and imagination. There are some who are still active sexual predators but only a few of those are still actively trying to keep a youthful figure full of vim and vigor and strength and energy. Ironically in society in general, those older male sexual predators, especially those who hunt for young girls—like college girls—are often mocked or derided as being, well, somewhat deviant or even comical. You hear it all the time in the halls of university. Co-eds snickering at the poor hair-dye job of one of the slimmer professors, well over sixty, trying to fake the looks of a man in his mid-thirties and catch the fond attention of the co-eds. And that same press assumes that young women who are the equivalent to older male sexual predators are usually not sexually turned on but are flirting just to trap an older man. That is the amateur, armchair psychologists, whether they are male or female, assume in the first instance that young women who appear to be chasing and flirting after attractive older men—men of power, accomplishment, influence, wealth (yes many times its mainly about wealth), and prestige are false gamers, and they can be disregarded as merely gold diggers, and nothing more. Their emotions and feelings are dismissed as being insincere. I can't say that I saw anything like that in Cammy's relationship with Milos. Of course, I didn't see the two of them together very often at all—I didn't see if they smooched on their long walks together, or whether they merely made hen peck kisses when they met and parted. I was excluded from witnessing any of the little sexual signals and games that occur between a man and a woman at the start of their relationship building to love and coupling. And Cammy herself did not through our electronic conversations ever even remotely indicate what, if any, electricity and arousal occurred when they were together, and close one to the other. She never mentioned in the years that they were "dearest of friends", as she always said, if they even danced together—"a warm, embracing dance" in the words of Frank Sinatra's song about the start of a love affair that still is played on the radio and even as background noise in the halls of the big shopping malls. She never mentioned that she caught hold of the scent of cologne he was wearing. My close observation of them was that she apparently did not find him sexy and alluring. And that was very understandable. I never saw Milos as sexy and attractive. Yes, he was a fit, very handsome older man, and he could be charming and much as he said all the time about Cammy, his eyes sparkled when he was in her presence. He looked at her as if he were caressing her with his eyes. How I wish there was a man in my life who looked at me the same way he did at her. I'd drag him to bed in a flash—especially if he was also so handsome.

So, the pop psychologists are at a loss, and they offer us only the explanations that you hear in gossip circles all the time when maliciously talking about May-December couples. Young women fall for older men and get into a relationship with them for ulterior motives, not for love and sexual attraction. They may feel some attraction to the man also, but the main motive is to get ahead in life or in their career. I noticed this in some classes at the Conservatory. Girls' fawning, flirting, moving close to a professor and stooping just a bit to show off their cleavage, I've seen it a number of times. And I never thought that there was love behind those actions. Whether love then ever develops in such relationships—maybe success in bed occurs and a wild passion develops in both the older man and the young woman, never can tell, love is so unpredictable—is hard to say. Again, at the Conservatory I knew of three older professors who fell for their comely young graduate students and then married them. In all three of the examples I saw, the couples had children and are still living happily together still, ten or fifteen years later. But I was not around to know who made the first move on whom, and I certainly can't offer any insight into whether the woman was sexually attracted and seduced the professor, or the more usual case where the professor, dirty old man, made a pass at her and then his desire and drive, well, one thing led to another until they were sexual partners. One couple was Professor X, a violin instructor whose first wife had died and at the same time his graduate student looked too attractive and was too consoling. He was not then rich and still is not today. He looks dowdy and worn out; this December professor is about seventy years old, and his May wife is maybe thirty-eight years old and also looks prematurely aged. Another is our Professor Y who teaches chamber ensemble playing and piano. He married at the age of fifty. to his student who was twenty-six at the time. The senior staff at the Conservatory still tisk-tisk about them. But I don't know the story of how they got together. The woman is not especially pretty, actually not pretty at all—but she had really big breasts which would have probably caught the wandering eyes and maybe attracted some wandering hands too. He was unmarried when their affair started. I've overheard him say that having a young wife and young family of children, reinvigorates a person and makes him feel younger too. And he looks like that has occurred. He is also not rich or imminent or powerful and can't even rightly say he is a huge success in his career. I don't think he ever concertizes. And the other example is Professor Z, the voice professor. He is now fifty years old, and she is thirty-four and she delivered a baby boy in my second year at the Conservatory which would make him now about six or seven years old. I don't actually know if they ever got married. But this professor does refer to her as wife, and she had and still has, a really knock-out figure. I can imagine there were moments when trying to coach her singing that he found ways to be very close to her, to touch her—"hold the diaphragm tighter like this"—or even wrap his arms around her to show her proper body posture when singing such and such. But it seems clear to me that old man Professor Z also is not rich and does not have a very good figure or appears at all sexy and attractive. In all three of these instances, I just cannot see the attraction that these Professors had for these graduate students. And I can't see that there may have been some ulterior motive, ambition, or some characteristic of the old professor that would have attracted the girls. And I wasn't around to see if the women fell in love and pursued the professor, or if the professor made the first passes and proceeded to seduce the girls. 1 suspect the latter occurred. But honestly, I don't know and will never know. But I do know that in all three of these examples where I've seen firsthand the outcome, the professors and the graduate students have ample opportunities to be physically close, often, and often for long periods of time, long enough for the young women to have their regular monthly ovulation cycle, when hormonal changes drive all kinds of feelings, and rushes of emotion. Long enough and close enough that the old men picked up all those faints, but invigorating, chemical signals from a ripe young female and couldn't help their responses then. Proximity, for women, is no doubt a major component of what is taken to be love. Women love men who are around them all the time, who make them feel their presence, secure, desired, and safe and protected. And I believe for men, just the slightest bit of proximity and sexual signaling, or the merest caress is enough to drive even the oldest and limpest, if you know what I mean, into wild erections, which are always mistaken for love. All three of these couples may be deeply and sincerely in love—it appears that way—but as I say I have no insight about how the young women felt at first, whether they felt love and were drawn to the Professors X, Y, and Z or if something else happened.

I have a little more insight in the case of a high school friend of mine, her name is Jennifer, who went to university right next door to the Conservatory, at Northeastern. We saw each other all the time in her undergraduate years. She studied biology and then continued into graduate studies. She told me one time that she had fallen in love with her professor, a senior, very famous microbiologist, who was supervising her laboratory work and was the advisor on her thesis. He was thirty-two years older than her and married. Jennifer confessed to me that she had been attracted to him for a long while, when one day at the lab he had made a pass at her, a caress and a groping. And she had totally and unexpectedly responded by turning to him and beginning to passionately kiss him and caress his male member. She said his first caress had awakened in her strong attraction and love for him. She surprised herself at how passionate she felt for him. They left together almost immediately from the lab and had sex on the couch in his office (door locked of course) for the rest of the afternoon. She said that she was attracted but also surprised to see him mostly naked, that he was really in good shape, even sexy, and he really moved her sexually from that first go. She felt like it was love at once—but of course she had been physically close to him, almost daily for four years already and felt that they had been ignoring their intimacy and affection for one another for a long time before that incident. After that they began to arrange sexual dates at places where they wouldn't be discovered. She was sexually experienced and said that she had had lovers before, but she acknowledged that the professor definitely held a position of power and control over her. If he had been just another dirty old man and ruthless predator, he could have coerced her or retaliated when he didn't get what he really wanted. But no. He said he truly loved her pretty much from the start of their affair, so after only a couple of weeks of passion, she told him to prove it. She gave him an ultimatum: get a divorce and marry me, was the way she put it, or the sex stops now. And he did. They got married five months later, even before she submitted her thesis for his approval. And she said, he sacrificed a lot to become her husband. His ex took revenge in the divorce court settlement and took most of his money. Only seven months after their marriage, she had twin boys, and she and the professor remained like starry eyed lovers—with babies crying in the background. That was the story she told me already a couple of years ago. Since that time, when the boys were still toddlers but after she had gotten her doctorate earlier this year, the professor had a massive heart attack and died. She told me not long ago that she had no idea that she could suffer such grief when he left her so suddenly. They had both thought he was robustly healthy, and they had begun making long term plans for their future life together. So that is really the only May-December relationship that I know of where I have some deeper insight into the woman's feelings from the start. I don't have even that much insight into the relationship between Cammy and Milos whatever it is because to me it is still not at all clear how she feels about him, and she does not want to tell me apparently. But Jennifer's story certainly demonstrates the risks that exist for the much younger woman in the relationship. Men die; on average they do not live as long as women, and even if they appear fit and healthy, they may die suddenly and unexpectedly if they are over the age of sixty-two, sixty-three. And the May wife or lover should know that; her December man will just not last as long as she will, and he could pass away in a flash.

All this contemplation and examination of what I have seen around me about May-December relationships is a little disheartening. And it didn't offer me any further insights into the case of my best friend Cammy. I still didn't see her for almost five months that year, and hardly heard anything from her, because we were both busy with our schedules. I was practicing for three auditions in August and September, one for the Philadelphia Orchestra, one for the Houston Orchestra, and one for Cleveland, and I was sure I wasn't ready for any of them, really, when the time finally came. So, I didn't pay too much attention to the messages Cammy sent me with news.

**Windows Chat Messaging**                                    **August 14, 2009**

HautBois Cam: Hey Maddie, haven't heard from you for a while. But I'm partly to blame. Been busy—aren't we always busy? Milosh has been teaching me how to play tennis and now we go out twice a week and play. He's really good. And that week in mid-July when we had that heat spell we went swimming together again in the lake. He's sexy you know under those baggy clothes he usually wears.

MaddyGirl: Yeah, I remember the heat spell. I was sweating bucketfuls while practicing. My apartment is inadequately air conditioned, remember? I wished I could have been swimming in a lake.

MaddyGirl: I fly off to Houston on Sunday. Wish me luck.

HautBois Cam: Good luck. Knock em out. Win that job. Which position?

MaddyGirl: Principal flute.

**Windows Chat Messaging**                    **August 19, 2009**

MaddyGirl: So, I only made it to the semifinals. Didn't get there. I think I messed up on the Debussy excerpt. But on to the next audition this weekend. Flight of the Bumblebee is a beast. One time I clinch it, and the next I miss every other note. And it sounds ragged, not rapid.

HautBois Cam: Sorry to hear that. But I have good news from Milosh. The Kronos Quartet is going to play his quartet based on my theme. Next month, in Carnegie Hall. Remember how to get to Carnegie Hall?

MaddyGirl: Yes. Practice, practice, practice. Preferably on 57th Street.

HautBois Cam: Right. He's invited me to come with him to hear the performance. It'll be the premier. On Saturday, the 12th. Would you be able to come along?

MaddyGirl: I'd like to, but I don't know my schedule yet with BPhil. I'll check. I wouldn't be a third wheel

HautBois Cam: No, not at all. Besides we're going there to listen to his music not to snuggle together in the rear rows. You and I could even share a hotel room together.

MaddyGirl: Oh. That works for me. Are you sure Milos won't be jealous of the missed romantic opportunity?

HautBois Cam: It was Milosh who suggested that I invite you along. He's had plenty of opportunities this summer to try and get me into his bed. And he hasn't pushed all that hard for that. Which is just fine.

MaddyGirl: OK


**Windows Chat Messaging**                    **August 27, 2009**

HautBois Cam: I have great news! The BSO is going to play Milosh's oboe concerto, with me as the soloist! Milosh told me today that

Levine looked at the piece and accepted that it needed to go into next season's program. It will be sometime in March next year. I'm so tickled.

MaddyGirl: Will Milos conduct it?

HautBois Cam: He doesn't know. But he says that probably Levine will conduct it. But we saw this summer that Levine's health is failing. Milosh had to fill in for him for four concert nights this summer because the maestro was ill-disposed. No one is saying what is wrong with him. But he cancels usually a day in advance and goes to the doctor and is gone for four or five days.

MaddyGirl: That IS GREAT news. I hope I can attend. I am so glad for you and will be so proud to hear you perform it.

HautBois Cam: And you know what. The BSO appointed Milosh resident composer for the next three years. I don't know which decision came first, but being a resident composer makes it easier to schedule a premier of a new work. It can be said to be his output, even though he finished it earlier this summer.

MaddyGirl: When are you coming back to Boston?

HautBois Cam: Probably in that week just before we go down to NY for the Kronos concert.

MaddyGirl: Maybe we'll see each other then.

HautBois Cam: OK, CU. I've looked at the score of the concerto and it has a really difficult oboe part. I'll be working on it all winter.

MaddyGirl: You'll do fine, I'm sure.

HautBois Cam: So, you think you'll join us in NY?

MaddyGirl: I still don't know. Got to run.


And I didn't decide right away. Because the date for the Kronos premier was near the date of my last audition in Cleveland. And I was thinking of flying there the day before, just the day after the Carnegie Hall concert.

And as it was that I only got to the semi-final of the Philadelphia position, I wanted to prepare even harder than I had earlier in the summer and reach the final. But at the last minute I decided I would go with them anyway. I was glad I did.

I made arrangements so I would fly from New York to Cleveland on the Sunday before my audition, staying the two or three nights in Cleveland and then flying back to Boston. I would go to New York with Cammy and Milosh—taking my flute with me, along with the music I needed for the audition and which I had by and large already memorized and practiced enough. As it turned out they had decided to go down to New York on the Saturday, the same day as the concert, so I asked if I could join them. It looked a bit expensive for me, and I must have muttered something about how much extra it was going to cost me to go to the concert and then fly to the audition using one-way flight tickets.

**Windows Chat Messaging**                    **September 10, 2009**

MaddyGirl: Have you already bought the train tix?

HautBois Cam: Nope. Not yet, but we're thinking of taking all reserved express trains. I forget what Milos said it was called, Allegro or Assela, or something like that.

MaddyGirl: Okay, can you get me a one-way ticket seated with you?

HautBois Cam: Sure. And I'll pay for it, Maddie. Don't worry, I'll pay for the extra cost. Maybe if this route costs you more—we all know that two one-way air tickets cost a lot more than two separate one way tickets—I'll buy that for you too.

MaddyGirl: No. That's really nice of you but you don't have to.

HautBois Cam: Why not? I'm going to pay for your hotel room—I mean we'll share a room, and I'll pay for both of us. I kinda have money to burn just now. What else are friends for? I wouldn't let

Milos pay for my expenses because he is often just a little short of funds. So just relax.

It was then that I remembered a message conversation that we had had a few years earlier.

**Windows Chat Messaging**                    **November 28, 2007**

HautBois Cam: I'm rich! I can't believe it. I had no idea that principal flute players were paid so well. With my new position starting this January, I am getting another 50% raise.

MaddyGirl: Wow. That sounds unreal. So, what is your current salary as co-principal, if I might ask?

HautBois Cam: It's 138 thousand. And I thought that was a huge raise for me when they told me about it last year when they took me on. I mean that was a 68% raise over what they paid me at the BPhil. I've been paying off my student loans real fast.

I was using the calculator function while she was typing and saw that not only would she be making more than two hundred thousand dollars, but also that she had been earning about eighty-two thousand at the BPhil. Quick calculation here: She was making twenty six percent more than I was—I am now—at BPhil. At the time that made me see green.

MaddyGirl: I would never have thought. So, you're going to be making more than $200k?

HautBois Cam: More than $210k. I'll have to get a tax accountant to do my tax filings and keep from paying too much income tax. I have to pay a lot of taxes to Massachusetts, you know. As I said, I'm rich. Now I just have to work hard to get tenure, and I will have arrived.

I remembered all that. I was truly impressed. But also, as I said before, a little envious. How was it that Cammy was paid so much more than I've been at BPhil? Is she really that much better than I am?

But I am not too proud. I'm often short of funds. And I was tremendously curious to hear Milosh's piece performed by the famous Kronos Quartet. So, if there was any way I could go to New York to hear the concert together with Cammy and Milosh, and still make it to my audition by Monday in Cleveland, then I wanted to do it. That is what I told Cammy. I couldn't go to New York—and go on to the audition—without Cammy's help. She was more than a friend. More like an older sister— even though she is not older than I am. Simply more accomplished.

We met Saturday morning at the South Station for the first train. I got there by the T; the Allston stop is only a few blocks from my apartment on the Green Line. And I wasn't too over-burdened. Just my flute bag with scores, and an overnight bag with my performance dress—which I intended to wear to the Carnegie Hall concert—and two changes of clothes, toiletries, and my cosmetics. When I saw them in the central hall, they were traveling even lighter than I was. Instead of overnight bags, they had large handbags. That was all. "Less to lose and less to carry," was Cammy's only comment. "We're going only for two nights and then right back on Monday morning, so we hardly need anything. We'll go to the concert dressed as we are now."

I have to admit that surprised me. Milosh was dressed in smart casual clothes which included clean blue jeans and a white long sleeve shirt— what we always see avant-garde artists in New York or San Francisco wearing—topped with a navy-blue wool blazer jacket that had Gucci brass buttons I noticed. No tie. And I have to admit I thought in the moment when we met in the station that he looked attractive and, yes, even sexy. He's tall and slender and he has this lively face, but he accentuated his good figure by wearing tight pants and a tight-fitting shirt and jacket. I kept thinking during the ride down on the train—I was sitting opposite him with Cammy next to him—that he was a really good-looking man who didn't look anything near his real age. He must work out to keep that flat belly. Cammy by contrast was wearing very plain, even dumpy clothes, a pair of faded and frayed blue jeans and a red loose fitting knit top over a white stretch top. She also had a light, sand colored jacket. She really looked like a college student out with her father going to a weekend football game. It's a strange thing I noticed over the years in Boston, which is a huge college town, but college age girls do everything to make themselves look dumpy and unattractive. Cammy for example on this day who is beautiful and has a knock-out figure, always hides her figure, except in concerts of course, by wearing shabby, frumpy clothes that hang loosely on her. By contrast I had brought my black formal dress for both the concert and the audition—even though there's not a lot of sense in that, I know, because the audition is supposed to be blind. If anything, my concert dress exposes that I have a little too much fat around my mid-section and on my derriere for my liking. I mean, I'm only twenty-eight, not a forty-two mother of three. My travel clothes were smart casual like the mail catalogues always show their models in new black jeans, a printed top and a black long raincoat. While they were boarding the train, I noticed that they touched each other, hands to hands, hands on hips or upper arms, several times, more than usual for a father-daughter combination. I felt a bit self-conscious initially because I thought people on the train might notice that they were a good-looking May-December couple and show their dismay. If so, what was I doing there? But no one took any notice of us at all, even at the hotel lobby.

After we sat down, Cammy handed me the one-way ticket for this "flight" on the Acela (which is the actual name of that express train Cammy had tried to recall a few days earlier). I was surprised that the cost was $170, and in the small lettering it said reserve seat only. I thanked Cammy profusely and Milosh broke in, "No, we wouldn't have it other way. I really wanted you to come, even if it is tight for your audition schedule. How else would get the opportunity to hear a premier performance of one of my pieces played by the foremost string quartet in the world?" We were going first class—and it was a fast train. The ticket said it arrived in much less than four hours—in time for lunch in New York. And the car was laid out and furnished very nicely—I had never been on such a nice train before. Always previously Cammy and I had taken the shabby, dirty trains to New York which grind on slowly forever it seems—and here there was this huge difference. I have never been able to travel first class because I just don't have the money for it. So, this was a real treat. And then the hotel stay in New York was also a treat—and also really first class. We stayed just a few doors down from Carnegie Hall on 57th Street at the Le Meridien, a French business class hotel. Again, I was surprised and frankly delighted at how nice the hotel was. French taste and style. For $300 a night I guess you would expect no less.

As we got underway and were just leaving the inner suburbs of Boston, Cammy looked at Milos and smiled.

"The weather is so nice," said Cammy as she looked out the window. "Maybe it'll be as nice in New York." They had to turn their heads to look at each other. During the whole trip Milosh was half turned away from the window so it was easy to look directly at Cammy and only have to turn his head a little to look at me.

"I hope so," said Milos. (I think at this point in their story I can call Milos, Milosh. Although I didn't call him to his face, Milosh even once, because he never asked me to address him that way. In the remaining years he continued to be Milos to me. Milosh seemed to be too much the personal name that was the sole property of Cammy, so I didn't use it. And unlike in Czechia, no one in America had switched over to calling him Milosh, not even James Levine.) "Because we can exercise our favorite activity. Namely a long stroll through Central Park. I hope you don't mind walking a few miles with us, Maddie?"

I was startled. A few miles? "I usually don't walk that far in a week." I said.

"Don't worry Maddie, Milosh doesn't walk too fast for us."

"And I would propose that we have lunch at the famous Tavern on the Green. That is not even a twenty-minute walk from our hotel."

"And what hotel are we staying in?" I asked.

"Le Meridien." said Milos. "It's a French hotel. Quite near Carnegie Hall and Central Park."

"I looked it up on Google," said Cammy. "It's really quite luxe, as the French say. Our room will be across the hall from Milosh's. You don't mind that we share a room? Not share a bed, just the room." Cammy smiled at me and then at Milos as if there was a little joke in that.

I played along, addressing Cammy. "I thought you would share a room and bed with Milos."

I noticed out of the corner of my eye that Milos blushed right away, apple red.

Cammy giggled. "I think Milosh would like that, but just now, not yet." Then she glowered at me, as if I had said something far too offensive and uncalled for.

"Of course," said Milosh half stammering. "I would like that, Cammy. But you already know that." Then more directly addressing me, "We're not ready yet."

So, we left that line of discussion. Well beyond the Blue Hills south of Boston, Cammy started again.

"Milosh's music for tonight's concert has been accepted for publication."

"Yes, that's right. Schirmers have accepted both the quartet and my oboe concerto. So, I'll be earning some royalties tonight. Every little bit helps keep me alive."

"Oh, come on," said Cammy. "You have lots of money."

"Maybe, but that is wealth, not income. I live on income. Good thing the NEC pays me to teach. That's my income from which I scrimp and save. I live comfortably by conducting and teaching at Tanglewood. I learned that early on here in America. If I only had income from my compositions, I would starve to death. Haydn once said that whenever he ran out of savings, he knew it was time to write another symphony. And mean another one beyond the ones that Esterhazy was already paying him for."

I was feeling mischievous. "So, what you're saying is that you maybe don't have enough income to support Cammy as a wife."

Cammy almost burst out of her seat. "That's enough! Maddie. Change the subject."

Milos was blushing again. Then he stammered again. "I don't know. You'll have to ask Gus that. I don't think it would take too much money to keep Cammy a happy wife. Besides, she has a very good income. Better than mine. At least, until I write a best seller and royalties can float me away."

It was easy to change the subject, because as Milos was pink in blush, and Cammy's face red with anger, I noticed for the first time the garnet necklace that she was wearing. It was set in silver and at just that moment it glistered in the sunlight reflecting off an expanse of water outside and flashing in through the train's windows. There on her upper chest this large square silver and blood red piece was hanging on a silver chain around Cammy's neck.

"Is that the necklace that you wrote me about that Milos bought for you in Prague? Are they rubies?"

"Yes, it is. No, they are not rubies, but rather they are garnets. Kind of like the national gemstone of the Czechs."

"That's right," said Milosh. "We have only garnet mines in Czechia. No rubies. And rubies generally are pinker than our dark blood red garnets."

"I like it. It looks really pretty around Cammy's neck, just at the beginning of her cleavage."

"I like them too," said Milos. "But you have it wrong. Cammy makes the garnets look prettier than they ordinarily would. I'm really happy that she likes them enough to wear them publicly."

"And why not?" said Cammy. "They're the prettiest and nicest gift I have ever gotten, from anyone."

And it was only then, for the first time, that I noticed that Cammy was not wearing her diamond wedding ring. I didn't say anything. And I don't think either Cammy or Milos noticed that I had looked at her left ring finger. The small diamond ring hidden in a rather ugly setting was not there. It had been there at the beginning of the summer. But actually, her hand looked better without it. I kept my mouth shut. Sometimes I can be intentionally discreet.

We were pulling into Providence where the speaker put out in a stentorian, black man's voice that this stop would be for only three minutes. The sunlight was a little muted by some high white clouds now. After the train departed, Milos turned to me and asked:

"Cammy tells me that you have an audition for the Cleveland Orchestra on Monday. Are you all prepared for your audition pieces?"

"Yes, I think so."

"What is in your repertoire for the audition?"

"Some excerpts from Brahms, the first symphony and the fourth symphony. Debussy's Afternoon of the Fawn, Ravel, Daphnis and Chloe. Stravinsky's Firebird Round of the Princess. And also, an excerpt from Dvorak's eighth symphony. And of course, the scherzo from the Midsummer Night's Dream, by Mendelssohn."

"Well, I don't know the Brahms parts at all. But I am familiar with all the rest. Tomorrow morning before you have to leave for the airport, if you'd like, I can go over them with you and offer my comments and maybe some helpful insights. If you think it might help. I don't think the other hotel guests will mind."

"You will? Yes, yes. That would help me a lot, I think. No one has listened to me, so I don't know if I sound right. Milos, that would be a super favor."

"Then let's do it. And maybe Cammy can sit in and referee. She's pretty good at auditions, you know."

"Yes, yes. I would like that very much. Of course, it will help me."

"If nothing else, maybe I can help to raise your level of self-confidence."

"Isn't Milosh generous?" said Cammy while at the same time she stroked his right hand. "I just adore this man."

Milos blushed again. I didn't say anything, but thought again that he was indeed a very nice sweet man who did not appear to be old and decrepit.

Not long after that Cammy took out her iPhone and began fiddling with it. She half excused herself by saying that this train we were riding was supposed to be equipped with wi-fi service. And she was trying to find out how to get connected. "Ah ha. I see the user site. I wonder if this is the correct password? There I'm connected." And then she was moving her fingers around the screen trying to connect to different websites. I couldn't connect to the wi-fi at all, and I put my iPhone down in disgust on the table between us.

"I told you, you had to get the latest model, Maddie. Yours is archaic."

"But it is not even three years old."

"Obsolete by design." said Cammy. "But in Milosh's case, he just is not interested in IT technologies. He has only an old Nokia—not a smart phone in the least."

Milosh smiled weakly and shrugged his shoulders. "I just don't need all the features that Apple has, not yet. Certainly not for the price they demand. Forgive me, Cammy."

"Well one feature your phone doesn't have, Milosh, is this nice camera. Maddie, could you take a picture of us together?" She handed me her phone and pulled Milosh closer to her and snuggled against him. She put on a false smile, and I took three photos. Milosh looked extremely happy.

Somewhere, deep inside Connecticut, a dark-haired bearded man in a wrinkled black jacket came down the corridor and stopped next to us.

"Cammy, is that you? Imagine, bumping into you on this business class train to New York." He spoke in an effeminate voice with a catty, not at all genuine tone.

"Samuel, is that you Samuel?" asked Cammy in surprise.

"Yes, of course it's me, darling. Are you still married to that loveable old man, Gustave Christoph?"

"Yes, as a matter of fact I am. But as you know he's always in Frankfurt. You know the concertmaster there."

"So, he's left you, just like he left me for another lover?" Samuel's tone was sharp and nasty.

Cammy shifted uncomfortably. "Are you still with the New England Quartet?" she asked. So that was it, I thought: the fiddler-on-the-roof look of this man named Samuel.

"Yes, we found a replacement for Gus. No problem really. And just now off to New York to hear a concert of the famous Kronos Quartet. Perhaps you've heard of them?"

"And so are we." Said Cammy. "But we're going especially to hear the premier of a string quartet written by our good friend here, Milosh Nowak. You might know him. He teaches at the NEC."

"Oh really? I may have heard his name before." said Samuel. "My name is Samuel Goldenweizer. Glad to meet you." he said as he extended his hand over to Milosh to shake it. He pointedly ignored me. "As Cammy mentioned, I play in the New England Quartet. Second fiddle."

"If your group plays modernist music," said Milosh calmly. "I have written earlier three other string quartets that you may want to try out."

"Maybe. Why not? Your name is Novak? Well maybe we'll see each other at the concert tonight. Got to go. Bye Cammy, I see you're as sweet looking as ever." Samuel said in a voice dripping with ice and insincerity. He then passed on down to the next wagon.

"He's a specimen. Isn't he?" I said.

Not long afterwards, Cammy excused herself to go to the toilet. I couldn't help making a comment to Milosh about the accidental meeting with Samuel.

"Not a pleasant guy, that Samuel. I got the impression he's gay, and maybe a former partner with Gus."

"I got the same impression, Maddie. But he's been like that for a long time. It seems that he does not remember me. He was in my conducting class at the Conservatory, sixteen or eighteen years ago. He was a bitchy queen then. Maybe he chooses to ignore me because I gave him no attention back then. Or maybe he just doesn't remember. He looks a lot different from what I remember of him."

"Really? He was in your class?" I realized almost at once that I sounded like the students who don't realize that life and achievements existed at an institution before they had arrived.

"Yes." said Milos. "He was touted as the prodigy violinist of the time. But his professor, I seem to remember, didn't think so highly of him. And I could care less about his sex life. But he does seem to advertise his orientation."

After Cammy came back, I went back to what Milos had said. "Really you've written other string quartets?"

"Yes, four others to be exact." said Milos. "Years ago. In my serialist days. They sound very contemporary, but I think no one likes that sound. They are seldom performed by anybody, and no one has asked to record them. There was a period in my music when I still wanted to sound like John Cage, but I don't want to make music like that anymore. People in the know may be surprised to hear my piece tonight."

"I'm dying to hear it." Cammy cooed. "Reading it off the score just doesn't give to my mind's ear the atmosphere and texture that a performance gives."

"Tonight, there'll be some people who will call my latest quartet neo-romantic, dismissively, just because they can recognize some fragments of melodies and harmonies that feel familiar. But it is not. I hope both of you like it."

We took a taxi together from Penn Station to the hotel on 57th Street. I was a little cramped because I always carry my flute bag with me. I never put it in the trunk of any car I 'm riding in, especially not a taxi. Cammy follows the same rule. The hotel lobby is like a bright high-ceiled cathedral and the room we had on the fifteenth floor was really super. I don't like leaving my flute in a hotel room, unattended, but sometimes you just have to trust the security of a hotel. We left almost at once for the Tavern on the Green. I was curious to see Milosh and Cammy and how they "strolled" together. Cammy after all had said it was the activity that they most often did when they were together. And they did not have a fixed way. On the sidewalks over to Central Park, they walked close together but not touching, a bit too rapidly to be called a stroll. Crossing 59th street over to the park, they walked hand in hand. But they let go of each other once in the park and slowed down. And after only a couple hundred yards, Cammy slipped her arm around Milosh's, and they were very close. I walked next to Cammy. They don't fit very well together, arm in arm. He's six foot two and she's only a bit shorter than I am at five foot six, so I said, they don't fit all that well; the top of her head comes up only to his chin. It's interesting, I thought at the time: girls and boys go out on first dates, just don't join together closely when they walk together. Side by side. Lovers on the other hand do all the time, walking hand in hand or arm in arm, close and snuggling. And of course, a man's arm around his woman's shoulders or waist is a sure sign of possessiveness—if they are not already lovers then he wants to show other men to stay away from his woman.

At the restaurant, we sat at an outdoor table on the covered terrace. In the view from the terrace there was still no sign that summer had loosened its grip: all the leaves on the trees were still green. Milosh was excited by the Fall menu—wild mushrooms were on offer. So, he ordered a side dish of sautéed wild mushrooms as a main and spicy pumpkin soup. Cammy ordered the salmon, and I asked for the lady's filet steak.

"Not that I am a vegetarian," apologized Milosh, "it's just that since my childhood I have loved collecting and eating wild mushrooms. And I cannot always find them or buy them. So, when they are on the menu I go for them. Makes me think of Fall weather in the forests outside Prague, think of my youth."

For a moment, because Cammy had the fish, I felt almost as if I needed to apologize for eating meat in front of them. But then I let it go and asked for the pumpkin soup as well. I'm not a skinny fashion-walk model, but I'm not plump either. And I like an occasional steak. The food was delicious. Cammy asked her Milos if she could try the wild mushrooms. And he was quick to hand his plate over to her—it was a generous portion, not merely a side dish—and pointed to one orange mushroom. "This is a chanterelle—it's especially delicious. In Czechia we called them Lishky."

Cammy chewed on the mushroom. "You're right, Milosh. But I can't tell whether the nice flavor is from the mushroom, or the sauce or the herbs."

"Well, yes. There are a lot of mushrooms like that. It would be nice sometime in the Fall if I could take you mushroom hunting in Bohemia, Cammy. And maybe you could come as well, Maddie. But it would have to be in early September. Wouldn't you like that?"

Cammy at once said, she would, just say the date. I concurred, although I am not sure I like eating mushrooms, however they may be prepared.

"Does this mean that you don't eat meat?" I asked.

"No, I eat meat and like it a lot. But wild mushrooms are very special. A grilled steak is always nice too. Especially served with mushroom sauce."

"Do you cook much for yourself?" I asked. Maybe I was trying to make trouble, I don't know, but as asked I was looking at Cammy, knowing that she doesn't cook much and never did for Gus.

Cammy jumped in. "I've been to Milosh's house twice when he's cooked me dinner. And both times it was wonderful. Really delicious. And not as heavy as I thought the food in Prague was."

"No, I don't cook dumplings, or knoedle, or spaetzle."

"Whatever. But I remember tender sautéed veal in vermouth and another time broiled salmon in a teriyaki sauce. And your salads were delicious too—although I don't remember what was in them. I can only cook what goes into the microwave or gets heated from the can."

"If you like to eat tasty meals," answered Milos, "it doesn't take long to learn how to prepare them. The motivation is all there. And the most important part is good quality fresh ingredients."

We all had white wine with lunch—Milos ordered a whole bottle of California Chardonnay—and we were definitely a little happy and lightheaded by the end of the meal.

"You know so much about food, Milos. But you look as if you don't eat at all," said Cammy.

"You know that I do. I am just a bit abstemious—that's the right word, isn't it?—never eat big portions and don't eat anything between meals. Most restaurants in America seem to serve monstrous servings, so when I eat out, I usually have leftovers for two more meals. I'm not ashamed to ask for the doggy bag—and you can understand I am the doggy who gets the leftovers or the bones."

I wanted to ask if they started living together whether Cammy would cook, but I thought better of it. I had already been too mischievous that morning. We did not have desserts, and Milos paid the bill which came to $70 each with the wine. He left a $45 tip. Cammy didn't protest, and I certainly didn't—I'm just not accustomed to eating out at such an expensive place. I know I floated out of that nice restaurant, and Cammy and Milos seemed to be snuggling together more than earlier as we continued our now longer circuit around the middle of Central Park. We got back to the hotel at almost 4. Milos asked if anyone wanted a nap—he admitted right away that he did. And the wine had certainly gone to my head so I asked if I could. Cammy excused herself and said she'd look through her Facebook in the lobby, while Milosh and I took the elevator up to the seventeenth floor to our respective rooms.

"Do you want me to knock in an hour?" he asked me.

"Yes, that would be for the best. Otherwise, I'll sleep through the concert."

"We can leave here at seven thirty. As you know the hall is only two minutes away."

On the way to the concert and to our seats in Carnegie Hall, I noticed that Cammy was acting excited and animatedly. She frequently took hold of Milos's arm. He was also smiling nearly all the time through the concert. We had great seats, the seventh row away from the stage in the parquet section. Milos sat directly on the aisle, because he planned to go up onto the stage after his piece was performed. As composer of a premiere performance, he expected to be invited up and share the applause. "If there is any," he joked. As we were settling into our seats and checking the program, Milos told Cammy that the Kronos Quartet had many years earlier performed two of the four of his other, earlier quartets. He thought that they had even performed the second quartet several times, at least that is what the royalties he had received indicated.

I did not find the concert to be very satisfying. All five pieces—Milosh's was last on the program—were very contemporary and with the exception of Milosh's piece, all were militantly modernist, and avant-garde. They left me cold, as they were often screeching and filled with gimmicks, very disruptive gimmicks such as the use of electronic recordings of sounds, sirens, and just plain noise, or the use of minimalism with what seemed like endless repetitions or using the string instruments as percussion pieces. I couldn't find any melodic lines, and in no piece could I understand where the music was heading. I think Cammy felt the same way. Milos continued to smile broadly. Undoubtedly, he knew the context of the pieces better than either me or Cammy. The audience also seemed to find the music—disorganized sounds really which at no point used the virtuosic talents of the four players—also to be discomforting, because they squirmed in their seats and made lots of noises themselves. At intermission Cammy admitted that she did not really like the music, or understand what was going on, but she also confessed that maybe if she heard the three pieces several more times she could. "But I wonder how the score looks. How do you write notation for what we heard?" Milosh did not defend the pieces at all or attempt to explain them. But he also did not say that he liked what had been played. He just said, "Kronos often performs compositions like those, but they also play tremendously good works, like those by Gubaidulina, Denisov, or Auerbach, or Charles Ives or George Crumb. They even play Piazzolla, and his music is very popular." Not long after Cammy turned on her iPhone: she said she was looking on the internet for Gubaidulina. "I've heard music by Piazzolla." I said to Cammy. "It's all tango music." "Yeah, I know. I like it."

In the second part, finally, came Milosh's piece at the end, and it was so completely different from everything else that had been played. It had plenty of tonality. The program called it Quartet No. 5 on a theme by Camille, a world premiere. It put Milosh's name as Milos Nowak, not Milohs. It sounded modern but there were clear melodic lines that broke up, abbreviated, and passed around the four instruments. As we had discovered when we looked at the score, the theme started in the viola part in the first movement. That was restated but put into a minor key variation in the final movement led by the cello and the first violin. I thought it didn't sound at all like I had thought it would from our looking at the score back in June—but then as I say I'm not so good at solfeggio. It did sound like music from early in the last century, like something Richard Strauss would have written, not Schoenberg. I liked it. Cammy nudged me when she recognized her theme, and I think she liked the piece as well. Milosh whispered to her that it was wonderful. Milosh kept looking at Cammy seeking her approval. She gave it to him by nodding her head and smiling, and again she took his arm and squeezed it. As the applause started, Milosh got up and went to the proscenium and then to the left and up the stairs onto the stage. The Kronos first violinist who was also standing, reached over and shook Milosh's hand and then held it up in triumph to accept the adulations from the audience. Then Milosh bowed together with all four members of the quartet. And he accepted a bouquet of flowers which came from an usher at the front of the stage. Milosh said something into David's ear, for that is the name of the first violinist and co-founder of Kronos, and the latter nodded his head. Then Milosh came back down off the stage, as the applause began to taper off.

"He looks younger than David Harrington." I shouted to Cammy. She nodded her head vigorously. "You're right. Much younger, even though he's five years older."

Milosh came back to find us standing in the aisle as most of the remaining audience were just clustering and looking at the wonderful interior of the hall or talking about the music they'd just heard.

"So, let's go next door. We'll meet the quartet in about forty minutes at the Russian Tea Room next door after they drop their instruments in their hotel. You liked my little composition, Cammy? Recognize your theme?"

"How could I forget it? I liked your piece very much. You're a genius."

"I doubt that. But I did feel as if waves of inspiration came into my mind when I met you."

We left Carnegie Hall and walked a very short distance to the Tea Room. I don't know about Cammy, but I was blown away by how ornate and fanciful the room and its décor were laid out. It was magical. The coppery ceiling is what struck me first. But the shining samovars were also impressive. We asked for a table for ten and the maître took us to a large round table surrounded by bench divan seats in crimson red. The painting on the walls and ceilings was primarily in red highlighted by white and gold—all really elaborate. Breath-taking. Only as we sat down did I notice the brass firebirds that flew down on friezes between tables.

"You've been here before?" I asked Milos.

"Yes, several times. Usually after concerts at Carnegie Hall. It is like entering into a Russian fairy tale."

"Seems that way. It's beautiful." Cammy agreed.

"And the food is very good—Russian fare. Maybe I can get mushrooms again." Milos grinned. We waited about twenty-five minutes for the Quartet members to come. A stout waiter kept coming to us to ask if there was anything we liked as we waited. He reminded me of a corpulent waiter in one of the earlier Disney classic cartoon movies, I thought maybe in Pinocchio or Lady and the Tramp. Definitely Lady and the Tramp. And here they were Cammy, the Lady, and Milos, the tramp—maybe not—and the stout waiter singing to us, That's Amore. Funny how memories can draw up imaginations like that. As the four men of the Quartet entered and snaked through the narrow restaurant toward us, other diners who obviously had been at the concert began to applaud them. Seemed as if everyone else in the restaurant recognized the casual funk and lean figures of the Quartet musicians.

David Harrington led the way and as they were introducing themselves to us, shaking hands and taking their seats, he said. "We've performed four times in Moscow and have never seen a restaurant as kitsch as this one. But it is fun. Not so appropriate for modernist music. You'll have to excuse us. Less than half of our band are here—the sound engineers, and lighting specialists are taking things down still at the hall. They won't be coming."

"The champagne is good, and the creamed mushrooms in cocotte are authentic enough for my tastes." said Milos. "Unless you want to spill out a fortune on real Russian black caviar."

The waiter brought the bottle of champagne and opened it and poured it out. I was surprised that two of the quartet members declined to have any. David Harrington said simply, "Tomorrow's a travel day and another concert. Want to keep my head clear."

I saw quickly that John Sherba was the talker in the group, at least he spoke his mind. While the others held back somewhat. They all seemed tired. Sherba asked Milos if Cammy and I were his students. "No, this is Cammy, my muse for that quartet you just played. I met her as if in a flash of brilliant light and sound." "So, she is the Camille in the title?" "Yes. When she is not inspiring me, she plays oboe in the BSO. And her friend here is Maddie, her good friend and great flutist, who, on her way to an audition, decided to drop by and hear you all for the first time. And of course, to hear my composition."

"So, she's your girlfriend," said Sherba. "Old composer seeks young female inspiration to re-invigorate his career. We've seen lots of examples of that."

Milos blushed. "I guess you could say that. You mean like my countryman Janacek? Or Bartok the cradle robber? Or Kodaly? I know them."

"So that could explain why your music has changed so much, Milos." said David. "It was hard for us to believe that you could write something so radically different from your earlier quartets. And frankly hard for us to decide on whether to perform it or not in this concert."

"I'm really glad you decided to." said Cammy, defensively. "It is great music."

"But it is not like something by George Crumb, for example. Our reputation and experience with avantgarde music almost prevents us from playing music that doesn't conform."

"Nonsense." said Milos. "You've played a number of works from India which display extremely old traditional and conservative musical forms."

"You're right, Milos." answered Sherba. "But I have to say we were all very much surprised when we tried it on to see if it would fit. I, for one, enjoyed playing it. You quote a lot of musical predecessors. don't mind if it is filled with tonal passages."

The Dutt offered a funny comment, "Here's the headline: Old composer finds rejuvenation through beautiful young muse, and starts composing tonal music after a lifelong career writing in serialism and minimalism."

"You could be talking about Penderecki, you know," said Milosh, "or Bartok for that matter. They changed their style completely in their old age."

Around the table there was laughter, but I was a little confused. It was kind of an insiders' joke. Because I did not really know the ins and outs of modern, avant-garde music. I've never actually listened much to it—most of the works of the last century—and in the BPhil, the music director never scheduled any. I could say that what I have heard, however, I have not liked much and would never choose to listen to it a second time.

Cammy protested a little; "But so much of modernist music sounds like the works of insiders composing for insiders."

"You put your finger on it exactly, Cammy." said Milosh. "Have you ever listened to any of my earlier works?"

"No. I can't say that I have," she answered.

"Me neither," I chipped in.

"There's not much of my corpus of works that is published on CDs or otherwise. But there is some. More has been recorded in Czechia and occasionally I get some royalties from there, which would suggest that there are some sales now and then. But those Czech CDs are hard to find or acquire. I bought six titles while we were in Prague. Remember?"

"Oh. No, I don't remember."

"And have you in Kronos included any of my quartets on any of your discs?"

David answered, "I think we have. One anyway, more than fifteen years ago. But I don't remember the title. I'll have to look for it."

"If you have time, and would like, Cammy, you can come over to my place and listen to what I have on discs."

"Yeah, I could do that. Our season doesn't start as you know until the end of September, so I have lots of free time in the next two weeks."

"It'd be great to get your reaction," said Milos, "but don't worry, to love me, you don't have to love my music. Especially my earlier, misguided music."

I noticed that Milos did not include me in this invitation. Up to then he had often been careful to include me whenever he invited Cammy for something in front of me.

"Your mentor friend, Carl Husa, said he likes your music," said Cammy. "and so did your friend Jiri."

"And I like your quartets, Milos," said Hank Dutt lifting the last of his champagne to his lips. "All of them."

It was an evening, after a difficult concert program, of lots of camaraderie and good feeling all around. It was one of the most memorable days in my musical life up to then. But I felt as if I were falling away from Cammy, even as I was coming to know Milos—or should I say Milosh—better than ever.

# Chapter Four



MaddyGirl: I'm flying home in a week. Have to return to Cleveland on 2nd January. Got plans around Christmas?

HautBois Cam: Actually yes. On the 22nd I plan to go to my parents' house and celebrate Christmas there. My sister and her family will be coming too.

MaddyGirl: Sounds good. Maybe we can get together before you go to Salem, in Boston, or at your place?

HautBois Cam: Yeah. Maybe in the week after Christmas you can come up to Salem to visit and eat some Christmas leftovers.

MaddyGirl: Okay. It's been a long time. And I haven't really eaten so well while I've been away.

HautBois Cam: You've lost weight as a newly minted professional?

MaddyGirl: Yep.

HautBois Cam: Any plans going forward?

MaddyGirl: Well actually I'm getting together with some of the flute girls to play some Xmas music at the Cambridge MIT mall. Before Xmas. It's good money over two days.

HautBois Cam: That sounds promising. I'm taking Milos out to dinner for his birthday on the 28th. I've bought him the latest iPhone for his birthday present. I'll have to teach him how to use it.

MaddyGirl: Sounds good. I got the latest model for myself too. Still having trouble learning all the glitches and changes in apps. I'll call you then when I'm back in town.

HautBois Cam: Do that. You probably have a lot to catch me up with.

MaddyGirl: Yep. Ciao4Now Dying to see you.

HautBois Cam: Me too, you.


I got home, or let's say, got to my apartment in Allston, on Christmas Eve Day. So, I had missed the opportunity to see Cammy before she had run up to Salem. Unlike Cleveland everything around Boston looked so depressing and bleak. There was no snow on the ground, and there were almost no Christmas decorations up around Allston. The streets were slick, wet and the sidewalks sticky and cluttered with litter. I had forgotten how rude and harsh the taxi drivers in Boston are. I had delayed my return flight to Boston so I could spend a few nights with my new boyfriend there. As I dumped my stuff in the apartment in Allston, I saw how empty my life was there; no friends nearby, no work, and the accumulated dust of more than three months being outside the apartment. There was in the mail an inquiry whether I wanted to renew the rental agreement in February—along with an announcement of a rent increase. Merry Christmas. I decided then I would go out to my mother's house in Worcester for Christmas, but I had to move fast, before the public transport closed for the day.

Through the holiday I called my boyfriend, Justin, several times. He missed me. As I did him. I had a hollow feeling clawing inside me. I wanted to jump back in bed with him. He's a wonderful lover, we rubbed each other raw with sex in the previous week, and we both wanted more.

So, as it happened, I decided to fly back to Cleveland on the 29th. And I didn't get to see Cammy on this short visit. The only thing I had to do was to confirm with the manager at the BPhil that my seat was still held for me, until mid-February when my temporary appointment with the Cleveland Orchestra was set to expire. With that business done on the Monday after Christmas, there was nothing keeping me in Allston, or keeping me away from Justin and his tender and vigorous embraces.

**Windows Chat Messaging**                    **December 29, 2009**

MaddyGirl: Sorry, but I have to dash back to Cleveland. I won't be able to visit with you this time. My BF is dying to have me again. Be back in Feb

HautBois Cam: Oh, that's too bad. I took Milos out for his birthday dinner last night. At Durgin Park. You know the place in Faneuil Hall where everyone sits at the same long table. I had schrod and he had coke braised short ribs—nothing very glamorous or fancy. The whole place sang Happy Birthday for him when they brought the cake out with candles. And then things got rowdier and friendlier. I'll send you the photos. But delicious. His dish especially. Some of our neighboring diners took lots of very good photos. My favorite one I'm attaching. He's kissing and hugging me, as we stood up. I nearly fell into his cake. It reminds me of that famous photo of the sailor kissing the nurse in Times Sq at the end of WWII. You know the one?

MaddyGirl: Lol, yeah, I know it. Where's his sailor's cap? Ha ha ha.

HautBois Cam: He drove me back to Slummerville afterwards and we continued drinking. It was really funny. I was giving him lessons on how to use his new Smart Fone, but our fingers were fumbling over the keys, we were so drunk. Drank until we both fell over drunk. Passed out. But this morning he cleared out real early—after fixing me a breakfast. Gus is flying in later today. Milos left behind the Apple box and instructions on the living room table. Got to hide them away.

MaddyGirl: Maybe I'll see Gus in the airport on my way out. But maybe not. I probably wouldn't recognize him anymore.

HautBois Cam: Doubtful you'll see him. He's flying in on Lufthansa from Germany.

MaddyGirl: What's he coming for?

HautBois Cam: We're still married, FBOW, and he owns this place. He's got time off.

MaddyGirl: Worse I think rather than better. Alright. See you in February.

HautBois Cam: KIT. Bye

MaddyGirl: Bye bye. Don't forget to post the photos in the Durgin.

I got back from Cleveland around Valentine's Day. I no longer had Justin hanging around my neck or petting my private parts. We broke up over the winter: he is saying that I wasn't doing enough for him (I think he only meant sexually, but I'm not sure as we had a huge roaring fight before he stormed out of my life and stopped answering his messages.) I was devastated for about four days, but then in the end you just have to carry on. I think I'm over Justin now. In the interim six weeks or so Cammy and I wrote rarely. She wrote briefly to tell me that Milosh was so busy composing that she was afraid he was going to have a breakdown. And that to make matters worse he had subbed for Levine also four times so far this season. She really liked how he led the orchestra as a conductor. I had to start preparing for a concert on the next day after I landed, for a Thursday concert. We agreed to meet after rehearsal on Wednesday because she also had an afternoon rehearsal.

But Cammy did not talk much about herself or "her Milosh" except to say that he was very busy composing and she was very concerned about him, overworking himself. Instead, I told her the whole story of my audition and my supposed success in Cleveland. I believe Milos's help on that last Sunday before the audition made a lot of difference: it was the first time I had gotten to a final of a major orchestra's audition.

And they made out that I had won the final, but a week after I got back to Boston, they told me that I had won, but that they wanted a five-month trial period for me to see if they would accept me, if I could, please, start the very next week. This was for the second seat—Jesus! For second seat they could not decide and would only give me a try out. They did pay me the regular salary—and that was nice, a lot more than I make at the BPhil, but I blew my chances I think because of that torrid affair with Justin. Men believe they are in love when their penises tell them that they've got enough. And that meant he came after me almost every night for a month. Toward the end of my stay in Cleveland I was worn out and over-tired and not practicing nearly enough. So maybe the quality of my playing fell off—I think I can definitely say that. And come mid February they told me sorry it wasn't going to work for them, and they'd be in touch if they had any other needs. At least they paid me in full, as they had promised, sixty percent more than what I earned in a year with the BPhil. And it still looks good on my resume.

It was that Sunday after the Carnegie Hall concert with Kronos, that was the first and only time I worked with Milosh. It was a life changing experience for me. I'll remember it forever.

Milosh, as he had offered, came to our room in the Meridien after breakfast. He had me play all the pieces that I had been required to prepare. On the Debussy especially he told me to tone down the tremolo I was putting in. He had said, "try to think of the sound of the flute at the beginning of Smetana's Ma Vlast. You want this passage here to sound like gurgling water, but in Debussy the waters are in an ocean, so it cannot be a heavy tremolo." I'll remember that all my life. He also pointed out some improvements I could make in the Mendelssohn. Approaches I had not thought of. So, we ran through this piece, and I repeated it maybe four times to get it to his liking. He also made a suggestion that I had never gotten before in any of the master classes I had paid so much money for. He asked me to hold my flute up a little bit more. "You'll project your sound better that way." He came near me and gently put his hands around me from behind and lifted my flute, so it was a little above the horizontal—I apparently had been playing it at about eight o'clock, as he said, well below the horizontal. I felt an immediate electricity as his arms were around me and I could feel his warm breath. Cammy was in the room with us, and she agreed that she thought my tone was now really good after those changes. And she liked my technique too. I don't think she was jealous at all the close attention he paid to me. All this flashed by and by one o'clock, we went down to the front lobby, I checked out, they said goodbye, standing close together as if they were my parents seeing me off to college or something, and I left by taxi for LaGuardia. The next day, I started the audition all excited, but also confident.

**Windows Chat Messaging**                    **September 16, 2009**

MaddyGirl: Hey Cammy. Believe it or not I won! I WON THE AUDITION. I was the last man—or girl standing. HURRA! I'm so HAPPY I'M SO HAPPY. I COULD BURST.

HautBois Cam: Congrats Maddie. I always knew you could do it. When do they want you to start?

MaddyGirl: I haven't been told the details yet. And they haven't told me just what I won. But they did say I was picked as the top. At the starting line there were 110 girls and boys who qualified for this audition. Can you believe it? I was better than 109 of them.

HautBois Cam: That's amazing. I'm so proud and happy for you. I must say, though, I think you deserved it.

MaddyGirl: Yeah. Got to dash to the plane. CU.

**Windows Chat Messaging**                    **September 18, 2009**

MaddyGirl: Bummer. I just got their offer letter. The Cleveland people are only offering me a trial appointment. For only five months. They will make another evaluation and decision then.

HautBois Cam: Sorry to hear that. That seems really deceptive.

MaddyGirl: Yeah. And they want me only if I agree to start on Monday, in three days! Can you imagine? I hardly have enough time to pack. But still I'm going to accept. So many things to do before I leave.

MaddyGirl: Could you come to my place on Saturday morning and help me pack? And help me close up the apartment.

HautBois Cam: Yeah. I'm not working yet. I can come. How about at 11?

MaddyGirl: Maybe 10:30? That would do me better. Also, I'm a little short on money now. No income for almost four months is rough. Could you lend me airfare and maybe $200 more so I can live in Cleveland? They'll pay my hotel for a week until I can get on my feet.

HautBois Cam: No problem, sure. Maybe we can go to Nordstrom's and buy you a new concert dress too, after we're finished in your apartment?

MaddyGirl: That'd be nice.

HautBois Cam: Don't worry. You can take it as a loan as well, pay me back later, when you can.

MaddyGirl: Okay. I have to run down to the BPhil office now and ask if they can put me on leave until the second half of February. And then I'll send these characters in Cleveland my answer. I can't really negotiate anything with them.

HautBois Cam: They do have a strong hand in all these arrangements.

MaddyGirl: And they take advantage of it to the extreme. Ok CU tomorrow.

Strange I wrote that only in the morning of the day when Burt made an advance on me in his office at the BPhil. Talk about taking advantage of someone. I told Cammy all about it the next day as we were packing in my place. I was there to ask him if I could take five months leave and not have to resign from the orchestra. Burt is a hunk, and he knows it. He's the orchestra manager, and apparently, he likes his job because for a long time he's had his way with young females (high school and college age girls) trying to get into the orchestra or get promotions. Anyway, as I was telling him about the circumstances, he seemed very agreeable and understanding. No problems. We were standing somewhat close together and then suddenly he took my hand and placed it on his male member—which was already erect—as if to suggest that if I sucked him off there in the office, or something more, he would agree to my request. Well, I jumped as I gasped. Didn't really scream, but I should have. I couldn't believe he'd do such a thing. He said simply, "Relax, calm down. No need to make a scandal. Just a small transaction." The thing was I felt immediately aroused by him—and also very angry, intensely angry. I didn't know what to do or say. Finally, I said. "You're not getting anything. Something for nothing won't go, buster. I'll send you my request in writing in an hour or so. And I'll copy the music director. And you'll agree." And I stormed out. Cammy chuckled when I told her. "Yeah, as I said, they have a strong hand, and they take advantage of it." "To the max, you know." Cammy then told me how she'd been approached by guys in the BSO in almost the same way. Apparently, there it occurs a lot as well. But the rumors were that the worst offender was Levine himself, with boys and young men trying to get into the orchestra—at Tanglewood especially. And then she told me that not long before the first trumpet player, a married man named Dan, had groped her, actually pinched her teat. And then seemed to ask for more. She told Milos about that incident.

"And you know what? The very next time he was rehearsing us—it was a hot and humid day and everyone was dressed minimally, you know, tank tops and shorts, so there was a lot of bare skin exposed especially among the women players—he stopped the orchestra and addressing us said something to the effect that we were not teenagers any more having fun exploring each other in summer camp, but we were professionals and responsible adults. And that "it had come to my attention that there are some predatory people, I am not saying whom, who feel it was alright to touch or make sexual passes at the women." But it wasn't and he said he would not abide by it, nor would the management. So those who feel it's alright to grope a woman here should cut it out or leave." He said all this quietly but sternly, all the while staring directly only at Dan. Cammy continued, "I think everyone got the message. Dan maybe was too thick skinned to react or to even blush—maybe he thinks he had done nothing wrong. Or maybe he had already forgotten about the incident with me. I was trying hard not to blush as Milos said these words, so I occupied myself by cleaning out my oboe. Later when we had a private moment, Milos asked for my forgiveness for speaking out like that. He hated the idea of people making unwanted passes, especially when they were in advantaged positions."

"But Dan won't pay the price for groping you, will he?"

"No, I'm afraid not. But in the past two months he has not come at all close to me, he's definitely avoiding my presence. And I hope that continues. So of course, I do appreciate it that Milos spoke out and tried to shame him. Then again, Dan is a married man, and maybe if his wife was told…"

"And Milos has never made a pass at you?"

"No, he's very careful about that. Kisses and hugs maybe, in greeting, but he has never touched me sexually or caressed me as if to start something. He's said that he would not because I am a married woman, and I have not shown him that I want those kinds of advances. Which was true at the beginning but may be not true now. He's very gentlemanly with me. But I know for certain he loves me. But we don't talk much about his desires."

"Well, convey to him my thanks once again for the help he gave me last week. I've never had a master class that was near as insightful as his professional comments. And he's not even a flute player."

And so, we left it, when I was running out of town in a big hurry. At that time, I didn't know when, or even if, I would be back. Maybe after five months. Maybe longer.

As it was, by late that winter, I was very busy working again in the BPhil and back in my apartment in Allston—snug and warmer than the junky little apartment I had in frigid Cleveland. We performed ten concerts in the next two months, and in late March I was promoted to principal—meaning first seat flute—which meant I became more conspicuous, and I got a raise which was very helpful. With what I had earned in Cleveland and the increased income from the BPhil I was able to start paying off my burden of student loans from my conservatory days. I also paid Cammy back for her loans for the air tix and my new concert dress. Paying down my debts was a good feeling. I was beginning to stand on my own feet, and I was getting acknowledgement of my talent.

Cammy and I met four or five times over lunch in those two months— on days when we both had afternoon rehearsals on Huntington Ave. She told me the news that her premiere of the Milos's oboe concerto was scheduled for the first weekend of May, actually three concerts on April 30th and the 1st and 2nd of May. Furthermore, she told me that she had started rehearsing her part which was difficult enough and that 'her Milosh' was going to help her practice the part at his apartment, in his piano room on the first floor of his brick three-decker. She told me that Levine was not going to conduct those concerts—he was receiving some sort of treatment and by March had taken leave for the rest of the season—but instead a guest conductor was scheduled, a man named

Gilbert whom nobody had heard anything about. Milos was already busy conducting a number of the spring concerts, and the principal assistant conductor was going to cover all the rest of Levine's schedule. We checked my concert schedule to see if I could attend her concerto premiere. Right then and there I whipped out my iPhone 3S (I had finally bought it at Cammy's urgings) and I looked at BPhil's concert schedule for the spring. And we were in luck, I did not have my own concert obligation on Sunday, the 2nd. So, sitting in Pan Asian, our favorite meeting place, I googled the BSO ticket office and bought myself a ticket for them. No way I was going to miss Cammy's solo performance and Milos's concerto written for her. Cammy tried to stop me, suggesting that I first ask Milos where his seat was and then buy a neighboring seat. But I already had sent my order in and so I was booked. I probably wouldn't be sitting next to Milos.

During one of these pre-rehearsal lunches Cammy told me that she and Milos had started a new tradition since the New Year: Milos would meet her after evening concerts and take her home, either by metro—which required a good long walk from Central Square—or by his car. This was working out to two or three nights almost every weekend since the beginning of January. They still got together for lunch or dinner once a fortnight, usually followed by a long stroll down the Back Bay and over to the Boston Public Garden.

She told me that during one of those concert evenings, in late January, it had started to snow hard and by the time the concert had ended the snow had socked in the city, and all transport had ceased moving, including the T, which as we all know has a lot of its lines running above ground. In the backstage area, Milos met her that night as he usually did that month with a look of grave concern. He said to her that it was impossible to move around town because the streets were uncleared and full of drifts and there were white-out conditions, and that as much as he would like he couldn't escort her home to Somerville. But she would certainly be welcome to come stay in his house overnight. It was only a twelve—or fifteen-minute walk away on a gentrified section of Tremont Street. He had even brought a kind of woolen poncho to wrap her up, because the temperature had fallen so low and the winds were icy cold. Cammy said: "Milosh is always looking after me and thinking about what I might need. He is the nicest, warmest man I have ever known." And on this foul night she needed just what he was proposing. So she went with him to his house. She was surprised because it was so close to the Symphony Hall but it seemed to take forever to get there, as they were stumbling and having a tough time advancing through the drifts and against the wind. When they finally got there, he said to her, "You see? It is only eight hundred meters away." Cammy told me that this really struck her. After forty years in the U.S. Milos was still figuring distance in meters. But inside, his house was warm, and no windows leaked. He immediately offered her a hot chocolate and asked if she would like anything else to eat. When she then said that she did not, he then gave her a tour of his house—it was the first time she had stepped inside, he had shown her the outside before on one of their walks. She was most impressed with the bare piano studio, as he called it, which occupied almost all of the first floor. There was only a baby grand piano with a bench, and a very large computer screen standing on a computer table, and several floor spot lamps. Other than that, the room was empty, nothing hanging on the walls even. "Don't want anything that would soak up the sounds," he had said. They sat in the main room on the second floor on two couches that were facing opposite each other while she drank her hot chocolate. She asked him how he liked the concert to which he answered that he had heard it on Friday night and had liked it, but he wasn't sure he liked how the conductor led the third piece, a composition by Ravel. Cammy said as they were talking that she was worrying that for sure, unlike in New York or in Prague, he would try to take her to bed with him that night. And she was a little tense. She admitted to me that she, at the same time as she was worrying, wasn't sure if she wanted to make love to him or feared the prospect. She had feelings throughout that evening that she wanted him to make love to her, but she thought the circumstances were not right. Milos himself was acting a bit funny and uncomfortable. He asked if she would like a cognac or a slivovitz, but she suspected that he was trying to get her a little drunk as preparation. And then she became even more suspicious when he showed her where she could sleep, in a large bedroom with a double bed which was already made up, and he took out from a drawer a clear plastic bag with a woman's flannel night gown in it. She said that Milos embarrassingly explained that he had bought it for a girlfriend he had had more than twenty years earlier, but that she had never worn it, and he had never thrown it out. He even had a new toothbrush in its original sales cartridge, unused. But, Cammy said, the real let down was when he excused himself asking if she drank coffee or tea with breakfast and backed out of the room with a soft "Good night, Camille." Not even reaching for a kiss. She recalled to me that she did not sleep at all well that night. The wind continued to howl around the house so that the windows ached and whistled, from time to time she heard him stepping gently around his room next to hers, and that as she slept, she kept thinking of him sneaking in and caressing her as he slipped under the covers with her, wearing nothing at all. But all that was in her imagination—maybe her dreams were filled with such desire—but by morning she was still warm and alone in the big double bed in a large bedroom.

When Cammy finished telling me this story, I couldn't help myself, "Cammy. It sounds like you need a man in your life. And Milos is the one." She didn't say anything to that. But she also didn't glower at me or frown. Eventually she said, "Maybe."

"But the next weekend, after the concerts, we resumed just as we had before. But without the weather interruption. I even went out one morning and bought a bottle of cognac to be able to offer to him when he took me home by the T, so that I could offer him a nightcap. He's always accepted—except of course on the nights when he has driven me home—and then always he says goodnight and returns home."

"Aw come on, Cammy. Can't you admit it? You love this guy Milos—Milos. And you want to reciprocate his love for you. So, what's holding you back? Don't you think you have to make the first advance on him? Open up, for God's sake."

That conversation was in early April, I seem to remember. Most of the assaults of winter were long over, and even the kite flying weather—windiness was over when on Monday the 19th I got a message from Cammy.

19 April 2010

**CammyFB**

HELP! Catastrophe! Maddie, can you come over
early this evening to my place? I need you and your
advice. BAD!

**MADDIE**

Sure. What's wrong? Something so serious?

**CammyFB**

I got a letter from Gus. Bad news. I'll show you
when you get here. Much tears.

**MADDIE**

I'll be there

So early that evening I went over to Somerville by the T, walking up from Central Square in a hurry along the narrow brick sidewalk, almost stumbling several times. Cammy did not come down to the door to let me up as she had before. Instead, she rang the door-phone to let me in, saying "Come on up. I'm in the main room on the third floor. The door is open." Remember she was still renting out the first and second floors of the three-decker to other young families. When I saw Cammy, she looked like a wreck. She had been crying and obviously throwing herself around the room. Her laptop was standing open in the middle of the table in the middle of the room, next to a music stand that had no sheet music on it.

"Here come read this, Maddie."

I looked at the screen. There was a word file, a letter, which bore Gus's name at the sign-off at the bottom of the page. It went like this. I was surprised by his poor spelling and I have noted his errors along the way—it is obvious he doesn't know how to use spell check or he doesn't have it for English text. I of course had forgotten that as a German who had come to the Conservatory and to the U.S. for advanced violin training only at the age of 19, that his command of English was never fluent. And as he was spending most of his time in the past four years back in Germany, it is not surprising I guess that he made misspellings.

My dear Camilla (sic), my love and my wive, (sic)

I regret needing to write this letter, but the time has finally arrived when I cannot defer (sic) it any longer. It can come as no surprise to you to understand that our marriage, started so promising, is now a complete failure and so it should (sic) be terminated. I am asking you for a divorce, to be completed as quickly and painlessly—although divorces are never painless—as possible.

I would ask you to initiate a divorce proceeding (sic) there in the state of Massachusetts (sic), as soon as possible. We should take the path of no-fault divorce process. I do not blame you, and although I probably bear some blame, I won't go into that. Probably our marriage from the beginning was a mistake, a dreadful (sic) mistake. I want to release you of all further obligations to me, so you can happily and freely carry on with your own life. As you may have understood, I have really no desire to come back to live in Boston.

Please let me know of your desires in this case, how you wish to go forward.

I am yours truly,

Gustav

Well, that about said it all; I could see why Cammy thought it was an awful catastrophe. She no doubt was blaming herself, facing up for the first time what had no doubt been quietly gnawing away at her inside for five years. That her marriage was a mistake, and very likely a mistake of her own making. She had fallen for him. The older man, worldly with an educated accent, a successful music career—even well-renowned. She had fallen for that, hard.

"And I should have known almost right from our wedding night," Cammy said more to herself half out loud than to me.

"What should you have known?"

"My father knew or at least suspected. But he kept his mouth closed."

"He knew what? I don't understand, Cammy."

"When I first opened this letter and read it, I was furious. And I raged for an hour, and then I sent him an email right back as a response to his letter. I told him, 'Skype me'. He almost never called to talk to me in the past four years while he was in Europe. Well, he did. I took the call and let him know that I was angry as hell at him. I was shouting at him on the line. 'You bastard, you fucking bastard, you can't even tell me—you don't have the decency to give me any reasons for your wanting a divorce.' He said at first what was the point, he wanted a no-fault divorce why probe at things they all knew to be true and that their marriage had failed and had been a failure from the start. I kept shouting at him. Called him all kinds of names. And then finally he calmly told me: 'Cammy I want a divorce so I can marry my life partner here, Albert, the true love of my life.' Now calm down and set out the terms for our divorce and we can get on with our lives."

"So, I should have known. On our wedding night, we made love alright. Like normal couples. I was full of passion and desire. But even before the week was out, he was trying to butt fuck me. And I wouldn't let him. Not even get close. And his reaction was to withdraw from me completely. We had almost no further love life—I mean no further sex—after that first week of our marriage. And after that he began steadily sliding away from me, European concert tours where he did not want my presence, until he decided to move permanently to Germany. And now he wants to carry on, with his real character. Why did he ever agree to marry me—when he knew his orientation? And stupid me, I thought it was just a momentary aberration. Hoping for a long time that we still had a marriage and a future love life together."

"What should I do?" asked Cammy, having trouble holding back the tears.

"Divorce him," I said rather too flippantly. "Take him for every penny. And only through a divorce with fault. Maybe if you got a divorce lawyer's advice, it would be best."

Cammy then started to cry. I didn't know what to say. She had never really related to me her feelings for Gus, and I had known nothing about the early days of their marriage. I can say that from the very start of their relationship—which I think she pursued, much more than he had—I didn't like the guy. Not at all. And I thought that their marriage was a big mistake. But I had hidden those feelings from Cammy. The heart moves in mysterious ways, as they always say. So why should I interfere and reveal my impressions—which could have been totally wrong.

Quickly I realized that in just a few days' time she was going to be performing Milos's oboe concerto, and that she couldn't help facing Milos because he was rehearsing her, as she had told me, in his house.

She certainly couldn't hide her feelings. Maybe she would be too unstable to be able to play the concerto. That would be very bad. But I didn't see anything I could do to help avoid that outcome. She'd have to pull through on her own. And maybe Milos could help her and support her. But I have to admit that Cammy has always been a very strong-willed girl.

After a long while, she settled down a little. I asked if she'd like me to fix her a cup of coffee. She nodded so I went off and barged and banged around her kitchen until I was able to come back with a mug of hot coffee with cream.

"You'll need to tell Milos, somehow."

"Yeah, I know. But I'm afraid he'll straight-away ask me to marry him."

"I don't see what's so wrong with that."

"I've pushed him off from that idea for so long, I think my chance has come and gone. And I don't know if I can love him."

"It doesn't seem like it would be too difficult. He treats you so nicely."

For the next hour or two her moods shifted from anger to sorrow, and to self-pity and then back. I mostly listened but she became more and more incoherent.

"You know, I could suggest that we step out and get something to eat. It's already nearly nine o'clock. Maybe your hunger is unbalancing you."

And I was right. We went to a nearby Indian curry house, and as soon as she ate some meat curry—"not too spicy please"—with saffron rice, she began to calm down.

"Cammy, you're upset and have every right to be. It's like you've been hit by a swinging bat that you did not see coming. But really, ask yourself: Does Gus asking you for a divorce absolutely change anything in your emotional life, or your day to day life and self-identity? I don't think so."

Cammy thought about that for a few moments. "You're right Maddie. It doesn't change anything, except maybe my relationship to Milos. And my life plan changes. I think I told you once that I looked to get a man, establish my career, and get a baby or two. So going forward I have only one of those goals, and likely cannot easily achieve the goal of having children."

"But you're still mistaken. Getting married is not a very worthwhile goal, in of itself. After all, you were married for what? seven years, and it was loveless and for the most part a lonely experience. Even that wedding ring on your finger does little for you, except maybe shoo away unwanted attention from guys you don't know or care to know. Getting love is a better target to aim for. I know that is what I want." "I hadn't realized you'd become a philosopher of female life, Maddie. Why aren't you eating your bamya?"

"I don't like bamya. It's too slimy—like a lot of guys."

"So when do you go to rehearse next with Milos? I mean the oboe concerto?"

"On Wednesday at three o'clock."

"So that leaves you time to go see a divorce lawyer before you get there. And I would suggest the lawyer my mother used. She's really good and her advice is always really sharp. She will prepare for you the terms and conditions that you might want from Gus."

"I don't want anything more from Gus. Just now I want him completely out of my life in every way."

"So you can start by taking off the wedding band right now, Cammy. But don't throw it away. You can probably sell it for the gold value."

"Yeah, so I could." and Cammy took the band off with some difficulty and then dropped it in the coin purse of her wallet. "There, take that Gus Tichon. I look forward to forgetting about you."

We parted late that evening in Inman Square; she was feeling somewhat restored, I think. I think she'll get over him quickly once she stops blaming herself for making the initial mistake of marrying that jerk.

**22 April 2010**

**CammyFB**

You were so right. I met with the lawyer you recommended and she was so helpful in clearing my mind of Gus. She's going to make up a term sheet for the divorce, and she also recommends that I sue him with fault. She thought of so many reasons: abandonment, alienation, adultery. To name a few.

> **MADDIE**
>
> Good, I'm glad that she's helped you Did you have your rehearsal session with Milos yesterday? How are you coming along?

**CammyFB**

Yes, I did. He had me play through the whole piece— it's 23-24 minutes long. And I play most of that time. He played the orchestral part on the piano. I don't think I'll play it from memory. But the sheet music is what Milos has printed out. All the parts will be from print outs. The orchestra manager is busy just now printing and taping together every part now.

> **MADDIE**
>
> Ha, ha. So how many pages is your part?

**CammyFB**

9 pages. It's no big deal. Apparently the publisher won't have the printed scores ready for another few months. Milosh used the neatest gadget: It's a score reader that he plays on the new iPad. He's becoming a fan of technology. He doesn't have to turn pages with this app.

**MADDIE**
Cool.

**CammyFB**

The hardest part is that I have to stand for the entire 24 mins. I've never done that before. Are you engaged in concerts this weekend?

**MADDIE**
Yes, gotta run now.

**CammyFB**

Our rehearsals start next Tuesday. The guest conductor flies in from Toronto on Monday and we have six rehearsals before our first concert on Friday. Big program: Mahler's 3rd, and Vaughan Williams' Lark Ascending. Pretty piece

<hr>

**27 April 2010**

**MADDIE**

I've got a date who is coming with me to your concert. Are you about ready? Is Milos pleased with your progress?

**CammyFB**
Very much. He was almost crying with delight when we finished the other day.

**MADDIE**

Have you told Milos about Gus and the divorce?

**CammyFB**

Not yet. I thought maybe after the concert. The lawyer said as soon as Gus agrees to the terms of divorce—the settlement between us—I can file for divorce right away. I think I'll tell Milos only then. But at the moment he is SO busy. He's working on a symphonic poem as part of his composer in residence requirements. And he just got a commission from his friend Jiri in Prague for an orchestral piece for next year's Prague Spring Festival, and he also has started work on an opera.

**MADDIE**

If he's so busy, is he planning on going to Tanglewood this summer? Are you?

**CammyFB**

I am. But he's so busy with everything that he might pass on the Tanglewood Academy and only drive out there for the concerts that he's conducting. Levine is definitely out for the entire summer. His health. It looks like this summer I'll miss him for weeks at a time.

**MADDIE**

Not good. So, I'll see you backstage after your Sunday concert.

**CammyFB**
Gladly.

Actually, a funny thing happened to me during late April. That orchestra manager, Burt, who made a sexual advance on me last fall when I was asking him to hold a position for me until I got back from Cleveland, he's actually a really good-looking hunk. And he wears his trousers tight which highlights his rather long limp dick. So, he was standing around backstage after we were wrapping up a rehearsal, I suddenly on impulse to give him back what he dishes out. I went up to him and approached really close to him before he was fully aware I was coming at him. I grabbed him by his hanging dick and I took it and squeezed hard. "Hey Burt, your manliness might want to go out on a date with me?" He jumped up like a started mouse and gave a loud squeal. I let go and said, "So what do you say Burt? Care to go out for a drink at the bar on the next street?" He was still trying to recollect his composure. And then he got really embarrassed. "Erh, I can't, Maddie. I'm a married man." "Well of course you are. So last time we met, you were just out fishing for some free girls' twat, in your spare time?" "What do you mean?" "Never mind Burt. But I think your wife wouldn't be pleased either to learn that you're groping the women in the orchestra. Not only that, you might be going out to drink with them." He was obviously dumbfounded. But maybe he'll learn something from my forwardness.

And afterwards, instead of heading straight home, I decided to go to a bar to have a drink and maybe meet a more regular guy. And for some reason I decided to go to the Cheers Beacon Hill—you know the place that was the namesake bar of the TV sitcom. Not that it is at all like the TV Cheers. But it was just on impulse. I've not done anything like that before, although I had visited this bar several times with groups of friends. I was sitting by myself at a small table when at about seven-thirty a small ensemble set up in one corner of the bar and began playing pop jazz pieces, not too loud. I decided to stay longer to listen to them, and so I ordered a second glass of cider, and the main course Boston baked beans with a small side salad. After about twenty minutes of playing or so, I thought the guy playing the saxophone looked familiar to me, but I couldn't place where I'd maybe seen him before. It bothered me so when they took their break and all of them filed over to the bar, I got up the courage to step up to him and introduce myself. And ask him where I had seen him before. Sounds pretty corny for a pickup line, doesn't it? He of course couldn't say, and he looked embarrassed. "Well, maybe at one of my gigs at another place, if not here." I said no, and then he said that he'd gone to the Berklee conservatory where he studied saxophone, jazz, and piano. That was a connection. I said that I'd gone to NE Conservatory, studying flute and that now I play in the BPhil. "Ah, maybe that's it," he said. "I play occasionally with the BPhil when they need a saxophone part." And that was it. He had a familiar face because maybe three or four times I'd seen him come to play his alto sax with us at the orchestra. So, I stayed in the bar listening to their second session, which finished at a little past nine o'clock. And then after he had packed up and said goodbye to his mates, he came over to my little table and joined me. We each had a beer, and we talked for an hour and a half. And when we were ready to leave, he with his big saxophone case, I with my flute backpack, we both headed to the T: he for the red line, and I for the Green Line. No invitations to home, no kiss at the doorstep. But we both agreed it'd be nice if we met again over drinks on an evening when he didn't have to play a gig. I suggested that he attend the concert we were giving in Jordan Hall on that coming Sunday, and we could go out to a bar afterwards. He said swell, and that he would. "Okay, so I'll see you there at the crew entrance after the concert," I said, not really feeling highly confident that he would show up. His name, by the way, is Jacob. He looked Jewish, too. But I have to stress, he looked really handsome, not anything like the boys who play the flute with me.

And I saw him a few days later after the concert waiting outside the crew entrance—without his big saxophone case—and we walked around to Mass Ave and went into a bar that we had used a lot during our conservatory days. Again, we talked a long time—he's really an interesting guy, travels a lot giving gigs—until it was late and then I invited him to join me in a regular date—namely going to the BSO concert on an early Sunday evening to hear my best friend play oboe in a premiere performance of concerto written just for her. And that's how Jacob kinda climbed into my life.

**30 April 2010**

**CammyFB**

Maddie, the concert was a smash success. I really topped myself with the concerto. I got two curtain calls. And Onjinian is a really good conductor. He had consulted with Milos and everything went just as we practiced and rehearsed. I'm so stoked for tonight's concert. The review in the Globe is glowing. The reviewer even mentioned my name. Look it up on their website. www.Globe.com1x/concertreview.

**MADDIE**

You're so right. I look forward to Sunday. See you at backstage entrance.
Our BPhil concert was not memorable. Lacked zip and zing.

**CammyFB**

We had the after-concert party last night. On Sunday, join me and Milos at his house afterwards for champagne.

At the concert Jacob and I sat eagerly waiting for the concerto, Cammy's piece. The Mahler was super, apparently Jacob is crazy about Mahler's music. As you may know BPhil doesn't play Mahler because it is too hard for us, and it costs too much. Cammy played her usual first seat in the Mahler, but after the intermission, she did not come out to play the next piece. The concerto really surprised me. It was so positive and light and airy. The opening lines on the oboe solo are a series of rising lines, like birdsong rising up into the air. After these lines play the rising notes five or six times, the flute and the English horn join in and play back or play a harmonic line matching the same bright theme. It reminded me of the Strauss Oboe concerto. I'll have to ask Milos if he intended that similarity, or if he was inspired by it. I read that for Strauss his oboe concerto was part of his twilight years compositions, his thinking of his own imminent death. I wonder if Milos had any that in mind. He says that he was inspired by the love he feels for Cammy and her joyful inner voice, both speaking voice and oboe voice.

I was really excited standing at the backstage door for Cammy to come out. Jacob hovered near me apparently wondering what to say. And before Cammy appeared Milos came and found us. I was a little surprised and concerned because it seemed to me that in the long time since I had last seen him, he looked as if he had lost weight, and his hair was now mostly gray, as if he had aged. He looked now like he was an old man, he resembled for the first time his own age, no longer looking like a man much younger than his true age. But I didn't say anything. I'd have to ask Cammy.

"Wasn't it wonderful? I mean Cammy's playing, of course." he said as he gave me a greeting hug and a kiss on the cheek. "I'm so pleased for Cammy—soon there will be requests from recording companies that will want her to record other concertos."

"Milos, that was a fine piece of music. I really liked it. When will the publisher get it out in print version?"

"They said by the end of the summer. But I suspect later."

"Milos, this is my boyfriend, Jacob."

"You'll come with Cammy and me, won't you, to my house for drinks to Cammy's premiere performance success? Both of you?"

But even before I could answer, Cammy came out the door. She looked completely different from her stage appearance. Instead of her deep cut, sleeveless black dress which tightly outlined her figures, she was in torn blue jeans and a plaid shirt with a light windbreaker. But she hadn't taken off either the garnet necklace that Milos had given her or removed the dangling garnet matching earrings that apparently were a more recent gift to her from him. Her make-up still made her look glowing—I noticed that Jacob was really taken by her, up close. She's really very pretty. Just as I remembered her from Conservatory days. And there at the rear service door of Symphony Hall, with her backpack and the black bag for her formal dress, she looked like she was still a student—maybe a graduate student.

We walked over to Milos's house, which surprised me because it was so close to the hall, and also because it looked so nice in what had used to be, as they call it, "a distressed neighborhood." A red brick triple decker, rather rare in the Boston area. We climbed up to the second floor to where Milos had set up his living room and there in the middle was a big bouquet of flowers which he handed to Cammy as soon as she put down her cases. "For the triumph of my lovely Camille." he said as he presented it to her. "A marvelous performance." Milos kissed her warmly on the lips even with the bouquet between them. Then he rushed to the open kitchen which was at the front of the living room separated by a large teak wood dining table. And he brought out two bottles of French champagne—Veuve Clicquot, the brand I've always wanted to buy and drink but which I could never afford—he placed one in an ice bucket and opened the other and poured out the bubbly into the champagne flutes which were already arranged on the table. While he was preparing, I looked around the living room. There was a bare hardwood floor, very shiny and clean, and a set of Scandinavian designs chairs and divan—brick red in color which were arranged around a low wood coffee table. There was a large rack stereo system in one corner next to the dining table which included a record turntable—

something I had not seen in a long time—filled with many records and flanked by four tall shelves for CDs and two big speakers. But what was most striking was that the walls were mostly bare, except for four large pictures, a photo of an old man with a moustache, another an etching of Dvorak—who I remember because he was so ugly—a second photo portrait of a very serious bearded looking man, obviously from the 19th century, and a color photograph of what was obviously an opera. I had to ask. But first Milos, after distributing the glasses, raised his, and said, "I raise a toast to my lovely muse, inspiration of today's concerto. May Cammy forever triumph like tonight." And we all drank the cold champagne, which of course tickled my nose—it was a lot drier than the stuff I occasionally drank. "Let's have another kiss." And then everyone stood around looking somewhat abashed. Cammy was glowing—her smile was like a lighthouse beacon. "Oh, I forgot." said Milos as he stepped quickly back to the refrigerator in the kitchen. He came back to us with two metal trays of sliced prosciutto and cheese which he placed on the table.

Jacob broke the momentarily lapse. "So, when did you write this concerto we just heard?"

"A little more than a year ago." answered Milos. "It just all came tumbling out in a period of one month. Cammy inspires me that way."

"Oh stop it, Milos." Cammy spluttered.

"And was it difficult for you to learn, Cammy?" Jacob asked.

"At first yes, but Milos helped me and rehearsed me over the past two months. I could've played it from memory. Effectively tonight, I did not need to even look at my score. I knew it so well."

"Well, I liked it enormously." said Jacob. "It rather sparkled, and especially the vivace part."

"So, you know music, young man?" asked Milos.

"Yes, I studied music at the Berklee Conservatory. Specializing in saxophone and piano. And I have a jazz trio I play with."

"Maybe I should write a concerto grosso for flute and saxophone, and you two could get together on the stage to perform it. That would be different."

"Oh no, I'm not as virtuoso as Cammy." Jacob said.

"And neither am I," I protested. "You know, like they say on TV, I'm 'not yet ready for prime time."

Milos did not know the expression—so he doesn't watch Saturday Night Live. Looking around his living room I then realized that he didn't have a flat screen TV anywhere.

Milos refilled the wine glasses with champagne.

"And who are in the photographs you've hung there?" Jacob asked what I was dying to ask.

"There, on the left the bearded man is Bedrich Smetana, the national composer of Czech, and then, you must know Dvorak. I'm originally from Czechoslovakia, you know, and was educated there in music under the watchful eyes of those two portraits. And then the big horizon photo is of a performance of Smetana's opera, The Bartered Bride. And finally, on the right, the mustachioed man is a photo of Leos Janacek, shortly after the creation of Czechoslovakia, after the Treaty of Paris, in 1919 or 20". Those are my champions that I always try to emulate."

I said I wanted to make a toast. "To Cammy, my best friend, and practically my sister in music. May all your music be filled with so much love and light." I think I was already a little drunk—giddy headed for sure. And we drank again to Cammy. By this time Milos was standing close next to Cammy, and he put his arm around her waist and squeezed her close to him as he drank.

Cammy was giggling a little, and as soon as Milos put down his glass, she swiveled around and reached up on tip toes and gave Milos another full on the lips kiss—maybe it was even a tongue in the mouth French kiss. His arms naturally fell around her waist and he embraced her close.

I was half hoping that Jacob would do the same thing, but he didn't. We hadn't reached that stage.

Rely on Jacob to break the lull that sudden private intimacy brings into a room. He said, "I think the sound of the oboe in that concerto was as sweet as I've ever heard. Much finer than any of the Baroque oboe concertos I've ever heard."

"You're nice. Of course, the Baroque oboe was played in an entirely different manner than today." Cammy said.

We all moved to the divan and chairs. But almost at once, Milos stood up again and opened the second bottle of champagne.

"Oh, I can't drink anymore champagne." giggled Cammy. "I'll pass out."

"Don't worry, my dear. You can lie right there on the divan, I'll bring a blanket."

I was also now feeling drunk. And couldn't think of anything more to say.

Jacob to the rescue yet again. "But it's curious. You don't have a piano here. How can a composer not have a piano?"

Milos was talking very excitedly. "Well, my composing piano is downstairs in my music room. It's a grand piano, a Steinway that the Conservatory bought for me many years ago. I used to have an electric keyboard up here, but I found I was playing it so infrequently that I moved it upstairs to my bedroom. I can fiddle around with little tunes while I'm dressing. Or after a shower where I sing the best."

Milos poured himself a fourth glass, but no one else wanted any more.

"No more for me, Milosh." Cammy muttered. I took some and Jacob had another full glass. The champagne didn't seem to affect him so much.

"Don't mind if I ask you, Milosh? But why does Maddie call you Milos, and even on the program it was Milosh? But Cammy calls you Milosh?"

"My birth name is Milosh, Jacob. But when I moved here to the States, people seemed to have trouble saying my name. I don't know why. So, I chose to be called a homonymous name, Milos, which people were familiar with and could say. And I've been comfortable with it ever since. But if you prefer you can call me Milosh, also. And I only wish that Maddie would call me Milosh too."

"Maybe people are more familiar with the name after the success of Milosh Forman's film, Amadeus." said Jacob. "So can I call you Milosh?" "Yes, please."

I hadn't thought of that explanation, but of course Milosh Forman became famous here many years after Milos emigrated to America. I'd already noticed that Jacob is so well informed about cultural things. And maybe people in the know now have no problem with saying the name Milosh, whereas more than 40 years ago, in upstate New York, it was too alien, and people were too ignorant to be able to accept and say correctly the name Milosh. "Perhaps," said Milos as if he were reading my mind and answering my thoughts. "My works since I emigrated are everywhere published as by Milos Nowak."

Then a little later Milos again turned his gaze on Cammy, "Cammy, Jiri wrote me offering a commission for a piece of music that he'd like to premiere at next year's Prague Spring Festival. He'd want me to conduct it. And I think you'll have to come with me again. I sent him electronically a copy of today's concerto, and he'd like to perform it as well. And it's only natural that you perform the solo oboe part. Wouldn't you like to go again?"

"Yes, of course I would. Especially if you're with me and you conduct."

"I think that is the idea," Milos said. He had been looking only at Cammy, that whole evening. I even thought of the tune, "I Only Have Eyes for You." It was so obvious to me that he did not once even look at either me or Jacob directly and held our return gaze. His gaze on Cammy was more than that of a proud papa. It was adoration.

"What are you thinking of composing for your commission? A symphony?" Jacob asked.

"Oh no, not a symphony. Something smaller. An orchestral piece. Maybe a rhapsody on a Czech melody. I've only just begun thinking about it. Because right now I'm already working on two pieces."

The evening broke up when Cammy almost nodded over on the divan. I was drunk and felt I could do the same. Jacob took up the call.

"I think we've finished drinking up to Cammy. I guess it's pretty much time to leave."

Cammy said she couldn't reach her home, and Milos said she could stay the night, because he couldn't drive her home anyway after so much champagne. "In your usual room here," he said. Milos alone took us to the front door; Cammy was already collapsed on the divan.

As Jacob and I stepped away from Milos's house to walk back to the T stop on Huntington and Mass Ave, Jacob asked me if Milos and Cammy were lovers.

"I don't know. It's a mystery to me, Jacob. He adores everything about her. He writes her love letters all the time, so I know he's mad crazy in love with her. But I'm just not sure about her. I don't think they sleep together, but in her own way, I think she loves him."

The thought came to my muddled mind as we walked to the T, arm in arm, that maybe Jacob would want to come to my place and go to bed with me. But when we got to the platform he begged out for the night, saying he had had too much alcohol. Of course, I felt the same way—leaden headed and numb legs—not at all suited for lovemaking. So, I was relieved as he put me on the first Allston bound train and himself, he stepped across the platform to the east bound train. Sex after a drunken spree just isn't love—it's an insensitive bumbling comedy. I don't even remember how I got into my own apartment and into my own bed that night.

## 4 May 2010

**CammyFB**

Maddie, I was so drunk after our little post-concert drink up at Milosh's place, I apparently passed out on the couch. What about you?

> **MADDIE**
>
> I was also pretty drunk. But I got home without too many people stepping on my hands! Ha ha!

**CammyFB**

And you know what? I woke up the next morning in the upstairs guest bed, in a nightgown. Not my own.

> **MADDIE**
>
> OMG! You mean Milos undressed you and carried you to bed?

**CammyFB**

Presumably. I was so disoriented. I didn't know where I was for ten minutes.

> **MADDIE**
>
> You mean, undressed you completely? Like naked? before dressing you?

**CammyFB**

No, I still had my underwear on. But you know I can hardly understand how he carried me upstairs.

I guess he's a lot stronger than I had thought. I was a lot more unconscious. He could've had me, and I wouldn't have known it. But he's too polite for that.

**MADDIE**

I should say so. He is strong for an old man. But you're not at all heavy I think.

**CammyFB**

He's seen me in a bikini before so I guess no great harm there. But enough to say I was really surprised out of my skin. But the hangover 's gone now. Will you be able to join me for lunch on Thursday or Friday? Usual place?

**MADDIE**

Yeah, let's do it. Thursday, if you can.

# Chapter Five

Love cannot survive a long separation. It needs to be nurtured by continuous physical presence, and touching—and of course watered regularly by lots of talking together. It is not enough to be sustained by love letters—whether perfumed or not—or by phone calls, or by email letters, regardless how flowery the language or passionate the sentiments—or explicitly erotic the electronic contents of such correspondence. I probably knew that from the very beginning. I could not hold on to my love for Jake while I was living in Cleveland and he remained in Boston. Needless to say, I was dying to get hold of him again, wrap my arms (and legs) around him, as the days before the Christmas holidays rolled down. He expressed his same desperation, he said that his visits in October were not enough for his appetite for me. My most important aim for my trip back to Boston was to re-ignite our passion—I mean our sex life—and to persuade him that his love for me would move him finally to move out to Cleveland and live with me there. So the expression that absence makes the heart grow fonder, is just plain bunk. Was never true.

We had separated when I moved to Cleveland in September. I had tried to convince him to move with me, but he resisted right down to when we kissed goodbye at the departure gate. I didn't get it then—I mean why he didn't want to move with me?—but I think he didn't understand why I was so strongly committed to joining the Cleveland Symphony full time. I can only guess that he couldn't think of me as a committed career girl. But I had to—I had to reach out and grab this once in a lifetime opportunity. To achieve my life aims. And I thought he would accept that and come join me. But in September anyway, he didn't. I mean he did drive out there with me with a rented truck full of my furniture, clothes and stuff, and after we found an apartment for me to dump all that in it, and he helped me set up all my things inside, and then we drove back to Boston to return the truck. The whole time he refused to understand how important it was to me to be an accomplished career girl in music. And from the time I got the invitation to go back to Cleveland with a three-year contract, back in early June, until the tenth of September when I left Boston again by air, we talked about it, and talked about it, but none of it sank it, I guess. So often, if we were at home—in his Charleston apartment—we would end up making love together either on the floor or in his bed, as if that resolved the tension. But of course, it hadn't. I thought I was so in love with Jake that of course he would stick to me. And I thought, or felt, that he was so in love with me that he would follow. But I was pursuing my dreams, and was getting well paid for that, doing just what I had wanted to do since I was twelve years old. Still that humid day in mid-September, I felt at the airport with Jake by my side—maybe for the first time—that affliction that novelists always write about: my heart ached with the pain of leaving Jake while also leaving to chase my dreams.

But on returning to Boston for the year-end holidays, I was also hoping to see Cammy, who I had not seen in even a longer time. Not since mid June. Absence makes the heart grow fonder, is the saying. But it doesn't work out that way, I think. With Jacob I ached to see him, but with Cammy, I did feel somewhat more distant—even with all the electronic communications. And she had invited me to join them at her parents for Christmas dinner and to stay overnight there in Salem. Of course there is no sexual love involved with my relationship with Cammy, but still I love her. Like a sister. We've been best friends for so many years now, since the beginning of high school. And I missed her terribly over the summer and in the fall while I was in Cleveland. So I was also really looking forward to seeing her again, as soon as possible. And I was still curious about her strange love affair with Milos. I was curious to know if they were finally a couple. By the time I flew into Logan all the conditions I think were set for the two of them to consummate their love. I mean I know that they were physically attracted and intimate too although if I believe Cammy completely, they still had not made love by the time Christmas rolled around, and both of them were still living alone in their own homes. I just have not been close enough to Cammy in the past six months to understand her motives and the degree of her love. Milos was continuing to be respectfully hands off, but according to her, he did want her badly.

After Cammy sent me that note in early May, the one about how Milos carried her upstairs and undressed her, I thought at the time, 'My God, what superhuman restraint he has.' I mean you read all the time in the press or the social media about guys taking advantage and raping girls who've passed out drunk on the floor of some fraternity house or dormitory. Some of the girls sue or raise a stink, but others try to pretend that they were in control of the situation, when of course they were not. So take those examples to show how little restraint and self-control young men have when it comes to the girls they can victimize and what they see as free sex. But even though Gus had cut her free, after May she continued to resist moving in with Milos. Because I assumed, if I believe Cammy, he continued right up to December to write her love letters which continued to proclaim his love for her and his overarching desire for her to fill the emptiness in his life. At least one of the letters that she showed me in June seemed to confirm that continuing desire. But I was beginning to realize by December, through our long separation, that Cammy was less and less confiding in me throughout our electronic correspondence. She was no longer telling me how she really felt about Milos—maybe just as well to keep discreet—or what happened between them. But she did say that Milos would be joining her up in Salem on Christmas day, and maybe I could hitch a ride with him in his old Volvo. (Which I really wanted to do, but instead I went out to my mother's for Christmas and spent Boxing Day and the day after. I had asked Jake to come along with me, but he declined.)

May just stormed past me. The BPhil had a large number of end-of-season concerts, and there were lots of rehearsals. And starting in that second weekend in May, Jacob (I called him Jake by then) and I became lovers, and we made love to each other so vigorously and so often that I was rubbed raw down under by the end of the month. But with him I always wanted more. I was, as they say, mad with love for that guy. He also became my Jake; I was the only one to call him that. To everyone else he remained Jacob.

I didn't get to see Cammy that month—after our drink up at the beginning of the month at Milos's house. We had agreed to meet, but it didn't happen after all. And by the middle of the month, I had moved in with Jake in his large flat in Charleston. We pretended to act like newlyweds– sex and exhaustion, and passionate caressing, often in public. When my schedule allowed, I went to hear some of his gigs, I think twice during that month. Then on the 20th, I got a letter from the Cleveland Symphony offering me a three-year contract starting in September. They are really screwed up there—administratively. First, they hire me then they tell me it was only a temporary hire, they then tell me they do not need my services any longer, and then the person who was the second chair resigns and they turn around and offer me a three-year, tenure track contract. With a great salary. I responded right away, saying that I wanted it. But I didn't consult with Jake about my answer. That was a mistake and he was hurt, because I hadn't consulted him first, and he knew that my acceptance meant that I would be moving there. It began a long series of arguments about our future together, and my future with a top orchestra, that ran right on through the summer. I did consult with Cammy and she was very supportive. She wrote, "Go for it." And of course that's just what I intended on doing.

Then as the end of the month came Cammy sent me this message:

**24 May 2010**

**CammyFB**

Coo coo. Do you remember that my birthday is on the first of June? Milos wants to make a party for my 29th. He would like you to come, and for you to bring Jacob too. Maybe we'll invite a few of our colleagues from the BPhil and BSO. He's thinking of having the party on Friday, June 4. You'll come of course?

> **MADDIE**
>
> Wouldn't miss an invitation for your birthday. Where is he planning on having the party?

**CammyFB**

At the W Hotel, on Stuart Street near Tremont. You know, named after President Bush. It's a really trendy new hotel with a swank restaurant.

> **MADDIE**
>
> Alright. I'll ask Jake. Hopefully he doesn't already have a gig for that evening.

**CammyFB**

I hope so too. I've already checked the concert calendar and neither of us have concerts that evening.

> **MADDIE**
>
> CU then, if not sooner.

Jake was all for going to Cammy's birthday party. He liked good food and free flowing alcohol. And he liked both Milos and Cammy. I spent the next week thinking of what kind of birthday gift to get Cammy. But I kept coming up with a blank—not least because I was so distracted by practicing for my concerts—my work actually—and not least after that the distraction of sex with Jake in all the spare time outside of work.

At the last moment I bought Cammy four CDs recordings of oboe concertos, half from the Baroque era, but also the Mozart concerto and the Strauss concerto. I didn't know whether or not she had them in her collection. And actually I did not know if she even listened to CDs. If she had the time. I did know that she listened to music when she was practicing or learning a piece for orchestra through the internet. She showed me this technique. And it was very helpful for my auditions. Jacob said he had not gotten her a birthday gift because he said he did not know what Cammy would appreciate. We arrived at the W on party day a little early and we spent the time looking at windows. And that is when I noticed that he had a small package with him. "I found a suitable birthday gift for Cammy." he said sheepishly. "Why didn't you tell me?" I asked, half annoyed. "I wanted to surprise you. And anyway the courier delivered it only today." When we finally walked into the restaurant we were no longer early. Milos was waiting at the entrance to greet people, and two of the three other girls were already seated at a large round table. They were Cheryl and Serena from the BPhil, and a girl she liked from the BSO. Cammy had also invited her parents and sister to come, but they had declined to drive all the way down from the North Shore. The restaurant was dimly lit, but it was spacious and modernist looking. In style, like Scandinavian design, all teak wood, glass and stone, with a round stone fireplace and chimney breaking up the middle of the room.

"Oh, I'm so glad you both could come. Cammy was counting especially that you would come Maddie," said Milos with a big smile on his face. "We're going to have entertainment tonight."

Cammy was at the table, beaming with happiness, and dressed even nicer than her usual concert dress—in other words not in black but in a colorful patterned dress that looked like some sort of expressionist work from a museum. She wore her garnet and silver necklace and garnet pendant earrings and lots of makeup on her face, including lipstick (which was rare with her). But it was an important party after all. She looked beautiful—I could think what an ordinary looking girl I am by comparison, and dressed—well let's say, not so classy or pretty as Cammy was. I have to admit that in almost everything about her—music performance, dressing up, haircuts, classwork—she does it better than I do, or ever could do.

When everyone was at the table—Jake sat next to me, and close, almost rubbing against me—Milos stood up and asked the waiter to bring the champagne and pour it out. Milos was going to run the party tonight, as toastmaster and master of ceremonies. And it was obvious that he was enjoying his role. We all raised our glasses and drank the bubbly to Cammy's continuing success and happiness. Little did the others know that Cammy was well on the way to much greater happiness, once she completed the divorce from Gus, and—this was my assumption—she would be free to reciprocate Milos's love for her. I didn't say anything about that at the party. It was not my place to say anything just then, but I looked at Milos and Cammy and saw a future couple, happily wed and living together in the brick three-decker. Maybe Cammy would even achieve her life goal of having children. And on that evening, at the party, anyway, it certainly looked to me that Cammy through her expressions and gaze was showing her admiring love for Milos, and not just gratitude for a good friend and mentor.

We all hurrahed the toast, but we did not have a repeat of the celebration the month earlier for the success of the concerto. This was a real party. Shortly afterwards the waiters brought the dinner to the table in three courses, soup, salad, and filet mignons —"ladies' steaks"— which were exquisite, buttery and tender. And then the surprise — Milos had hired a violinist to play some pretty rhapsodies for us—almost like a gypsy entertainer. Starting from the meat course, this violinist—maybe he was from the BSO, but only Cammy and Milos would know—he played beautiful romantic little gems that I mostly recognized as being familiar. But there was only one piece that I recognized by name: it was Fritz Kreisler's Love's Sorrow. It's very pretty and romantic, but Milos didn't like that selection and he called out to the violinist. "No, no. You have to play Liebesfreud, not Liebesleid. For this occasion, please the Liebesfreud." That wasn't a problem actually. No one at the table knew what he was referring to. I of course knew that Love's Sorrow was the name of that little piece, but I didn't know that it was actually called Liebesleid. I don't know German, and I didn't know what Liebesfreud meant, and couldn't say that I knew that piece of music. Cammy didn't know either what Milos was talking about. And she asked Milos what he meant. "Don't worry, I'll tell you later. Just that Liebesfreud means Love's Joy." This interruption ruffled the artist only a little bit. He thought for a moment, seeming to mutter the melody under his breath and then started again with a different piece. When he had finished that Milos said for the entire table, "At this party we are only going to talk about the joy of love." Cammy made an even broader smile. Jack nudged me and whispered to me, "Yes only the joy of love." In all, the violinist played for us for about twenty-five minutes.

It became apparent to me during the party that the other three girlfriends at the party were not aware of the depth of the relationship between Milos and Cammy. She shared much of her feelings for Milos and the more intimate details of their relationship with me, but not with these other girls. But it occurred to me that there was still a lot she did not tell me about this relationship, and her true emotional reaction to Milos, her feelings for him. She kept a lot of that to herself. For example, she had only shared with me one of Milos's letters, but had revealed that he had written many others over the years. And she never actually said whether she answered Milos's letters or discussed them with Milos, I have assumed that she did not write him back answers to most if not all of his letters to her. But then we communicated primarily through electronic chats and messenger services–and she never put the most personal or intimate information in those communications.

After the meat course, and when the violinist went away, Milos stood up again, had the glasses refilled with another bottle of champagne, and offered another toast to Cammy. "I want to toast Cammy for her tremendous musical talent. May she continue to shine. And continue to inspire me in making music about love."

That was easy enough to toast to, and everyone clinked glasses together. "And now, I would like to start the presentation of birthday gifts." Milos sometimes spoke strangely, or a little stiffly. "I want to be the first to give a gift to Cammy." And he stooped over and took a package out of a small backpack that I had not noticed up to till then. He took out a flat rectangular package wrapped in silvery paper. Cammy clapped her hands together with delight—almost the stereotype of how young girls react to getting presents. She tore off the giftwrap and saw a pale green box with a small latch on one end. She opened this and lifted the lid. And then she let out a muffled whoop and a loud "wow!" She jumped up and on tiptoes reached over to plant a kiss directly on Milos's lips. It did not linger. Milos took the box from her hands and carefully extracted the long loop of a pearl necklace and gently put it around Cammy's neck and latched it. I have to admit it was stunning; a beautiful chain of midsized cultured pearls that glowed with a faint pink and cream sheen. "Milosh, this is the most wonderful gift I have ever gotten." she said. We all took our turns oo'ing and aah'ing over this necklace. "I'm not sure you be allowed to wear it to a concert when you are performing," said Milos. "Probably only the orchestra's players' union can answer that. But I think we can find plenty of other occasions when you can wear it."

One of the girls had quick thinking taken out her iPhone and took a photo of Cammy wearing the pearl chain. All the rest of us then took out our iPhones and began to take photos also. I asked to take a photo of Milos with his arm around Cammy. They both promptly complied. I looked at it in the back screen, and it became the icon portrait photo of the two of them that I have kept ever since then. I've printed it and have hung it on my bedroom wall. Then the others presented their gifts. Everything else was something related to music or oboe. My pathetic offering was a four-disc set of oboe music recorded by Heinz Hollinger. One of the girls presented Cammy with oboe earrings—you can't give that gift very often. But the real champion of the evening was my Jake. He surprised me and Cammy with a present of rare value: it was the score of a concerto for oboe and flute by none other than that famous villain, Antonio Salieri. I was amazed and said so. "Is that the same Salieri who tried to murder Mozart in the film Amadeus by your namesake, Milos something or other?" I asked to the general table. The others all knew the film too. Jake protested: "Milosh Forman. And no Salieri did not kill Mozart. Salieri in his time was a famous leading composer, and teacher to Beethoven, Hummel, Schubert, and even to Mozart."

"That's right, Jake," said Milos. "You even pronounced Milosh correctly. That nonsense about Salieri doing in Mozart all started in Russia with Pushkin writing a play—pure fiction—about their relationship. But in Mozart's time, Salieri was the top composer of Vienna. And his music was everywhere acknowledged. This has to be today a rare piece."

"Yeah and I got it, courier delivery, especially for Cammy, with the hopes that maybe Cammy and Maddie could play it together."

"That would be a great spectacle," said Milos. "We'll have to see how that could be arranged. Maybe with the Boston Philharmonic? I'll have to have a talk with Benjamin."

He meant of course the music director and founder of the BPhil, Benjamin Zander.

"Maddie, I would love performing this with you. How about you?" Cammy said as she was scanning the score. "It looks not too difficult and it is in the classical style—straightforward and melodious."

"I don't know. I'm not as virtuosic as you are."

"Oh come off it, Maddie." said Jake, "I've heard your playing."

"Well then, it's settled." said Milos. "We'll try to get you two girls together to play this in front of a discriminating audience. Next season. I think it would be a great success. And people will come from all around to hear the pure music of 'that villain,' Salieri."

Cammy thanked Jake profusely. "But wherever did you find the score of such a rare piece?"

"Through the internet of course. There's a website that produces and sells scores and sheet music of pieces that are out of copyright. They even sell scores, which are only available as photocopies of scores held in libraries, which have been out of print and unavailable for scores of years."

"That's a funny pun." I said. "Scores out of print for scores of years."

Then Milos said we had now come to the 'moment musicale' where we'd have to sing. He gave a signal to the waiter who disappeared into the kitchen. Twelve minutes later he reappeared with a large white cake with sparkler candles blazing. We all began to sing 'Happy Birthday' to Cammy as the cake approached. As it turned out it was also a rarity: it was a baked Alaska cake, that unusual mix of meringue, white cake, and ice cream all baked in the oven at the very last minute. It's very delicious–I had heard of it but had never eaten such a confection before. It is every bit as good as its reputation. Mischievously I took a photo of Cammy eating it as some of the meringue was sticking on her lips. It's also hard to eat neatly in a proper lady-like way.

After the dessert there was coffee and tea. When Cammy excused herself from the little girls' room, I went with her. I asked her if as it appeared Milos was going to pay for this party, she said, "Yes. He insisted on it. Even if my family came." "But he doesn't have that much income. How can he afford it, and that expensive gift too?" "He has money, lots of savings. Thirty-five years where he had low income but even lower expenses. So not surprisingly he's got a lot of full bank accounts and investments. He tells me that I'm the first person that he's been able to be generous to almost since he left Czechoslovakia." "Well he's certainly generous. And has a nice taste too." I said as I looked closer at the pearl necklace under the brighter light of the powder room. "Are you going to stay together here tonight?" "No, don't be silly. Why be so extravagant, when it's only a thirty-minute walk to his house? I'm going to spend the night there."

Back at the table, the other guests were finishing off the coffee and the wines. Jake was talking to the girl sitting to the other side of him who played violin with us in the BPhil when Cammy was there. When the waiter asked if anyone was for a digestif, I was feeling light headed from the champagne and dinner wine, so I asked for a Bailey's on the rocks. Jake said he would like a Grand Marnier which he usually only consumed on vanilla ice cream. Not long after we started with our drinks, Milos stepped away—maybe to the toilets, maybe to make payment arrangements discretely—and I leaned over to Cammy and asked her in a low voice: "Have you told Milos yet, about Gus's request?"

"Shh. No. But I don't want to talk about that here." And that was the last we spoke together face to face until Christmas. It was a great birthday party though. The entire party hung around for another hour and a half. Milos ordered for himself a cognac, but no one else wanted a strong drink. The party broke up after that. Cammy and Milos started walking in the direction of Milos's house, up Tremont, away from the center. All the rest of us headed for the T stop to head for home.

We both had concerts scheduled on the next two June weekends, and then Cammy headed off to Tanglewood. My summer was filled with Jake's attentions and love-making; I am certain in hindsight that I had fallen completely in love with him—and it was the passionate sex which sealed the issue for me. But not to the extent that it deflected my ambitions and commitment to bettering myself. I had decided to move to Cleveland and all summer that decision was the underlying theme of our relationship. We argued and discussed, I trying to convince him to move with me, and he tried to show me it was better for me to stay, living with him. Neither of us understood the other's arguments. I could not until the very end understand why he couldn't relocate to Cleveland. He made vague arguments about his life being based on the Boston area, but I think what really set him in his ways is that he could not accept the humiliation of needing to move in order to follow his woman's career. And he was still one of those men who cannot accept that their women make the money in the household, or at least make an awful more income than they do. But he wouldn't say that. He did offer to help me move my stuff to Cleveland and to find a new apartment there. He would drive in a small rented truck and we'd drive together–it was only a full day's drive away.

The summer was very busy for him–it was always his busiest season for gigs when he earned the most cash for the entire year. For instance, he was a regular player at the Boston Pops annual Fourth of July concert on the Charles embankment. He'd been doing that for ten years when I met him. I remembered then where I had seen him first. He played the saxophone solo a couple times for us at the BPhil in the Ravel version of Pictures at an Exhibition. He was good–and he played the tenor sax in addition to the alto sax

By contrast, as usual for me, the summer time was mostly empty. I had no auditions to prepare for, although in August the orchestra did send me the music to prepare for the first concerts in September. That was good of them. I would be ready for the early season concerts anyway.

Jake, who also played piano and had a small electronic keyboard in his apartment, decided to teach me some songs that we could play together. So in addition to regular, vigorous sex we regularly played together on days when he didn't have gigs. I have to admit, it was fun. He thought we could be working toward something where I could join him in a jazz gig with his small band, but nothing came of it and to me it did not seem to offer much prospect of work. I didn't add much to his or his band's repertoire and my playing did not get him any extra gigs. I did take up the nice house-wifely duties of cooking meals for us to help fill the time, although when he worked evenings at a restaurant or bar, I didn't need to fix dinner for the two of us. I actually lost weight over the summer—whether from the heavy sex or from eating less on a more 80 regular schedule, I'm not sure. But by the time September rolled around I looked a lot better—I had lost 15 pounds if you can believe it. What love can do—all consuming love, as the saying goes.

**22 May 2010**

**CammyFB**
I got by return mail Gus's answer. He's accepted the
terms of divorce that your lawyer wrote up for me.
I had agreed not to demand alimony, but I will get
the house. I will file tomorrow.

**MADDIE**
Sounds good. How long until you're officially done
with him?

**CammyFB**

They'll schedule a trial–so to speak. A court date.
His lawyer will plead guilty and then it's all over.
I won't even have to see him. I will get the divorce
decree the same day.

**MADDIE**

But you'll have to come in from out there?

**CammyFB**

For the court hearing? Yes at the minimum.

**MADDIE**

Having fun out there in Tanglewood?

**CammyFB**

Yeah, but I miss Milos, really bad. Like I ache all
over for him. We call each other often, but I miss
his presence.

**MADDIE**

Ah love

Then a few days later, Cammy wrote again:

**28 July 2010**

**CammyFB**

So I filed my divorce claim and the court hearing
will be in late September. I can hardly wait.

**MADDIE**

Okay, I guess I will already be in Cleveland by then.

**CammyFB**

126

Oh I nearly forgot that you're leaving soon. Has
Jake agreed to go with you?

MADDIE

Not yet. I'm still trying to convince him. He'll drive
me there though.

**CammyFB**

Milos is coming out this weekend to conduct two
of our concerts. I'll be so happy to see him again.
You can't believe how much I miss him.

MADDIE

I suppose he misses you too? Have you told Milos
yet about the divorce?

**CammyFB**

No, but I think not until it's completely finished
and the divorce decree is in my hands. Otherwise
the wait will just torment him and distract him
from his work.

MADDIE

You think he might straight away ask you to
marry him?

**CammyFB**

Yes, I do think so. His letters suggest that that is
what he is thinking.

MADDIE

But why don't you ask him to marry you? You want
that don't you?

**CammyFB**

I'm still not sure. For my next husband, I want to
be able to start a family.

MADDIE

And you're still afraid of his age? That he won't be able to do it?

**CammyFB**
Kind of like that. Say, why don't you come to this weekend's concert? Maybe we could drive out herewith Milos? I'm sure he wouldn't object. You can stay with me.

**MADDIE**

Hey, that's a great idea. I miss you too, you know?

**CammyFB**
Okay let's do it then. I'll tell Milos.


So that is how I finally made it to Tanglewood. I never would have gone there just on merit. And I've never been able to go out there in the summers to attend one of the concerts because I couldn't afford it and I never had a car of my own to be able to drive out there. Milos was quite gentlemanly about it. We left Thursday morning from his house—I wouldn't let him come to pick me up in Charlestown, that would've been too much of an inconvenience. And throughout the almost three hours it takes to drive out there, Milos was talking happily about music and the upcoming program. I was a good girl the whole way. I strongly resisted the overpowering urge to ask him about his feelings for Cammy and whether he loved her enough to want to marry her. That would have been a gross intervention—and just not my place to ask. He only briefly spoke about Cammy, and that was about the part she was going to play in the Debussy piece, La Mer. "It's a part made just for her; her sound and dynamics perfectly suit the piece."

But then I do not have a will of iron, shortly before we arrived in Lenox, I had to ask.

"Don't you love Cammy?"

128

He looked briefly at me and then put his eyes back on the road.

"What can I say, Maddie? Deeply, fondly, madly. Like they always say in the Hollywood movies. She hasn't told you?"

"So you miss her this summer?"

"Yes very much. I find myself wanting Cammy's presence to be all around me all the time. But maybe you can give me an insight into Cammy's feelings. Does she love me?"

"Yes, I think so. But I can't say exactly how much. I think she doesn't understand exactly herself."

"You know, Maddie," he said after a long pause, "I've noticed that young people seem to be mostly preoccupied with understanding how to do things, how to get by in life. Well, I have a similar question for you. Tell me, how do you think, can I get Cammy to love me?"

"I don't know, Milos. From what she's told me and what I've seen, you're doing everything right."

"She's shown you my letters?"

"No, only one, a long time ago." I should have lied and told him none.

"So then, I can only try to continue to be as close to her as I can, all the time. But a composer has to spend lots of time by himself working at his craft. I suppose it's the same for a writer. But even as I write music, alone in my study, I ache to be with her at my side. I think that should answer your probing question."

And thus I was chided. Mildly. But as I said I could no longer resist. I was all the time asking Cammy the same questions. Maybe I needed to inquire of myself more profoundly about my feelings for Jake. Not long after that we drove up to a quaint old-fashioned house, a large house, where Milos was going to be staying for the weekend until Monday. "I have to see when they've scheduled rehearsal for today. Maybe we can meet altogether for a quick lunch, if it's not too late." He deposited his traveling bag in the front foyer and then took out his iPhone and called Cammy to ask where we should meet.

Then we set out on foot across what looked like a leafy green campus intersected with big lawns or meadows here and there. Milos was leading, I had no idea of where we were heading so I was just looking around. And I think I spotted Cammy first at some distance walking quickly toward us. Maybe Milos did not recognize her. She had the "teenager on holiday" look. She was in short shorts, frayed at the bottom, and a very revealing halter top and sandals. My hunch was right. Milos did not recognize until she was within shouting range. And then he stopped and stretched out his arms. And she surprised me, again just like in the movies, she ran up to him and jumped into his arms. He lifted her up in his arms and spun around once. She did have to jump up—remember he's quite a bit taller than she is. She tucked her head next to his neck. They didn't kiss until he put her down.

"I'm so glad to see you, finally."

"And I'm happy too, Cammy. I find myself always missing you these past weeks."

They stood for a long moment just holding hands and looking at each other, pouring out their affection for each other through their eyes. Only after that long reunion, did Cammy turn to me and say. "Hi Maddie, I'm really glad you could come. I'm always happy to see you."

"But I think we'll be busy for most of the rest of the day. I can't show you around, now. But let's go to lunch now."

"When does rehearsal start?" asked Milos. "And where's your oboe."

"Rehearsal starts at 2:30. I have to go back to my room to get it. So we need to hurry." And they set off, hand in hand to the canteen. She obviously was not cautious about showing her affection for Milos publicly—I mean almost everyone there on the campus knew both Cammy and Milos by sight, and I think they would have been a little surprised to see them walking together like young lovers. But then again, that summer's crop of students probably would not have known Milos. Probably they would only recognize him at the concert the next day. We had a quick lunch, and they were just talking shop. I couldn't participate much in that conversation. Then shortly before two, Cammy told me to come with her to her room so she could get her oboe, and I could drop my things off. We then headed off to the practice room—the "closed shed"—where she said they would be working until five thirty. They only really had to work with the guest pianist who was doing the Gershwin concerto. She apologized that she couldn't show me around, and suggested that maybe I would like to go swimming. It was, after all, a hot day. She pointed vaguely across the meadow to where the lake was. "I have to go to my room to change my clothes into something a little more presentable. We can meet there or maybe at the canteen at around six fifteen. What do you say to that?" My answer was strictly practical: "Where do I go for shelter if it starts to thunder and rain?" "That's a good question," she said, without answering my question.

Fortunately it didn't thunder or rain that afternoon—although by around five it did look as if a summer thunderstorm might soak the place. I did go back to Cammy's room and put on my swimsuit under my shorts and shirt and grabbed a towel and headed for the 'bowl', which is what they call the lake there. I asked a few people on my way and they all pointed me in the same direction. But I could hardly swim. It was a really hot day, but the water was frigid cold. I jumped in and thought I would have a heart attack; it was so cold. I jumped right back out. How could the water, in what was really only a large pond, be so cold? It gave me a headache for the rest of the day.

I met up with Cammy back at the room at five thirty. Walking back, I saw that already there were people arriving at the parking lots for the evening concert. She changed into a black and white casual top and pants—looked really classic and handsome—while I got out of my still damp swimsuit and into jeans and a knit top.

"You might want to take a hoodie along with you." she reminded me. "It gets chilly after the concert starts and the sun goes down." On the way out, I picked up my hoodie, and Cammy picked up her music bag with the oboe in it. She muttered as she left the door, "I hope I have enough reeds to get through the rest of the summer. No place here to buy new ones."

As we left the dormitory, Cammy said: "You know, Milos is such a good conductor. You wouldn't believe it. He communicates so well the real feel of the music. His beat signals are so clear and his change of tempi are also good. He's better than Levine any day–but Levine is the famous one. I think most of the orchestra members feel the same way. And he's so good looking, too."

As we walked back over to the canteen, she asked me how things were going with Jacob. Of course I was very frank with her. "We're having sex like chimpanzees in the treezes. In every free moment when we're together. I'm crazy in love with that guy. From the moment I met him, you can't believe how horny I've been feeling. But I'm filling up on him now, that's for sure"

"Don't make any accidental babies."

"Don't worry. We're protected."

"When we're not doing it, we try to play some music together—he introduced the idea—but usually I'm too exhausted from the love making to think clearly. Or to play very well. But he's very supportive."

"That's good. And he treats you well?"

"He's the best. The best man I've ever been with. I think of Tina Turner's song, every time we start doing it together. The only thing bad is that he's working most evenings, and comes home late, both really tired and smelling heavily of smoke. So we don't make love at night as much as we do during the day."

"What's he going to do when you move to Cleveland? Is he going to go with you?"

"No. But we're still talking about that. He says he doesn't want to go to Cleveland. Says he'd have to start over from scratch."

"But he'd be with you. Not exactly from scratch."

"Yeah. But he means it from a work perspective."

We met up with Milos at the canteen. He hadn't changed, but instead he had a suit bag with him. Obviously he would change in the dressing room behind the stage.

"You look lovely as usual, Cammy. I've not seen you in this outfit before." He leaned over and kissed her on the cheek. Can you imagine? To get a kiss every time they meet up? Even though they had been rehearsing together over the past three hours. He's such a gentleman. Of course, he hadn't seen her for six weeks. And I guess he couldn't get enough of her physical presence.

"I was only able to get you a comp ticket for the lawn seats, Maddie." Said Cammy as she brought her tray of supper back to the table. But I think you won't mind. Free is free and the sound is alright too. You can't see the orchestra as well, that's all. And if you go early you can get the lawn area closest to the overhang of the shed."

"Cammy, I haven't told you." Milos said offhandedly. "I finished my first piece for my residency. I've submitted it to Levine to review and think about scheduling. It's a simfonietta. I've played it through the simulator and it sounds good to me. I've also sent it off to my publisher."

"That's great, Milos. So, you like it?"

"Yeah. I do, not to sound too puffed up with myself. I like it a lot more than most of my earlier works. It definitely is not modernist. And it is not as monotonous as most of the composers working these days, you know, with endless repetitions of one rhythmic line."

"I can't wait to hear it, Milos. You'll play it for me through your simulator when I get back to Boston?"

"Of course I will. I will even ask for your comments, and suggestions for ways I might improve it."

"Milos, you're too modest. I'm sure it's perfect. Brilliant. And I think even Levine will be envious, as he sometimes claims to be a composer himself."

"Well, the important thing will be that he accepts it and schedules it soon. While he's still the music director. I don't think he's going to last much longer with the BSO."

"He's really sick?"

"Yes, seems seriously ill. The orchestra has already tipped me off on a lot more conducting work for me in the coming season. I've already been reserved for four concerts, and they told me to expect more. It's really too bad for him. But it's great for me. A real boost to my income, as you can understand."

"You think he's dying?" I asked, as always so blunt and awkwardly direct. Cammy hushed me. I also speak too loud about such things in environments where there are other interested parties, who love to gossip and to overhear others' conversations.

"I really can't say. I have no insight into his medical condition." said Milos. "But the last few times I've seen him, he looks awful. And he shakes uncontrollably."

"It's really a shame." Cammy said. "He has appeared to be suffering the last several times he led us. Poor man."

"But that's not the only news from me, Cammy. I finished the simfonietta and I've already started two other pieces and am making good progress on them. One is the commission from Jiri and the Czech Philharmonic. They won't take me long. Because I already have developed most of the ideas and themes I want to work with for both of them."

"You're brilliant, Milos. I can't imagine the genius that drives you."

"I've told you before. You're my inspiration, Cammy. And my genius comes from you. The fire of love that feeds my imagination."

"Wow." I said. Cammy blushed. "Not often you hear such expressions of adoration."

"But they are never enough." said Milos. "I got my idea in thinking about the pain of love and separation. And while I was walking around the Back Bay–without you Cammy—I also thought about the feeling of reunion. So that is the theme of my second piece."

I was sitting there as an observer, so engaged in listening to this relationship, that I hardly noticed my meal. It had no flavor, when compared to what Milos was saying. I think Cammy had a hard time eating her food, also. It looked as if she were flushed with emotions.

We walked over to the ticket office by the shed, and Cammy got me my comp ticket. Cammy and Milos walked hand in hand. Surely that was noticed by everyone in the orchestra–everyone that knew them. Then we separated, I to my spot on the grass, under the wooden awning, and then to the stage door entrance. I had not been sitting for more than five minutes before I began to feel uncomfortable, both the hard ground on my bottom, and the sadness that Jake had not been able to come with me and sit by my side. I could just imagine lying together, caressing each other and necking, while the darkness fell and the orchestra's tunes wafted up through the warm evening air. Ah me. Opportunity missed– forever.

The concert was very nice. I still can't remember the name of the pianist who played the Gershwin concerto, but he was good, looked young and lean, and he really put out the sound. The Haydn symphony was lightly, sunnily pastoral–and short. And the Vaughn Williams piece was also part of the great outdoors–I should have been playing the flute part. It's so uplifting. The concertmaster played the violin solo. It stuck with me more than the Gershwin concerto. Cammy's oboe could be heard in snatches through the Gershwin and the Vaughn Williams. But in total, the concert was delightful music, well performed, just suited for a summer's evening.

And afterwards, that was when I became a third wheel. We walked to one of the big Victorian style bed and breakfast houses right outside the Tanglewood area on the road to Lenox. It was still only shortly past nine o'clock and they still were serving wine and light snacks on the covered porch out front. We sat there and ordered three glasses of white wine. Mine was cold, and the glass immediately clouded. They both talked about the music. I had little to contribute except that I had liked the playing immensely, and that the choice of music was very appropriate for an outdoor summer music festival. Then suddenly I remembered the story of Tanglewood, and I blurted out:

"Can you imagine the noble looking Koussevitzky carrying around his bass viol, and trying to get the rich backers out here and Boston Brahmins to lend support to stage this festival for the first time, under a tent? You know, elitist European summer tradition?"

They both looked at me as if I had a loose nut in my head. After they moved to leave, indicating a long stroll was called for, I said good night and headed back to Cammy's room while they disappeared into the inky night, hand in hand, walking slowly. Cammy came in late, after 11:30. I was already in the sleeping bag she had put out for me.

"Tomorrow morning at 10 we have an open rehearsal." Cammy whispered to me as if I were asleep. "Do you want to attend? You said you wanted to head back tomorrow. There is one bus leaving at 11:45 from Lenox that is pretty much an express."

I said I would take part in the rehearsal and then go over to Lenox for the bus. And we said our goodnights. I was aching for Jake, but also I had spent a lot of time that day lying on the hard ground and there on the hard floor, so I was aching in my hips, shoulders, and neck. I needed a bed. As I fell asleep I wondered if the great George Szell had organized this European summer music tradition for the Cleveland Orchestra. I was trying to think where it might be, if he had, as I dozed off.

As I said, after I left Tanglewood that next day, after listening for one hour to Milos rehearsing the orchestra, I did not see Cammy again until the next December, just before Christmas. In the interim, as I was in Cleveland, I was working hard–trying to make the best impression possible so I could make my appointment permanent. Any new musician in a big orchestra understands this. Jake came in late October and provided both companionship and interruption to my intense practicing. I enjoyed the resumption of our love life, romping in bed together, but I was really trying to convince him again to move to Cleveland and resume living with me. Oh parting is such sweet sorrow, how I felt this in the airport when he left after only four nights with me. But in fact, the feelings were much more complicated. Yes, I ached for his physical embrace, I would miss the passionate sex, but I also would be able to dedicate more time again to practicing and preparing for concerts, so I was relieved in a way as well. Not in the least to catch up on the sleep I had not gotten in those four days while he was sharing my bed.

But there was an innovation that came out in the market that fall. Facetime–what a life saver that was. A fancy application that allows users to send and receive video conference calls on their iPhone. Cammy told me about it and we started using it on a few occasions in late

November and December, when we could schedule free moments. I also tried to introduce Jake to it as well. But he had only just bought a Samsung Galaxy smart phone and it was not compatible at that time. So until much later in 2011, we continued to rely on text messages and the less satisfactory Skype video calling. So only Cammy and I called using Facetime. And she was much more frank and open with me through this channel than she had been with through the chat messaging apps we usually used. Perhaps because it was more spontaneous than physically writing or typing, and also the visual angle adds to sincerity as both parties can see instant response and facial signals as they talk and interpret each other's statements—better even than telephone calls.

So I guess I can say then that I did see Cammy before Christmas, but only through the internet and not really face to face, as she was in her apartment in Boston, and I was all by myself in Cleveland. And our schedules still made it imperative that we first write ahead and schedule a call because otherwise our phones were switched off whenever we were busy with practices or rehearsals. One of our first trials for this was early in December.

So I called her the next day. Outside it was snowing like you wouldn't believe—it never snowed like that in Boston. I was going to be socked in for the day. But it didn't interfere with our connection.

## 24 May 2010

**CammyFB**
Maddie, Can we try out connecting on FaceTime tomorrow afternoon say around 1:30 or 2? I have something very important to share with you.

**MADDIE**
Yeah, sure? 1:30 okay? What is it, if I can ask?

**CammyFB**

Milosh wrote me another lover letter. I want to
read it to you.

**MADDIE**

OK. I'll call you.

Facetime

"Hey therem Cammy. How are you doing?

"Great. You wouldn't believe it, but I got another letter from
Milosh. And this one really knocked me off my feet."

"So is that good? Or bad?"

"No, it's so wonderful. You wouldn't believe it. I had to tell you.
I've got it here on my laptop. I want to read it to you. He's such
a wonderful guy. I really love him to death. I want to read the
letter to you. And I couldn't wait until the next time when we
could meet, like after you get back here in the Boston area."

"Okay. You're sure?"

"Oh, yes. Here it is:

"He writes: My dearest Camille—in his letters he always calls me Camille,
when we're together he just as often says Cammy—My beloved,

"I look around my apartment as I sit here at my keyboard
and I see the emptiness that has been my life for far too many
years. It try to fill it with music, but this is only a palliative. I
need a loving wife, I need children.

"Ever since I introduced myself to you, Camille, I have had
hope that my life could be fulfilled and that I could abolish this
emptiness. You are the loveliest woman I have ever known and

139

I have written to you countless times telling you of the depth of my love for you and how much you inspire me and please me.

"But now I realize that I desperately need to bring you into my life and to make you my wife, and that I believe you now feel the same way about me. But we both are reluctant to say this in words delivered in person. I have too long been too shy to tell you to your person of my feelings and desires for you–that is my way. And that was also because I feared that my love for you was unrequited and that you would be forced to reject me. I feared this so much that I let our relationship remain undeveloped and static, for far too long, years even.

"Over this past summer, when we were separated for a long time, you at Tanglewood and I here at my keyboard, I realized that this state in our relationship had to change. That I need you near to me too much to let my fear hide or extinguish my desire. I also began to feel that your feelings for me were also changed, that you actually loved me in a way that showed you too wanted to be my woman and partner in life.

"The time has come for me to pull together the courage to tell you, implore you, ask you to join me, in spite of my age, to join me in filling our life together, in making a family together, in publicly affirming our mutual love. I hope you can also be brave to find a way to answer me positively at this time.

Your loving Milos

[Cammy put the letter down. She must have printed it out before she called me.]

[All I could say was] "Wow."

"Yes, wow." [Cammy began to sob right there over her iPhone line.]

"That's a marriage proposal."

"Yes, I think so. Maybe as close as he'll be able to get to proposing."

"When did he send it?" "I opened it yesterday morning. He had sent it late the night before."

"And when do you expect that you'll see him next?"

"Well, the concert season is over until after New Year's so our usual 'dates' are not scheduled. I invited him to come with me to my parents' for Christmas day dinner. So, unless we arrange a get together, nothing is lined up right now."

"Well, maybe you need to call him and ask to get together with him."

"But, don't you think I will have to answer him definitively then?"

"Yes, probably."

"Even if he can't manage to make his proposal in spoken words?"

"Yes, even then. But, Cammy, you still don't think you're ready to commit to him?"

"I think I am. I find myself wanting him, wanting his embrace, his kisses all the time. I want to be near him all the time."

"So there you go. You love him. And want to marry him. So you know the answer."

"But I don't want to force him to say what he is not ready to say yet, I mean in person."

"I don't think you'll be forcing him to say anything he doesn't want to say. Face up to it, girl. You're both ready to commit your love to each other."

"I suppose so."

"What do you mean, suppose so? Of course you are."

"OK." [Now Cammy was sobbing again.]

"I'm so happy, Maddie. I can't control my feelings."

"Okay, we'll talk later then."

"Bye."

After that call, I began to realize that Jake and I also needed to talk more frankly about our feelings for each other. But that would have to wait until I got back to Boston. Iwas hoping that during the Christmas break we could.

It was less than a week later that Cammy called me again through FaceTime. She wanted to confirm that I was coming to Boston for the Christmas/New Years break and, especially pressing, she wanted to invite me to come to her parents' house in Salem for Christmas dinner on the 25th. "Milosh and I will be going. We can even offer you a ride. And if you're both still a number, you and Jake should come together, with us. I would really like that. You know, I kinda miss you Maddie. I think I've told you a number of times throughout chat line. Like there's a hole in my life without you Maddie."

"Cammy, have you spoken to Milos? Have you two gotten together in person?"

"No, I decided it would wait until Christmas."

Later she signed off, "Glad to see you Maddie. Talking to you always helps me. Also it makes me feel good to see you so happy with Jake."

I couldn't bear saying to her at that time that Jake and I were not really such a happy pair. And I wasn't at that time with him. We were eight hundred miles apart. We'd had a falling out as the Fall ended, but it was only over the phone and through online chats, so it was hard to tell just how he felt. I missed him a lot. That's to say the least. But doubts had crept in and I wasn't really sure when I took off from Cleveland if he would welcome me rapturously, and let me sleep with him in his apartment. I was still so crazy to see him and I was really ecstatic when he showed up at Logan airport to greet me when I flew in. Right away I began working on him, because he was acting as if he were sad at my coming, or at least not really so happy to see me. I insisted that we go together out to Worcester to my mother's house for two nights around Christmas. I had already told Cammy that we couldn't join them in Salem because I felt really obliged to spend Christmas with mom and my brother's family at Christmas. I had looked forward to going with Cammy and Milos—and also maybe with Jake—but it was very important that I go to mom's for Christmas, because I thought I might not have many more opportunities to visit with her. And although he was initially reluctant—I just really did not know what was bothering him—I convinced Jake to go with me. I even convinced him to prepare some Christmas songs we could play together to entertain my nieces and nephew. Now that's a combination you don't often hear playing together those timeworn Christmas carols–alto sax and flute. You had to have a sense of humor and playfulness in order to make them work together. But I succeeded in cheering him up and we went out to Worcester and enjoyed ourselves immensely. My nieces fell over themselves with laughter. And on Christmas day before the afternoon turkey dinner, we did a reprise of the music and everyone had a great time. Jake confessed in bed that night that part of the reason he was sad was because he was scheduled to be playing on New Year's eve in a hotel party–big band sound playing into the early hours of the New Year. But I told him that we'd just have to go to the party and invite Cammy and Milos to join us. And I also told him he'd have to make love to me even more to compensate for being busy on New Year's eve and morning. So he started that very night–comp time I called it. We rolled back into Charlestown on the 27th like the lovers that we had been in the previous summer. I had cheered him up and he had filled me with love too.

There was a chat message waiting for me on my computer when we got back and I opened my laptop up. Cammy wanted to schedule a FaceTime talk, a private one, where Jacob would not be able to overhear us. That was possible right away as Jake had stepped out, so I called her right away on FaceTime.

Facetime

"Hi Cammy. Are you back from Salem?"

"Yeah, I'm back here in my place in Somerville. You wouldn't believe what happened there. I'm still so excited. I had to tell someone."

"So tell me, what happened?"

"I made love to Milos. In my old bedroom. I climbed up on him and seduced him. And we made the most delicious love there under my father's roof. I'm mad crazy in love with that guy, Milos. He's not at all old and unfunctional. He was—well, super. It seemed like hours we made love together. I had to slow him down a bit, because I remembered that that bed makes too much noise. You know, it is the same bed where I lost my virginity eleven years ago. But that night with Milos after our Christmas feast, was far superior to that first time. It was the best love-making I've ever had. You could say it was a rediscovery of love, for both of us. He said over and over again that he loved me. He even said it in Czech. I now want him more than any man I have ever known. I want more."

"How do you know he said it in Czech?"

"I asked him to tell me he loved me in Czech and he did."

"Well, finally. It's about time, Cammy. But you said you seduced him?" "Yeah. I mean I led and kicked off the love making. It was kinda funny. Dad was so embarrassed when he said we could sleep in my old bedroom. As if I was still a school girl and he was giving my virginity away for the first time. And you know I then realized that Milos is older than my dad. Well, once we were in the bedroom, Milos became embarrassed again and he acted as if he didn't know what to do next. I told him that his last letter was a proposal for marriage and that I accepted. And then I went to him and began to kiss him, and started taking off his slacks and then his shirt. He helped a little. Then I undressed and pushed him on the bed and literally jumped on top of him and away we went. He was firm straightaway. And we were humping away until the bed complained too much. Oh, it was great. I love him so much. I didn't really expect he could be such a convincing lover. I sometime thought that maybe he couldn't do it. When he came inside me, ah it was ecstasy. I nearly came myself. I can't say I've had many orgasms in my life, but with Milos I am sure to have loads."

"Like she says in "It's raining men?""

"I almost couldn't breathe by the time we were finished the first time. Ahhh. Such passion. I have never known such passion. And we both kinda passed out after that first love making. Like I was exhausted and tickling with delight—buzzing all over— but completely worn out. And tired too. And dizzy from the wine at dinner. I don't know how much time passed while we dozed. And then we made love again."

"It's great isn't it? Like Jake and I did last summer."

"Great? No, it's the greatest thing in all the world, in life. Just awesome. Wonderful. Making love with someone that you love more than anything else in life."

"I'm really happy for you, Cammy. You deserve such a man, such love. Like, I mean, you and Milos belong together. I only wonder that it took you so long to get there and want Milos as much as he's wanted you all these past years."

"Yeah. It was kinda funny, because then afterwards we both slept so soundly, that mom had to knock on the door to wake us for breakfast. A late breakfast. We went downstairs to the table like two naughty kids."

"But when we drove back to Boston, we agreed we needed to go to his place, and make love again without any restraints or creaky beds, or wake up knocks on the door. I only got back here a couple hours ago. Had to get a change of clothes, to shower. And to rehydrate. And probably now to take a nap."

"Yeah, and in maybe a few days you'll feel like wanting to eat something too."

"Anyway, I just had to tell you. I'm your Cammy, madly in love, and still tingling all over but ready to collapse."

"You look like you're literally glowing. I'm really happy for you. And for Milos too. You'll join us for the New Year's Eve party at the Parker?"

"Yeah. We'll be there."

"Great. We got tickets for you. See you there."

"Okay. See you. And Jacob too?"

"Yes, but he'll be playing most of the evening in the orchestra."

"Okay, bye Maddie."

"Bye bye. Take a napp."

When I got off the iPhone connection, I looked around Jake's echoing place. It was cluttered and needed a thorough cleaning. Jake's presence was everywhere apparent, jazz albums lying on the floor, posters of sax players on the walls, dirty dishes stacked in the sink. A half-drunk open bottle of white wine on the table. The bed we had not made up before we left for Worcester three days ago. I thought to myself, maybe first love is the best and most passionate. And after that first roar of the flames of passion, maybe love-making becomes more like stirring the old embers. Still pleasurable, but not the highest heat and ardor. I wondered if we could resurrect our love, or if it was already too late for us. I would have to try harder that evening. But I think it is clear that neither he nor I have completely surrendered ourselves to the other.

# Chapter Six

Cammy and Milos met us at the Parker House ballroom sharply at eight. I had already given my winter coat to the coat room attendant, and Jake was waiting for me already because he had come at six to warm up with the band and set up their gear and change. Standing with Cammy and Milos at the entry to the ballroom were Cheryl and her date, and that other girl from the BSO, whose name I had forgotten, with a man she introduced as her husband, Bertie. I thought he looked kinda like a Sesame Street character of the same name. But that didn't matter. I didn't speak to them for the rest of the night. Cammy was dressed to kill. She wore a red ball gown, which bared her shoulders and arms, along with her pearl necklace and now matching pearl earrings. I'd never before seen her dressed so fabulously. She is a beauty, really. Movie star looks, I've always thought. Milos was in his frack coat with a white bow tie, which from the looks of it he used when conducting the BSO. I by contrast looked like a frumpy old nag dressed in last season's off the shelf dress. Jake was dressed in a black suit also with a bow tie, but as it turned out it was the costume for the entire band that performed that evening. I squealed and gave Cammy a big hug and two-cheeked kisses. I was so happy to see her looking so radiant. I knew too why she was so happy. Milos gave me a very formal peck on the cheek and wished me a soon to be Happy New Year. We had bought an entire round table in the middle of the floor, and a waiter showed us into it and helped seat us. Milos had wanted to pay for the whole table, as it had been his birthday only two days earlier. But Jake had gotten comps for the two of us, and Bertie had insisted on paying for him and his wife. Tickets weren't cheap either. $135 each, drinks included, but not including the champagne. Jake sat with us for about twenty minutes and then excused himself because the orchestra was supposed to start at 8:30. For me it wasn't much of a party, because I only got to be with him for fifteen minutes each time between the first three sets. As soon as we were all seated, Milos ordered a bottle of French champagne to kick off the celebrations. There was enough in the bottle for seven flutes. Jake passed on the champagne this time, because he had to play a lot during the evening. I sat on one side of Cammy, and Milos was on her other side. We stood in unison and after Milos gave the first toast to the memorable events of the old year, we sat down and I noticed that the ballroom was already deafeningly buzzing. It was decorated in glittering fashion, red and white foil bunting, shiny balloons, garlands and colorful paper streamers hung from the chandeliers. I had never been to one of these hotel New Year's parties before and it was all breathtaking.

Jake left us and then Cammy turned to me still before they began serving the festive meal. "Hey, Maddie, look at this." she shouted. She was brandishing her right hand at my nose. I focused in and saw a large, glittering diamond on a white gold ring.

"Does that mean, what I think it means?" I asked a little confused and surprised.

"Yes, sure does. He proposed to me on his birthday. We're getting married. I'm so excited!"

I squealed again and gave Cammy another kiss as I tried to wrap my arms around her bare shoulders.

"When? When?" I shouted. I took her hand to look at the ring more closely. Milos noticed but didn't say anything, just smiled.

"No set date, just yet, but we've talked about sometime in late May. We will go to Prague again right afterwards as a kind of honeymoon for two weeks starting around the first of June. Around my birthday. I'll be thirty."

"And then a married woman again. You will then have two of your life objectives in your hands."

Cammy started to giggle. "I'm so happy. I don't need any champagne tonight to feel so deliriously happy. Excuse me if I act giddy all night."

"You're excused of course. It's everyone else here who are acting giddy for no particular reason other than the change of the calendar who needs to be excused."

So, I thought. She's done it. She's in love with this older man who has worshiped her for the past five years or so. And they are going to get wed and make a family.

A while later she continued: "And Maddie, whatever you're doing out in Cleveland, in late May, you have to drop everything and come to my wedding. You will be the maid of honor. Promise you'll come."

"For all the world I wouldn't miss it."

The festive meal was beginning to be served. And still Jake couldn't partake with us, because the band was playing. But he had told me to hold a plate for him because they would break at 8:45 for twenty minutes and he wanted something to eat for the night. I did some little calculations in my head and it seemed clear to me that I wasn't going to get to dance with Jake that evening at all, because he was fully committed. I was glad for him that he was performing (and going to be well paid), but while we were celebrating a holiday, he was a working man, working hard. And that left me on my own. The food was super but predictable, roast beef and roasted potatoes. Nothing really all that fancy. I ate with relish but I noticed that Cammy did not. She was paying too much attention to Milos. I enjoyed the prime rib, but it was too much for me, and the potatoes on my plate were cold.

After the dishes from the main course were cleared away, all but Jake's, the band switched to dance music and couples began to stand up and drift to the dance floor in front of the bandstand. I stayed at the table, and three times had to ward off waiters who attempted to clear away Jake's food. Finally after twenty minutes of playing the band took its first break and Jake along with the dancers all returned to the tables. Jake was not in a talking mood, as he was eating fast–he had only a twenty- five minute break—and the canned music they put on the sound system was the infinitely repeated, faux—joyful winter holiday music, not suited for dancing. So we didn't dance together either. No one at the table addressed Jake and he spoke to no one, including me.

As the last hours of 2010 ran down I was sitting at the table feeling more and more awful. Cammy and Milos were gayly and ecstatically paying attention only to each other, and the other couples made conversation and gave repeated toasts to some past achievement for the year. The band howled out it second set of music, which was lively and upbeat, but I was feeling alone and devoid of mirth. Cammy had love and was going to marry the man with her, but I was loveless and isolated. Finally the New Year's countdown started. Jake was on the stage with the band which was silent and waiting for the countdown. Milos was pouring out champagne around the table. And then the countdown. And then a gong sounded and a huge roar rose from all the partiers, hurrays and cheers, and popping of crackers and confetti tubes, and the band started "Auld Lang Syne". Cammy was deep in a passionate kiss with Milos, and the other couples were also kissing. But I stood by myself with a half drunken flute of stale champagne and for a moment all I could think about was going back to my cold apartment in sad, poor Cleveland, its streets choked with dirty mounds of snow. After only one round of "Auld Lang Syne" everyone rushed outside to the front sidewalk of the Parker, some in their coats, most without, to watch the beginning of the giant fireworks display in the Boston Common just opposite the hotel. It wasn't particularly cold, maybe only thirty degrees, but it was a bit windy and I got thoroughly chilled by the time the last sparklers fizzled out and fell to the earth, the explosion echoing through the streets of the city. I was glad to get back to our table. The band started again playing a set of music suited for dancing, mostly the ersatz jollity of songs by Abba and other dance hits of the 70s and 80s. Cammy went dancing again with Milos and the other couples also were on the dance floor. In the meanwhile the waiters started serving out from the large white cake that they had rolled into the room just as the clock struck out the twelfth ring. The cake had a large burning sparkler sending up its brilliant flames. But by twelve twenty people were already heading for the cloakroom and beginning to leave, even though many remained dancing on the dance floor. Cammy came laughing back to the table pulling Milos by the arm. "This is the greatest party I've ever been to." she exclaimed breathlessly as they sat down. I had to agree. It was a very nice party, but I was depressed—or more likely feeling glum from being drunk on the champagne and wine. Jake had promised that we would dance together at the last break at twelve-thirty. And right on schedule the band stopped and the overhead speakers began playing disco hits. Jake came to the table, his bow tie already off, and he asked me to dance with him. It felt to me as if he had to drag me onto the dance floor, but we danced actively for the next twenty minutes until I was feeling absolutely leaden. When we got back to the table, Cammy said that she and Milos were going to start the walk back to his house. Jake began eating his piece of cake. But his coffee was completely cold and there were no more refills going around the room. I recalled that it was a very delicious cake, with lemon icing, and I wanted, in that moment, a second piece. We stood up and said our goodbyes first to Cammy and Milos—Cammy was flush in the face but still beaming with joy—and then not long after that we said our goodbyes to the other guests at our table who also took their leave. Cammy and Milos were going to stroll back to Milos's house. And afterwards Jake and I were alone at a large table for twelve. We kinda looked at each other—it was hard to talk because the music was so loud—and I think that expression of emptiness, the 'what's next?' look that Jake gave me—said all that could be said. We were finished as lovers. The New Year promised us nothing more together.

Yeah, sure, we went back to his apartment in Charleston well after two o'clock and we fell into bed together and we dutifully made love until we fell asleep. But I didn't feel like I loved Jake, and I'm pretty sure he reciprocated the feeling. It wasn't the wild passionate, sweaty sex we had had the previous summer—the wild spark had gone out. He no longer loved me much either it seemed. We had talked a great deal during the month of December about his moving out and joining me in Cleveland, but we had not reached a resolution on that. He remained indecisive. Before I had flown back to Boston I had extracted an invitation from the orchestra for Jake to audition on the tenor and alto sax for a position as the designated saxophone player. It was set for the twentieth of January and the invitation included a play list of the orchestral excerpts that he would be expected to prepare and play for the evaluation committee. It was really a very exceptional opportunity, because the audition would be a non-compete audition. He just had to impress the evaluators. But Jake did not respond with any enthusiasm, and although he accepted the invitation and told me, and then the people at the CO that he would come, it didn't seem to me as if his heart was in it. When I left on Tuesday to return to Cleveland, Jake did not escort me to the airport. He said he had other things he had to do—but he couldn't, or wouldn't, say what those other things were. So when the twentieth was approaching I called him to find out what he was planning on doing and how he was feeling with regards to the excerpts they would ask him to perform. He said all the pieces were easy and no problem for him, so he was ready. And the day before his audition he did fly in and come to my apartment. But that night he was cold and indifferent toward me both at dinner and afterwards. The only thing he said about moving to join me here was that he still could not figure out how he was going to make a living. I said that he could live off my income until he got on his feet with new jobs or prospects, but maybe that only made him feel worse. He was not a liberated man; he apparently could not face being supported by his woman. I also added that I was sure he would win the audition and the appointment was virtually already his.

But he did not impress the auditors of his audition. I have no idea what happened, or how he performed, and Jake wouldn't say, other than to say that they did not make him an offer. We did not make love that night either, and the next day after breakfast he left for the airport. I had a sinking feeling as he walked down the snow covered sidewalk to the bus stop that that was it with Jake; that I would never see or hear from him again. Shortly afterwards I saw one of the evaluators at a rehearsal and I asked him how Jake was at his audition. He did not want to tell me, but eventually he did. But what he said was revealing, "Technically he was accurate, his sound is good, but he played everything as if his heart was not in it. He did not understand the context or the feeling in the particular excerpt. We all agreed with that assessment." His heart was not in it—that pretty much summed up our little love affair. Through the rest of the winter and into the spring I did not hear from him, but I tried calling him a few times, but never could connect. I wrote him some emails, but didn't get any answers. We were finished completely, and I'm sure I'll never know what happened. I don't understand how men feel love, but it's pretty clear when a man does not love you. All communication stops and distances are both literally and figuratively built between you. I carried on with the work at the CO and was quite busy. The conductor there then was quite a bit more rigorous and demanding than what I had been accustomed to at the BPhil. I remember Cammy saying the same thing. Although in my case I think the conductor terrorized me and I worked so hard so that I would never make even the slightest mistake. That means I practiced almost every day for three or four hours. Always in preparation for the next concert—always music that was new to me. For the next five months after my return from Boston it was all work and no play. No dates, no boyfriends, no free time actually.

Cammy and I, without the possibility of meeting over lunch or after rehearsals, resumed our communications by chat and FaceTime. But not as frequently as in the years b efore 2011 when I still lived in the Boston area.

### 15 February 2011

**CammyFB**
Hey there Maddie, long time, no hear from you.
Can we FT this evening?

**MADDIE**
That works for me. Say about 8?

**CammyFB**
That works for me. I've moved in with Milos. I have
to talk when he won't be disturbed. And he has
some lessons this evening. We live like newlyweds
in this great big house. 7:30 would be better.

**MADDIE**
OK, I'll call you then. Love you and miss you.

**CammyFB**
Yeah I miss you too. A lot. But you know the drill—
really busy, and now I'm taking care of one of the
world's greatest musical geniuses.

**MADDIE**
OK bye bye. You'll tell me tomorrow.

I called her the next evening at 7:30.

February 15, 2011

"Hey there, Cammy. How are you doing?"

"I've never felt happier in my life. I'm already the wife to the smartest, greatest man alive and I'm so in love with him. The marriage will just be the confirmation of what we already are. Every day is like special. I told you I've moved in with him. And we're discovering both of us what life can be like as a couple. I never knew that love could be so ecstatic and joyful. Those are words I hardly ever used before in my life."

"That's wonderful, Cammy. I'm so happy for you."

"And I wanted to update you on our plans, before I totally forget, being lost in loving Milos."

"Okay. I'm listening."

"We've set our wedding date for Saturday May 28th. In the afternoon, in Salem. You can make that date, can't you? I mean you don't have to play a concert that evening in Cleveland?"

"Even if I do, I would come and miss the concert."

"And I want you to be my maid of honor. You know, best friend and that sort oft thing. I want the wedding to be really pretty and formal, and dresses, all white and pink. I'll send you what I've decided when I get to thinking about it. Maybe next month. The wedding itself will be in the Catholic Church there in town. That doesn't get in the way of your religious preferences does it?"

"No, are you kidding, Cammy? I was born into the Catholic Church. Remember, I'm ItalianAmerican. Even though I've not practiced religion since I was seven or eight."

"Good. And we'll have the wedding party at the Salem Country Club. It's really pretty out there. It won't be a large party. Milosh wants to see if his sister can't come. But we've only just begun to think about the party and who to invite. Ironically, Milosh is scheduled to conduct concerts with the BSO on Thursday and Friday, before that date. In fact he has lots of conducting work lined up in the next few months."

Cammy continued: "And we've decided that we will leave for Prague for two weeks the very next day, the 29th. We are both going to participate. Milosh is going to conduct one of his new pieces which the Prague Philharmonic commissioned from him. He's putting the finishing touches on it right now. And on another night, he's going to conduct a concert with Hura's works. But you know what he's arranged?"

"No, tell me."

"He's gotten his friend Jiri to agree to let me perform Milosh's concerto for oboe in one concert, and the Martinu oboe concerto in another concert. Can you imagine?"

"And why not? You're the best in New England, right? And you've already performed it with the BSO." I said. "He has a lot of confidence in you. I think he always has, since he first started paying attention to you. He loves you for more than just your good looks, you know"

"It seems he likes my looks too," Cammy giggled.

"I should hope so. Remember, it was your smiling, laughing, cheery face that he said first attracted him to you? Remember that day on the sidewalk café, when he first came up to us and introduced himself to you, professing his attraction?"

"Yes, I remember. It was a day that will always stand out in my memory."

"But, that sounds like you'll be taking a working honeymoon, right?"

"Yes, but I think it will be a lot of fun. Although I looked at the Martinu piece already and it's something of a challenge."

"But you have time to work it out, don't you?"

"Yeah, sure. But right now, Milos is working so hard. He's working on a symphony that he started last year, and he has started writing an opera. Can you imagine?"

"No, that must take up all his free time. Do you ever see him, besides when you're in bed with him?"

"Yeah sure. Whenever I have a free moment, he takes regular breaks and we take walks around the city, just like we did early in our relationship. But still he has these upcoming concerts he needs to conduct with the BSO, and he teaches two classes at the Conservatory this semester. He's at one just now, an evening class. And in every other moment he is working in his studio, composing or listening to his music. As I say, he is really working hard. Like he was a twenty something."

"You mean like Mozart or Beethoven?"

"Yeah, almost you could say he's working himself too hard. But he denies it. He says he has never enjoyed so much composing new pieces as he is now. And he tells me it is because I now love him that he has become so happy."

"He's always saying the nicest things to you, Cammy. I'm envious. But really. You are the luckiest girl alive to be connected with him."

"I think so too. But speaking of working hard, why don't you have a concert tonight?"

"We've been performing a festival of concertos by Bartok. And the conductor is Loran Maazel. We gave concerts this week on Wednesday, Thursday and last night. So tonight is a cold night. And we'll perform a matinee tomorrow followed by the evening festival closing concert tomorrow evening. That's a lot. Don't you think?"

"Yeah, you'd never get the BSO to work so hard."

"Yeah. But our music director is really a task-master. We work really hard for the concerts for our Miami residency, which is coming up soon. And otherwise I have to make sure I prepare everything so that I don't make even one mistake. Because he's rather unforgiving. So, I'm working hard to make sure I've got everything down cold."

"Well, that's not bad."

"No, but it means I'm an all-work, no play girl now. I practice, go to rehearsals, and go to perform concerts, eat, and sleep–and not enough sleep–and that's all."

"Doesn't Jake occupy some of your time?"

"No, I guess I haven't told you. We're finished. He just couldn't face coming out here to live with me. Too much of a sacrifice for him."

"Didn't he go out there and audition for Cleveland?"

"Yeah, he did. But he didn't impress the committee listening to him. So that was that. No appointment—and maybe he felt ashamed of that outcome. But I haven't heard from him since. And I don't think I will again."

"Oh, I'm sorry, Maddie."

"No need to be. I guess it really wasn't love. Or at least he didn't love me. He loved only the sex, and when I left for here, I guess he figured he could find sex there in Boston, without me. So you don't need to invite him to the wedding party."

"I guess not."

"Where are you Cammy? I don't recognize the room that you're in."

"Oh, I'm in the second bedroom. We've converted it into my studio so I can practice and it doesn't interfere with Milosh's work. He's on the first floor. You can stay here when you come for the wedding. Don't worry."

"Oh, but that'll only get in your way. Don't you think? I could just as easily stay in your Somerville apartment."

"No, I no longer live there so I've rented it out–the whole building is now rented out to three families. So you can't live there for even one night."

"Oh wow. You really have changed your life already."

"Yes–complete transformation. And I already feel like a married woman. No longer a little girl, no longer married to an absentee and indifferent man."

"Well, I've said it before, Cammy. You deserve the love of Milos, and happiness."

"I don't know about deserve, Maddie. But I'm thankful for the love from Milosh and I'm indeed happy. He treats me so well, like his 'little treasure' as he often says, Like I've never been before in my life."

"It makes me really happy to hear it, Cammy."

"Don't worry, Maddie. Love will find you too someday. I know it. [She said that as if she had heard the depressive sound in my voice. I had been trying to hide my feelings.]

"Well, that's all I have to tell you. We haven't really talked about what's going on with you, Maddie."

"Nothing for me to report. My colleagues in the flute section are all really super–they've given me a lot of support and really consider me an important part of the group. I get on really well with the first flute. Can you imagine? She's a super woman. She has five kids from teenager on down. How she ever manages that and playing superbly all of our repertoire, I can never imagine. I don't think I could do that. And she's still really nice and she looks like she's closer to 25 in age than to 50. I think I need to start taking better care of my skin–like she does. Other than that, nothing to report. No boyfriends, no dates."

"And no one is making unwanted passes at your ass, either?"

"No thank God for that."

"Well, I'm glad for you, Maddie. We should talk together like this more often. Remember? Like we used to, when we were both in the BPhil?"

"Yeah, I remember. I kinda miss those days, you know. I miss gabbing with you over nothing in particular. Those were the days."

"Weren't they?"

"I have to go now. Milosh is due back any moment now. And we'll have a late supper that I whipped up. So bye now."

"Bye Cammy. Remember, your Maddie loves you."

"I do you too. Bye bye."

Initially I felt overwhelming sadness after Cammy got off the FT. So alone and so empty–forlorn and far away from all my friends, even from my mother. And outside my window the wind moaned, it was so cold and dark on the streets under mounds of snow. I almost cried. I heard dirges rising in my mind in response to the complaints of the wind around the windows–almost like the Andante by Barber. But then I started thinking about all the changes that have occurred to Cammy in just the past few months, and the happiness she now visibly displays, and I began to feel really much better. Cammy was in love. What a beautiful outcome to her story. And I've witnessed most of it. If it was possible for her, maybe it would be possible for me too. I thought then of the love songs and the positive feelings of Bizet's Carmen and it made me feel better. I went to the kitchen and took a Vitamin D tablet. Maybe I haven't been getting enough of that vitamin. But then I remembered that in two weeks we would all be going to Miami, so I felt certain my vitamin D deficiency would disappear there in the sun and warmth of south Florida, and maybe even my depression.

3 March 2011

**CammyFB**

I forgot to tell you the last time we spoke, that James Levine is finished here at the BSO. In February he told the orchestra that he would be conducting for the rest of the season because of illness. And then yesterday he's terminating his contract effective immediately and that he would not be conducting at Tanglewood again.

MADDIE

> Sad to hear that, of course. But I gathered that he was not too popular with the players?

**CammyFB**

Not really popular. But in fairness, in the past few years, since I've been working here, he has missed so many concerts. He doesn't rehearse us much when it is his turn to conduct. And he doesn't communicate much. You can see him shaking at times.

MADDIE

> Yeah, we have a rocky relationship with our music director. It seems like he is trying to break into the orchestra.

**CammyFB**

So that means that they've asked Milosh to conduct six times between now and September. Four times until June 20th. And they've invited a new man that they want to try out as Levine's successor. Milosh is worried about the added stress on his work schedule. And also worried that they might terminate his residency.

**MADDIE**

That would be bad. But he doesn't want to be considered as a successor to Levine, does he?

**CammyFB**

No, he stresses that from now until he dies–God forbid not soon—he is a composer first and foremost. And he has so much more yet that he still wants to write. I have to run now. Bye.

**MADDIE**

OK, bye for now. Maybe we can Facetime soon?

**CammyFB**

Yeah we can set a time. Ahoj—that's Czech for bye. Milosh uses it all the time.

I was right about Miami fixing up my mood. The sun and warmth was great, but even more reassuring was the encouraging reception I've gotten on the beach here in my new swim suit. The young men, it seems, really like my figure. That's reassuring. There's no one even noticing me in the least in Cleveland. Of course, most of the hooting fans on the sand are Cuban, so they're really macho and I don't pay too much attention to them. Anyway, when we returned from Miami I was feeling refreshed and restored, and the winter blues did not return for the rest of that winter—my first in Cleveland.

Facetime

14 March 2011

"How are you doing Cammy? Still loving Milos?"

"You bet. I love him to death. He is such a wonderful man. Last month we bought a new king sized bed and not only is it comfortable and quiet when we make love, it is also so soft and spacious that we are both sleeping soundly without disturbing the other."

"I'm back from Miami about a week now and it was great. I understand why the Canadian snowbirds fly down there in the winter. It's really perked me up."

"I have good news to tell you, and some bad news also. Milosh got word that his younger sister died late last month. From cancer. She was only sixty two years old, and her illness came on suddenly. She was so nice to me when we last went to Prague. Like a sister to me. Milosh told me that he really loved her when he was young, but that he spent most of forty years without ever seeing or hearing from her.

And then last week Jiri told Milosh while he was informing him about the preparations for the Prague Spring Festival, that his wife had also died. She was the same woman who was Milosh's first wife, but who left him shortly after they fled Czechoslovakia in sixty-eight. Milosh was really sad for two days when he heard the news about his sister. But he told me that he was actually somewhat relieved that we don't have to meet his ex—on this next visit to Prague. But he was consoling to Jiri."

"So that was the bad news, I presume. What's the good news?"

"Milosh got word from this musicologist, a well-known fellow who teaches at Oberlin Conservatory, that he would like to write a biography about Milosh—he already knew about the difference between his name Milos and his real name Milosh—and also he would complete the catalogue of all his music. Can you imagine? He came over last week for a preliminary interview with Milosh. He already had compiled most of Milosh's oeuvre but of course did not have any of the works that Milosh has completed in the past four years. Most of those have neither been published or performed publicly yet. Well Milosh agreed to cooperate with this guy, Dr. Reginald Spann—he's English, very proper, and Milosh showed him the scores of the pieces that he had missed in his compilation. But Milosh was surprised to find that Dr. Spann had catalogued even works that Milosh had forgotten that he had written. Milos said it was a very friendly interview, and he told him that he could get more information also from Carl Husa, his mentor. And this Dr. Spann then said that it had indeed been Husa who had recommended to him to write a biography of Milosh Nowak. It seems that Dr. Spann has already written and published a biography of Husa, and he presented Milosh with a copy. Milosh was amazed. And he had forgotten that Husa was so much older than Milosh was. Apparently in working on the biography for Husa, Dr. Spann learned that Husa had been both a sponsor and mentor to Milosh and that there was a correspondence between them. Milos was again amazed because he had written all those letters in the years before the personal computer came about, he had typed them, and he did not have copies of any of them. Dr. Spann asked his permission to read them. Husa had declined to show him the letters unless he got first permission from Milosh, so he was asking Milosh's permission. And Milosh of course gave it to him. And Milosh also mentioned that he had written letters in the early years to his friend Jiri Beloslovacek. And Dr. Spann asked him if he couldn't have two or three more interviews, one especially for the years of Milosh's conservatory years and then escape from Czechoslovakia. Milosh told him that he was going with me—to the Prague Spring Festival in June and that he could find for Dr. Spann copies of his first published works which he had composed before nineteen sixty-eight. Milosh told me that Dr. Spann was ecstatic about that."

"How fascinating. You did not attend the interview?"

"No, but Milosh would like me to sit in and attend the next two interviews. As a way to learn more about him. About when he was young, a time in his life which he has not yet told me much about. Dr. Spann learned at this first interview that Milosh and I are engaged to get married, and that was huge news to him. So he wanted to meet me and of course include me in the next interviews. Can you imagine? Am official biography to appear about my Milosh?"

"It's very exciting, Cammy. Seems like that certainly counts as good news."

"Yeah, and it will probably get the word out broadly about Milosh's music, more of it will be performed. And publishing houses might be a little more likely to promptly publish his new scores. That is certainly good news. You can imagine how pleased that interview made Milosh. He was walking on air for the past week. He said to me in bed the other night, "You know, Cammy, this biography will mean everyone will know about my love for you, and how important you have been to my life in the past five years." Yes, Milosh said that."

"I'm not too surprised that Milos says such things about you. He worships you."

"And I now am wildly in love with him too. You know, we're already working hard to make a family, too. He really wants a son, or daughter. Before it is too late."

"Too late? What do you mean? Do you mean there are fertility issues?"

"No, we checked. And the tests confirmed that we're both fertile and capable of conceiving children, normal, healthy children."

"Thank God for that."

"And you know what else? I got the score of the Martinu oboe concerto. The second one that I'm scheduled to play in Prague this June. It's not too difficult at all. I can kill it. I've already started practicing it. Milosh is supposed to conduct it, and he says he has already memorized it, but he'l conduct it from the score anyway, just to avoid embarrassing Jiri, or Martinu for that matter."

"But I am only talking about myself and Milosh. What about you, Maddie?"

"Oh, I have no news here about myself. The Orchestra is busy, and in three weeks' time we go again for a ten-day residency in Miami. I really like that. And it will be spring when we get back. I'm looking forward to that. But you know, it's just work, and back home for me. But you know it really pleases me to hear that about your love with Milosh. And I really look forward to your wedding. It works out fine for me, because that weekend is a cold weekend" for Cleveland. I don't have to miss any concerts."

"Well maybe you could think about coming to Prague, if you have free time. I mean after the wedding."

"Thanks, Cammy. That could be fun. But I do have concerts in the first half of June. And besides I couldn't afford to go to Prague and stay in a guesthouse. I would like to see you and

Milosh perform. But it's kinda out of my budget, with the airfare and room and board. You know."

"Okay, I understand. You know, on an unrelated topic, if you don't have time to meet any interesting people or potential boyfriends, maybe you could try a dating app to meet someone compatible, to keep you company."

"You think?"

"Yeah, they seem to work. Do you remember my friend Charlene? She met her current boyfriend through one of those dating apps. They seem to really hit it off."

"I'll look into it. Thanks."

"Anyway, we should talk again like this in about ten days or a week."

"It's always so nice to be able to talk face to face through this medium. Almost as good as being there in person. I miss those times."

"Time to sign off, Maddie."

"OK, bye bye."


So FaceTime was the foundation of our new relationship, between Cammy and me. We used chat lines less and less, but of course conversed on FaceTime less frequently than we had with messenger chat. It was clear to me, also that Cammy spoke more frankly over FaceTime than she did when writing on Messenger. I got deeper insights into her feelings and her thinking and her relationship with Milos. It helped being able to see the reactions on her face, and presumably it helped her too seeing my reactions.

While I was in Miami in late-March early-April, I got an email from Cammy. She was planning her wedding and in it she sent me a photo of the dress for the maids of honor. She indicated where I could get the dress—it was an online dress shop where they custom made dresses to order. I had never bought a dress online–I bought my small needs for dresses off the shelf. Cammy told me to order the dress right away as they said they usually took four to six weeks to finish and deliver their dresses. So I did just that one evening shortly after I got back to Cleveland. But it wasn't so easy. First of all I needed a measuring tape and had to run out the next day to buy one. Then of course it wasn't so easy taking all of the measurements by myself, the tape would slip off, or creep up. I must've looked crazy standing in my underwear contorting myself in front of a mirror trying to measure my waist and my hips with a twelve foot long measuring tape running around me like some stiff serpent wrapping me in its coils. I finally succeeded and put in the order. It wasn't cheap. Five hundred and seventy dollars before taxes and delivery. I had never bought such expensive clothes before. I wondered how much Cammy's wedding gown would cost. I hadn't asked her how much her classy, sexy dress she wore at the New Year's party cost, but I could well imagine that she spent more than I was going to on this dress. And that the wedding gown would cost more than a thousand dollars. I had trouble imagining that if I ever got married, I would ever buy such a dress. I began imagining the huge cost that Cammy's wedding party would come to. But then I had no idea how many people would be attending, so I stopped thinking about it. By and large Cammy and I never discussed money or expenditures. Except maybe we talked about and compared our salaries. I wondered if Milos would be paying for the wedding and wedding party. I had no idea about his income but I was inclined to think that it would be a burden on his income.

Facetime

5 April 2011

"Hiya Maddie, I just wanted to talk to you briefly about what's going on here. You got my note about the dress, right?"

"Yeah, and I ordered it. Should come early next month. It looks really pretty. And very feminine. I hope I got the measurements right and that it fits me well."

"Good. We are so busy here. In fact, Milosh is working so hard, I really worry about his health holding up. The man has tremendous stamina and he works ten hours every day on his compositions, in spite of his work obligations at the Conservatory and with the BSO. He conducted last weekend's concerts and they were really well received. By coincidence it was a concert of Czech music, Dvorak and Smetana. Really pretty."

"This weekend the orchestra is going to perform his second work that he's written for his residency. A guest conductor will lead us, a guy named Gilbert. Apparently every orchestra around America wants him as a conductor. He's being tried out here as a successor to Levine."

"Never heard of him. Have you had rehearsals with him yet?"

"No, we will have our first rehearsal with him tomorrow. Milosh will be there to assist the interpretation of his piece. It's a big piece, kind of a tone poem, almost forty-five minutes long. Really flashy. And Milosh included a really good part for me in it—intentionally. And my parents are going to come down here for the Saturday concert. I hope everything goes well. It's a brilliant piece, lots of catchy themes and some unusual rhythms."

"And can you believe it? Before he's even finished with this piece—he hasn't given it a name yet, so it is just symphony in one movement—he's working hard on this opera and at the same time composing what he calls a concerto grosso."

"An opera?"

"Yeah, haven't I told you about it before? When he was young he wrote two operas. But they were both in the Czech language, so they haven't been performed much at all. This one is in Czech too. He wrote the libretto himself, last year. It's a story of the failed love affair of Leos Janacek. Milosh really admires the music of Janacek. He wrote the libretto after he read this book called Intimate Letters, which included the love letters that Janacek wrote to his lover, a young woman named Kamilla. Milosh recently had the libretto translated into English and he gave it to me to read."

"And what do you think of it? The libretto I mean."

"Well, it's about unrequited love. Very interesting story. He's shown me some of the music he has written already. It's super, you know. Just super. But I told him that it seemed like it was our story."

"What do you mean? I'm not familiar with Janacek's love for Kamila."

"Well, Janacek was much older than Kamilla when he first met her and he fell in love with her. And even though she was already married and even had a child from her husband, he wrote lots of love letters and arranged clandestine meetings with her. And her love reanimated his composition. Milosh says that after Janacek met Kamilla his musical compositions became better than anything he had written earlier in his life. You see? A story like ours."

"Yes, maybe, but you're going to marry Milos, right? You love Milos, right?"

"Yes, yes of course. And that's just what Milosh said. He said that I reciprocated his love and we're getting married. So ours is a different story. And that Janacek's Intimate Letters revealed a tragedy. A love affair that never was fulfilled. And he said besides, Janacek was really too self-absorbed in himself to ever really love anyone, regardless of what he wrote. Milosh said that he hoped he was not anything like Janacek, in his love for me. I think that's right. So the opera is a love story, but also a tragedy. Because Janacek fell dead before his love for Kamila was ever consummated, or requited. Anyway, he's trying to finish it by the end of this summer."

"Sounds sad, Cammy. Love unfulfilled. I suppose with those letters written by Janacek, that Kamila didn't write answers, or if she did, that her letters in reply were not preserved."

"I don't know. I'll have to ask Milosh. I didn't write answers to Milosh's letters. How could I?"

"I don't know. Maybe he rarely asked you anything for you to reply to."

"Yeah, well. It turns out that this Dr. Spann also wrote a biography of Janacek, and has a book where he translated many of those "Intimate Letters". Maybe a coincidence. But also maybe his interest in Milosh and in Karl Husa before him lies in the Czech connection, and the musical legacy of Janacek."

"Sounds reasonable."

"By the way, he came again for another interview—Dr. Spann I mean—with Milosh. They talked for four hours. Milosh was so frustrated afterwards. Missing all that work time. He's coming again at the end of next week for another interview, and this time he wants me to be there as well. He also asks me if I can find other students who have studied composition with Milosh, if I know of any in the Boston area. He'd like to speak to them. As well as to his students of conducting."

"So Milos will miss more work."

"Yeah. It seems so. But you should see him work. He is amazing. I think Milosh is a genius. He knows by memory all kinds of music. Avant garde as well as the classics. And he can bring up a line of music on the keyboard and start playing with it. He knows so much. He played an excerpt from Lutoslawski the last time I was there in his study with him, and then he compared it to another piece. I've never heard of Lutoslawski's music. And the other piece was by Berio. I didn't know anything about him either. And then he played a piece, with full harmonics, that he said was his merging of these two excerpts. It sounded great, but I couldn't hear how it was related to the two other pieces. He said to me, "Don't worry Cammy, I'm still playing around with this idea, to see whether it can make a theme that supports sonata treatment." And before I could comment, he then played a passage from Smetana. I've heard Smetana and his music before. He said, "Did you hear that?" Those other two excerpts seem to have been lifted straight out Smetana with only minor changes. That's what I hear. It seems like almost every week I learn more about how brilliant Milosh is. And talented. I just had no idea until after I moved in with him."

"Cammy, I'm really sorry that I can't come to hear the concert this weekend. The one with Milos's premiere performance. I'd love to hear it. You know, up to now, after most of the last five years I haven't heard any of Milos's compositions in live performance."

"Well, I've only heard three pieces of his. One here at the BSO, and the others in Prague. So if you get to know a man through his music, I'm just a beginner too."

"And I don't suppose there are any recordings of his works available either?"

"I think there are. But they're only available on the Czech label, Supraphon. I'm planning on finding what I can this next time in Prague and I will buy them and bring them back with me. I'll try to keep this secret from Milos and make them as a gift to him."

"Maybe you can buy some extra copies for me? I'd like to hear them."

"Okay. But now I have to go."

"Me too. I have a date this evening."

"Maddie? Really? Did you use the dating app I gave you?"

"In fact, I did. Having my first blind date tonight. Going out to an Italian restaurant. I guess the guy figured with my name being Martinelli that I would like Italian food. Well I do. So, Ciao for now."

"Bye, Maddie. Have fun."


As it was, that date was not too successful. I ate too much pasta and felt stuffed. And also self conscious about feeling stuffed and appearing to be too plump. And the guy on the other side of the table was a real dud. He had nothing to talk about. And he didn't know anything about Italian food or music, or just about anything other than basketball. Of course I know nothing about basketball. He also wasn't from Cleveland originally, and he also did not know anything about the city. Add to that, he was kinda funny looking. So, I wrote the experience off to a bad fit. But I tried again to make a connection. The second time my date was better—but I think the guy had lied about his age. He could just barely hold up his side of the conversation, but he acted bored by me. So that date didn't work out either. And we both amicably said farewell at the end of it. I think those first two guys had a similar outlook that was very much like Jake's—they were just ordinary blokes drifting through life, with no real goals or plans for the future, and no ideas of what they wanted out of life. Thinking back over my time with Jake, I think the only things he wanted out of life were to play saxophone, and to fuck with girls as often as possible. I tried a third time, but by this time it was already late April and I couldn't do a date on a weekend, because of our concerts schedule. The app took note of that apparently and found me on a date with a guy who said he liked classical music and also could date on weekends.

And wouldn't you know it? This third date, when I met him in the Fountain Park of Eternal Life at around two o'clock in the afternoon—what a funny name for a public park, I thought, very evangelical, was it maybe a converted cemetery?—as I was walking up to him, he looked very familiar to me. He was oriental looking, Chinese-American, short, slight and with short black hair. He turned to me and asked if I were Maddie Martinelli. And then he too reacted to me as if I looked familiar to him. "Are you by any chance a flute player in the Cleveland Orchestra?" he asked me. And it was then that I recognized him. He was a viola player in the orchestra. But I hadn't until then learned his name: it was Davey Chang (actually Dai wan, but no one used that name.) And indeed he played viola and had been in the orchestra for four years. And he was from Taiwan, but had studied in San Francisco and became an American citizen not long before. So we laughed together over the coincidence and began to walk down the downtown toward the Lake. He was not really good looking, but at least he could carry a conversation. And he had lots to tell me about how he got to Cleveland.

He admitted right away that even after four years he didn't know the city really well, and it didn't feel like home to him yet. Apparently while there are lots of blacks living in Cleveland, and lots of Hispanics, there are not so many Chinese people. He thought most of the Chinese people he met were in the orchestra, but not all of them spoke Chinese, and none of them spoke the dialect he had grown up with in Taipei. So we visited the Rock and Roll Hall of Fame. It was the first time for both of us to go there. I think I had a lot more interesting discoveries there—memories from my childhood listening to pop radio—than Davey did. And afterwards we walked back into the city and had dinner at a Tex-Mex place. Altogether it was a nice introductory get together, and we agreed to go out on another date. Of course we saw each other at Severance Hall both in rehearsals and concerts in the next four weeks. And we met together afterwards over coffee and talked—nothing structured. He was a nice guy, and an interesting character. He had already had so many adventures, some not so pleasant, and he was able to tell me about them with a good sense of humor. We went out on several dates in May and early June and I grew to like him more and more, and he seemed to like me too. Of course I saw him and spoke with him at every concert and every rehearsal.

## Facetime

2 May 2011

[Some minutes of preliminary small talk. I had called Cammy at around our scheduled time.]

"So have you prepared the two oboe solos that you're going to perform in Prague?"

"I'm ready for Milos's concerto. But I'm still working on the Martinu piece. It's not so difficult, but it is very complicated in areas. Milos has taken some time off to listen to me and offer some insights."

"He's still real busy, hard at work on his compositions?"

"You can say that. I think he tries to put in at least ten hours every day, except when he has to conduct or in the evenings when he has classes to give."

"And has been interrupted again by his biographer?"

"Yep, he came last week and we spent four hours with him. He asked a little about our romance, how it started, who initiated the relationship, and how I felt about Milos initially. Dr. Spann raised the issue of the difference in our ages, and whether that bothered me. He referenced specifically the story of Leos Janacek and Kamila Stossova. He was surprised to learn that that was the subject of one of Milos's current projects, an opera about Janacek's love."

"So what did you tell him? I mean Milos did not look or act his age when he first came up to you. Now did he? And now you have intimate insight into how or whether he acts his age, now that you're engaged to be married."

"I didn't want to dwell on it so much with Dr. Spann. But he apparently has done a lot of work on the young women who became the lovers of much older composers. I think he's thinking of doing a paper on it. Along the same lines he asked Milos if Cammy had acted as an inspiration to him and his composition. And Milos enthusiastically answered that inspiration was saying the very least. He said something along the lines that since he has met me that he has had an entirely new career. That musical ideas come to mind constantly."

"Dr. Spann said that in addition to Janacek who felt the same way about his Kamila, there were quite a few other composers who had affairs, fell in love or married much younger women. But not all of them claimed it made any difference to their musical output. He said the most famous of these cases was Wagner and Cosimo Liszt. But he said that it seemed from everything that has survived their love affair and marriage, that it was Cosimo who went after Wagner and seduced him at the start of their affair which was secret for a long time even while she was still married. Wagner wrote a long birthday piece that he famously played at the bottom of the stairs of their house as a wake up message, but other than that there is not any real evidence or statements that Cosimo inspired any works of Wagner."

"Spann mentioned the case of Bartok, who seemed to fall in love with his teenaged students and seduced them. He married his second wife who was twenty-three years younger than him, but apparently he did not get any inspiration from their love, although after his death she became his greatest promoter of his music, especially outside Hungary. But the real champion on the May-December lover affair it seems was Kodaly's with a nineteen year old student of his while he was seventy-seven. They married but did not have any children together in the six years remaining of his life.

"Spann gave us several examples of the elder composer falling for a young woman who became his wife. Most of the young women were musicians, and Bartok's wife was good enough on piano to play the piano part of his concerto. But most of the May-December affairs and marriages did not bear children. There was another famous Czech émigré, Martinu, who also worked for a while at Tanglewood. His affair, he told us, was really deepened by an injury he sustained after a fall there. Fascinating stories. Frankly, Maddie I didn't want to tell him much about how our love developed. I didn't say a word about the love letters Milosh wrote to me. He didn't say anything about them either. And I didn't tell him that I really want to have Milosh's baby. We're trying really hard, you know. I don't think that needs to be in a biography about Milosh the composer."

"I agree with you, Cammy. Those kinds of details are more for gossip sheets than for serious biography studies."

"Milosh and I had already decided before he came that we are not going to invite him to our wedding or the wedding party afterwards. What for? Anyway, he got enough information about our relationship over the past five years. He can make comparisons to the experience of all those other composers as he likes, but I think our case is unique. And it's way too early to say how our love will work out in the future. It's enough that Milosh says I have inspired his recent music. If Dr. Spann wants to know how specifically he can ask Milosh. But he didn't. From what I gathered from what he told us about those other examples of June-December loves, is that Dr. Spann can't put his finger on how the younger women inspired musical creativity."

"Remember, Cammy, we learned in Nielson's class at the Conservatory of the love message that Brahms sent the still married Clara Schumann? It was just the notes and words written on a postcard for that beautiful theme at the end of Brahms's First Symphony. Remember that?"

"Yeah, who could forget? Nielson even sang it for us. Definitely inspired. Very romantic. But Brahms didn't pursue his love and attraction for Clara, as you know."

"This guy, Dr. Spann, really knows a lot about composers of the last century. I mean the twentieth century. He knows his stuff but he doesn't connect one composer's music as inspiration to another's unless it has been stated by the later composer. And Milos has never mentioned to me that he's gotten inspiration for his music from another composer's compositions or orchestration. Dr. Spann asked Milos if he had felt inspired by the works of Martinu or Husa, and Milos was unable to say that he followed the musical ideas of the other men's works. But he left it, that Husa was a true mentor to him when he first arrived in the U.S. For a number of years. He even helped get some of Milos's works in front of conductors and performed."

[Cammy paused a long time and looked away from the camera on her screen—very pensive.]

"I don't think I would recognize whether structures or themes enter into Milos's pieces from others' compositions unless he specifically pointed them out to me. He doesn't quote, he changes things beyond easy recognition."

"Oh, by the way, Cammy. I got the dress yesterday. And I've tried it on. It is charming and it fits me nicely. I'll try and take a selfie of me wearing it. And if I can, I'll send the photo to you. Otherwise you'll have to wait until the wedding to see it."

"Okay. I'm finishing up most of the arrangements for the wedding party. All the invitations went out early last week. The caterer has been contracted. It's so much effort, but I am making progress with it. Milos has suggested that a small ensemble from the BSO might be put together for the wedding music and for the wedding party too. But we'd need to instruct them what pop music they would need to play, and how to play it. Also Milos has bought our air tickets and booked our hotel for Prague. So much to do yet. And we have less than a month left."

"Actually, Cammy, it all sounds like fun. You know what I mean? You're working on the wedding you always wanted, and didn't get from Gus. And arranging it just as you want it to be. By the way, how many people are coming?"

"Maybe twenty-eight, but possibly up to thirty-four. It seems that none of the people Milos would like to come from far away are coming. Jiri can't make it, because he's directing the Festival of course, and Milos's sister has died. And it seems that Karl Husa can't come because his health is failing and it would be too difficult for him to travel. All of my family will be there. Friends and girlfriends from Conservatory days are coming, but I don't know how many will be bringing boyfriends. By the way, do I understand right, that Jake won't be coming with you?"

"No, he won't. We're through. I haven't even told him about your wedding plans. Although he knew at New Year's that you and Milos were engaged to marry."

"Have you booked a flight here yet?"

"No, I need to get around to it."

"Well, Maddie, I've got to run."

"Yeah, me too. Have to practice for this weekend's concerts."

"Okay. Send me a note next time you want to gab."

## 16 May 2011

**MaddieFb**
Cammy, I bought my air tickets. I'll be arriving
on Thursday afternoon, the 26th. And I'll leave on
Sunday afternoon. Should I book a room in Salem?
How do I get there from Boston?

**CAMMY**

No, you can stay in our place in the South End. We'll drive up together to Salem on Saturday. And we'll figure out how to get you to the airport on Sunday.

**MaddieFb**

Where would I sleep at Milos's?

**CAMMY**

The third floor bedroom which I use as my studio. There's a nice comfortable bed in that room and I won't be needing to practice there for those days, as you can imagine.

What time will you be arriving? Maybe Milos can pick you up at the airport?

**MaddieFb**

Are you sure? That'd be great. And can I send your wedding gift to your parents' address by courier? If yes, could you send it to me?

**CAMMY**

Sure no problem.

# Chapter Seven



**CammyFB**

Maddie, I can't come out to the airport to meet you tomorrow. Could you jump on the T and come on out to my house on your own? There's just too much I still have to do.

**MADDIE**

Yeah, I can, no problem. Could you remind me of the street address again?

**CammyFB**

I'm at 1720 Washington Street about two blocks up from Mass Ave. Can I expect you by eleven?

**MADDIE**

No. My flight lands at 10:30, so closer to 12.

**CammyFB**

That's okay. We need to leave th1e house here, no later than 1:30. So see you tomorrow.

**MADDIE**

Is there anything that you'd like me to bring?

**CammyFB**

No. Just you. Be on time. CU.

**MADDIE**
CU2. Try to cheer up.

I got on the T and fifty minutes after landing at Logan, I was walking down Mass Ave toward Milos's townhouse. It was sunny but very breezy. I wondered how Cammy was feeling and how she was going to hold up.

It took me a long time to come up with a good idea for a wedding gift for Cammy and Milos. I quickly gave up the idea of something for the house: you know the kinds of things, fine linens, bath towels, silver service, or porcelain coffee service. They were mature and didn't need such things. Finally, as I was thinking about how they were both top professional musicians, I came up with the idea that maybe I could find some of Milos's recordings. Not so original, as Jake had done something like that for Cammy's birthday. But that led me on a search for recordings, and using Amazon and the internet search engines I found that there were three vinyl records of his works from twenty five, thirty years earlier—none of them were new, all used. There were also two CDs that had some of Milos's quartets on them. One of course was by the Kronos bunch. And once I committed to getting these items, I realized that I needed to get a record player—it was real' trendy to buy top quality record players and play antique or re-issued records on them. So that was how I arrived at a wedding gift. The three records and two CDs plus a stereo system including a state-of-the-art record player and top quality Bose speakers. A combination that should be in the living room of every top musician—or so I thought. When I went to buy them, I found out that the records and the stereo set were really expensive. And the records being rare were going to take a long time to be delivered. Maybe not even by the time of their wedding. But I ordered them anyway. "Hell, I thought, recordings of Milos's music were only going to get rarer and harder to find in the future", and thus much more expensive. That's the way a marriage should grow with time, rarer and more valuable. I put them down for delivery to

Cammy's parents' house. The delivery service promised they would arrive by the 27th of May.

I was hugely surprised when I arrived at Logan Airport to find that Cammy was waiting for me at the gate. She hadn't told me that she was going to pick me up and when she said my name out of the crowd, I nearly shrieked, it was so unexpected. We hugged and kissed and giggled. She looked great. She was dressed in a pretty blue dress—while I was dressed in my usual grungy jeans and a plain printed shirt—traveling clothes for warm weather. I was carrying a small travel bag and my maid of honor dress in a suit bag. She insisted on hiring a taxi to take us to Milos's place. She was so excited and told me all about the last-minute arrangements that she was making. She had picked up that morning the wedding corsages and boutonnieres that would be given out the next day. And she still had to confirm the florist would be decorating the church and the country club ballroom the next morning as they had agreed.

"You can't imagine how excited I am, Maddie. I wanted a big formal wedding. And making it happen has been both frustrating and really fun. Milos has paid for everything. He's really such a doll. You can't imagine how excited he is by the event. He's put together the musical ensemble from players in the orchestra and from the conservatory. It's a great music program, both for the church and the party. We've even practiced waltzing together for the first dance. And you'll really like my wedding gown—it's pearly pale pink with white lace worked into it. Most everything is done. The caterers are making the wedding cake just now. Everything else is ready and waiting."

"Sounds great. Sounds to me like this all costs a fortune. Can your parents' pay for such a fancy shebang?"

"No. As I said, Milos is footing the bill. On everything, because—you're right—it's out of my father's league. Beyond his budget. But I've been surprised to learn that Milos has saved a small fortune over the years.

He's rich. And he wants to spend his money on his future family. That's me, and our future kids."

"So this is the wedding that you really wanted and didn't get with Gus?"

"Exactly right. I had dreamed of it since I was in high school. And saw the possibilities at my sister's wedding. Her's was more traditional. You know, a virginal wedding—the young bride—she was only twenty-one when she got married. Two inexperienced young lovers dying to fall into their wedding bed after the party. Honeymoon to Cancun. So I wanted a really nice fancy wedding. But I never spoke about it. Now it seems I'm about to get one. Even though I am divorced, thirty years old."

"You could say, it's another enormous gift Milos is giving you."

"Yeah, you could say. He's so wonderful. I just love him to death."

"Uh ugh. That's the promise you're supposed to make publicly tomorrow, Cammy."

That evening, because their schedule required them to go to Salem on Saturday and to the airport flying to Frankfurt on Sunday, they had decided to eat out. We all strolled over to the pan-Asian restaurant that Cammy and I used to haunt to order a simple dinner. Cammy was super excited. Milos was strangely quiet. He apologized later, saying that he was working out a theme that he wanted to include in one of his current compositions and he couldn't get it out of his head.

"I just hope all the arrangements we've made work out. The florists need to arrive early tomorrow to decorate the church, but someone there needs to unlock the door for them."

"Remind me, what church is it?"

"It's the Catholic Church, the main one, in Salem. Ironic actually that such a historically Puritan city has a large Catholic Church."

"Are you both Catholic? I was born into a Catholic home, but I can hardly say I'm a practicing Catholic."

"I'm the same way," said Milos. "But I was raised in a Communist country that banned Catholicism."

"When I was young," said Cammy, "our family went to this church. I even had confirmation there. I sang in the choir when I was a teenager. But I can't say that I'm a believer. A few months ago when we declared that we wanted to have a church wedding there, we had to go to the priest and he ran us through a number of pledges and instructed us on what a wedding meant in the Catholic Church. We have to baptize and raise our children for instance in the Church."

"It was funny that he inspected our divorce documents." added Milos.

"Mine was written in Czech and he couldn't read it if he wanted to. He just waved that off, and said that was good. The document could've said I was a certified loony who liked mushroom farming for all he knew."

I continued with the sarcasm, "Be glad he didn't ask you for a document certifying that Cammy is not a witch; it's Salem, after all."

"I think the Essex County marriage registry asks for that." Cammy laughed

"My first marriage to Martina wasn't nearly so bureaucratic." Milos continued. "We were two twentyyear olds who had been sleeping together for two years already and we just went to the civil registry and made it official. All it took was submission of our passports, internal passports. Took five minutes. Almost no questions asked. So I was a little surprised that this interview took so long and he was so solicitous about our marriage. And the long instructions too."

"But I was most surprised when he asked at the very end of the interview if we loved each other." Cammy said.

"I never thought that the Catholic Church concerned itself about love." I said. "Was he also concerned that you are not a virgin and that both of you were divorcees?"

"He didn't explicitly address those issues, but he stressed that marriage is a holy sacrament and it is meant to make a family. He then suggested that Milos'hs age might not make procreation and family possible and had I considered that? Well, we had that one covered, as we had completed both of our fertility tests only shortly before–not at this priest's urging but out of our own concern. After that he was fine. And that's why his question at the end about love seemed so strange."

I had a good laugh over that. It reminded me that if I ever got married—who knows when now?—that I would avoid the church I was baptized in.

Then Milos again cut in. "One thing he told us that made me laugh: The priest said that he noticed that we were both musicians so that we might be appreciative of his concern that people often request music that is inappropriate for marriages, holy sacrament that it is. He said he always asked young couples—then he said "Excuse, couples getting marrie."—to appreciate that musical works often had deep meaning that was inappropriate to the occasion. And then he said we could appreciate this as musicians. He said that he always asked people to think carefully about the selection of pieces, and that he especially requested that we not use the old chestnut of Mendelssohn's Marriage March, which so many people unthinkingly use. He said that the music was written for a Shakespeare play representing the scene where a fairy married a human who had been transformed into a donkey. He said further: "Now, such a marriage is an abomination—between a fairy and an animal—and Shakespeare made it appear as a comedy spoofing carnal love, not sacred marriage." I really hadn't thought about it, but he clearly was right. It was easy for us to forgo using that march. I proposed using Clarke's Trumpet Voluntary to which he had no objections. Besides, the Mendelssohn piece is played so often it has become hackneyed."

"I'm not sure I know that piece of music." Cammy said. I had to agree I didn't know it by name.

"You will recognize it, I'm sure." said Milos. "You should remember it. It was used as the processional for Princess Diane's marriage to Prince Charles, a long time ago. After that it was played everywhere at weddings."

"Milosh, darling, I wasn't born when Diane got married."

"Oh, sorry. I forget how long ago that was."

He continued: "But you'll probably remember the recessional music I've chosen. It also uses a trumpet with an organ. It was the theme music for many years at Masterpiece Theater on WGBH."

"Nope, before my time also. I don't think I've ever seen Masterpiece Theater on TV."

"Oh, wrong again." Milos said and blushed. "You see I am so much older than you. Are you sure you still want to hook up with me? I am an old coot, you know, as they say in Maine. Come to think of it, I haven't seen Masterpiece Theater in more than fifteen years."

"I haven't heard of that expression either about an old coot. But I bet it was before your time, as well as mine." And Cammy leaned over and kissed Milos on the cheek.

"Anyway, we'll both be so flustered and ecstatic that we won't hear any of the music," he said. "I can guarantee you that." And he took her hand into his and kissed it, and made like slipping an invisible ring onto her finger.

"But after all that," I said, "The priest in Salem agreed to let the marriage take place in his church."

"Of course. It is after all a paying service, and in his interview, he could not establish any strong reasons why he would not marry us."

We all had a good laugh at that.

"But I'm still a little worried that the florists cannot get into the church early enough to set up the decorations, the garlands, and bouquets we requested," said Cammy. "Especially as after they finish there they have to go to the country club and set out the flower arrangements and bouquets there too."

"Relax Cammy," I said. "It'll all get done, and no doubt on time and just to your liking too. I feel confident."

"And you remember that you have to bring the ring for me?" Cammy said addressing Milos.

"I won't forget. The most important symbol of our love and devotion and our promises to each other. I never had one for Martina. I won't ever make that mistake again."

"Aren't you excited, Mili?"

That was the first time I had heard Cammy use that endearment with Milos.

"I can hardly breathe, my love. And I hope the musical program pleases you no end."

"I'm sure it will. But you're right. I'll be too excited to even notice."

"You said this was your childhood church, but this was the same priest you remember from then, not so long ago?" I asked.

"No, he wasn't. This was a new man. I didn't know him and he didn't know me. I guess some things do change in Catholic Churches."

"Even Popes." said Milos as he smiled.

"But coming from a socialist society," he continued, "very bureaucratic, I just wanted to say that the bureaucratic hurdles for a marriage license in this country—or at least here in Massachusetts—is just as confused and bumbling and frustrating as it was in Czechia, all those many years ago when I went through it. The Essex County registry required blood tests results, and if divorced, proof or some document proving that you're divorced. Again they didn't know how to read my certificate in Czech, so they required an apostille on a translation. That is a real nuisance and not at all easy to procure."

As we finished eating dinner and the waitress cleared away the last of the dishes, but before we were ready to leave, Cammy decided to lay out the plan for the next day's movements.

"Tomorrow, we don't have to get up early. But leave time for showers and clean up. I have already put some fruit and danishes in the fridge for breakfast. And I say we should aim to leave by ten. Okay? We'll go to the parents' house in Salem and we can all change there into our costumes for the day. And then we should plan to leave from there at twelve fifteen. The church is called St. Mary's in case anyone should ask you or you get separated." [She said this while looking at me.] "The wedding music starts at twelve thirty and the wedding march for the processional will start at one o'clock. Before we leave for the country club, we will have our wedding photos taken in the church and out front. The weather is supposed to remain sunny and warm. That should take about twenty minutes and then we leave straight after the service for the county club. Father will drive me there, and Mom will drive Milos and other maids of honor. Maddie you'll go with me, if you sit in the backseat. After we get there we should go straight to the dining room and the musical entertainment will start. Dinner will be served and when it cleared away Milos and I will do the first dance. We've been practicing waltzing together. Then I will change out of my wedding gown after that first dance, while the rest of the party dances. And then the cake will be brought out and after the cake, more music and dancing. Then coffee service. And before you know it, it will be heading toward six o'clock. We'll leave at six thirty for the Salem house."

"Excuse me, Cammy," I interrupted. "I wanted to ask: Why am I the maid of honor, and not your sister?"

"Oh, you don't know? Jenny is eight months pregnant and really big with her third child. When I asked her she already knew that she was pregnant. And she said being thirty-nine with two small children and a third in the pouch, she didn't feel she could be of any help at all. And she certainly couldn't be a maiden. But she didn't want to be called the matron of honor. So she declined. As it is, I think her husband is going to be on watch the whole day—and may have to dash off to the hospital if she begins—You know the drill."

"OK. I guess I understand. I'm only thirty and I feel already a little too old to be a maid of honor."

"Then after this, we plan to spend the night in the parents' house. And Maddie there is a room for you too. We probably will have drunk too much to drive back that evening to Boston anyway. And on Sunday, we will call a taxi to take all three of us back to Mili's house. And you, Maddie have to leave for the airport before two o'clock, and we have to leave by four-thirty. I understand you'll already be gone by then. All our traveling bags are packed and ready to go. And that's the plan."

"And we'll come back up to get the car after we get back from Prague." said Milos. "And we will pick up wedding gifts then and bring them back home in the back of the car. After which, Cammy will have a lot of thank you notes to write."

"And we're planning on heading for Tanglewood the next week, around June 20th or so."

And with that, like a well-oiled sports team, we set off for Milos's house, all prepped and eager with anticipation.

The wedding and party afterwards went off just as planned, just as Cammy had wanted it to. No hitches, no failures to deliver. But everything happened in such a whirl, I could hardly keep up with all the stimuli and impressions I got, the flowers, the music, the bride and groom, the perfumed women, the wedding march, traveling to the party venue, the toasting, the dances, the cheers. The musicians that Milos had selected performed marvelously, at the church and at the party venue. The trumpeter was fabulous—I guess I never noticed him before in the BSO because his parts were usually submerged into the orchestra. Being the maid of honor meant I was participating, but couldn't really observe too much. At the wedding I couldn't see Cammy's face except in brief glimpses like when she turned for the kiss and put on the ring. She was beaming with happiness like I've rarely ever seen her. So beautiful in her tight-fitting pearl pink dress and her make-up was also stunning. In fact she was gorgeous in every way. So in love. And Milos was also beaming with joy. He uncontrollably was smiling throughout. The happiness he exuded made him look years younger than his calendar age. Although when he danced with Cammy he looked earnest and concentrated. I didn't get to speak to Cammy from the moment we left Milos's house. She sat in the front seat and I was in the rear seat so I couldn't hear anything. And after we arrived at her parents' house things passed by in such a tizzy, so rapidly that there was no time to say anything but banalities. I think I squealed a lot, and giggled a lot—even before I had drunk any champagne. Cammy was the same. She was trying hard to control the bubbling over of her emotions even at the key pledges of fidelity in church that she ended up almost whispering her vows, so that no one in the church heard her. I drank too much, found a dance partner, and spent the final hours of the party dancing frantically. Cammy and Milos were slipping out and coming back after performing little duties all throughout the party. I remember I commented to Cammy how scrumptious the wedding cake was, and she replied that it was made by a high school classmate of hers who had not been a very good musician and had quit music to open a confectionery and cake shop in Salem. That was about as much as we said to each other all afternoon. At one point, after they had posed for more photos on the greens of the golf course, Cammy and Milos left the park altogether for a long stroll around several of the golf links of the course. I was so drunk by the time the party broke up, that I very nearly passed out in the car on the way back to her parents' house. I remember vaguely that by the end I was trying eagerly and sloppily to kiss my dance partner—which probably irritated his date. Next thing I knew I was recovering from a terrible alcohol induced headache at the family dining table after dark, dressed again in my grungy jeans outfit, with Milos and Cammy still babbling to each other—repeating their love and affection and their vows—while Cammy's parents were trying to serve us coffee or little snacks of leftover canapes. The whole day seemed like a long, uninterrupted dream and I was suffering the headache, but feeling otherwise happy. Later that night as I was finally dozing off, I heard the distinct thumping sound of a screeching and groaning bed coming from deep in the house.

It wasn't long before we were piling into a large taxi the next morning after breakfast and again I was in the lone seat—but up front this time. So again no conversation, and not even any eye contact with Cammy or Milos although I got occasional glimpses of Milos in the rearview mirror. I wanted to hear them talk about their honeymoon in Prague at the Prague Festival, but of course in a taxi, I couldn't through the entire hour it took us to get back to the South End. They were already packed—including Cammy's oboes and huge reserve of reeds—so that all we did was throw the wedding things here and there. I packed up my bag and put the bridesmaid dress in a suit bag to carry on the plane—almost certain that it would never be used again. And just like the day before everything was a rush. Cammy asked me at one point, "So you really like Bob? You were kissing yesterday like lovers there by the end." "Bob?" I asked. I actually did not know his first name. Or his last name. But I remembered that he was good looking and a great dancer. And I also seemed to remember that his hands had been all over me, touching, caressing, and stroking my private parts—really quite shameless to do that in front of everyone. But he had probably been drunk too. I know I certainly was—and I still had an awful hangover. And the ibuprofen didn't seem to help. Soon my taxi came and I was on my way to the airport. Cammy promised to write through Chat Messages. Milos and Cammy both saw me out to the curb and both gave me hugs, farewells, and cheek kisses as if they were seeing me for the last time. I fell asleep as soon as the plane pushed back from the gate and did not wake up until it touched down in Cleveland. My first thought was: 'I must look like a mess. Good thing there are no mirrors on the seat backs of planes.'

2 June 2011

**CammyFB**

Hi Maddie. It feels so different and a bit strange to be staying in a first class hotel room as husband and wife. We arrived here in Prague on Monday after a long layover in Heathrow, London. What a chaotic, crowded airport. We arrived here exhausted and collapsed into bed together even without eating dinner. On Tuesday we took it easy also. Last night for my birthday we went to a special restaurant, just the two of us. No party. And in place of a birthday cake, Milos ordered a Hapsburg treat called kaisersmarren. It was delicious and full of calories. And just like the meaning of the name it looks a mess.

My first concert is tomorrow. Milos's concerto is Saturday when he conducts. We might go to a concert tonight. Milos would like to hear it because it includes a major piece by Karel Husa and Jiri is conducting. We saw Jiri briefly on Tuesday for lunch.

He looks a lot older. He's still grieving for the death of his wife—Milos's ex. He didn't talk about it but it's clearly etched on his face, and he's lost a lot of weight and his skin color is wrong. Pale sand color.

**MADDIE**

I'm sad to hear that. I really can't imagine what grief is like. But he was pleased to see you as a married couple?

**CammyFB**

Very, he first thing asked to see my wedding ring and he gave me a little wedding present and apologized again for not being able to come. He's so gracious— like Milosh in a way.

**MADDIE**

Are you ready for the concerto?

**CammyFB**

Yeah, except that I have jet lag. Right now I'm feeling drowsy. Milosh seems to be holding up better. We both have rehearsals later today. But in separate locations. I don't know how that will work. I can't figure my way around this crowded city. The streets are so crooked and small, and there are crowds of tourists everywhere. Without Milosh to act as my guide—and of course I don't know a word of Czech except for ahoj which means goodbye, not real' helpful for asking directions—I can't get around. I'm supposed to go to a hall on Wenceslas Square, but God only knows where that is. I just recognize it because it is humongous and on a slope with a gigantic statue at the upper end. But really the whole city is like being in a fairy tale. Magical. Just perfect for a honeymoon. Tomorrow morning Milosh

196

says we'll go to the original theater where Mozart performed the Marriage of Figaro and premiered Don Giovanni. Next week they're playing Marriage again and we're going to go as it is appropriate for our marriage. Although ours was not a comedy. I love this guy so much—he knows everything about music here in Czechia and he seems to have boundless energy.

MADDIE

Everything sounds wonderful. I'm jealous of course. Wish I could be there (with my own man!)

**CammyFB**
The Festival is really busy. And everyone seems to want to meet and talk with Milos. But now, I gotta run. I'll write later. Bye.

I didn't get anything more from Cammy for a week. Apparently she was busy. But the next week another long note came from her reporting on their "honeymoon". I have to admit it was the most unconventional honeymoon I have ever heard about. But then they were in every respect a very unconventional couple, and in spite of the age difference they acted like young lovebirds, even more than most newlyweds I have seen.

8 June 2011

**CammyFB**
Hi Maddie. This past week we performed in three concerts, and went to two recitals. Lots of music. We took two days off to visit like normal tourists around Czechia. We spent a day and night at Czesky Krumlov. What a lovely, tiny place—very quaint, although a bit run down. The countryside is so

beautiful and green. And the Vltava is a river that fits the Smetana anthem.

I give my second concerto on Friday. And Milos conducts again. He took me to the old Conservatory and explained to me how he studied with the legendary Czech conductor Ancherl. I had never heard of him before, but Milos had nothing but highest praise for him. He studied together with Jiri in a classroom that is still there and still used for lessons. I insisted that we search for Supraphon recordings of Milos's works and we found a number of them. Mostly LPs, but in new condition. Now we have a top class record player so we can listen to them—me for the first time—thanks to you.

This Festival seems to be dedicated to Milos. In addition to the conducting and his concertos, the opera theatre is going to perform one of Milos's operas. One he wrote when he was twenty three—if you can imagine—before he emigrated from Czechia. It's on Sunday and we're going. It's a short opera, only two hours long. Milos says that try as he might, he can't remember it. Hard to believe.

Every day I learn new things about Milos. He is a superman. My superman. Amazing musician. And everyone here says so too. He's going to be on stage for the closing gala concert on Sunday evening. But not conducting. Introducing one of his new works.

We fly back next Monday, the 13th. Also via London. Sorry for such a brief letter. Love, Your Cammy Nowak from Prague.

I always forget about the time difference between Europe and here. It must be six hours to Prague. They're ahead of us. So, I get her notes when I must still be sleeping. And I can't answer her because she is out at concerts in the evenings, midday my time. I found myself thinking about Cammy, and wanting to talk with her, at least through FaceTime so I could see her too. But the timing was never right. Besides who talks to the bride on her honeymoon, besides the husband of course? But I was constantly thinking that she had again accomplished two of her life goals—a husband (which I still maintain really means love), and a top professional career. And unlike her time with Gus, she now had at least the prospect of attaining her third goal in life as well. But I couldn't talk to her. I wrote her an email letter in late June, saying all these things, and telling her how pleased I was that she had found love and happiness, and that my only regret now was that I did not know when we would next meet and we could hang out together again like we used to in years gone by.

While Cammy was in Prague with her new husband, I was wrapping up the Cleveland season—my first complete season with the orchestra. This period included two concert weekends, and a children's concert workshop at one of Cleveland's elementary schools. This kept me pretty busy, but it also gave me the opportunity to hang out with Davey without having a "formal structured date". You know, "after dates" so to speak, after rehearsals, after concerts. And I spent a lot of time with him in June, mostly talking and learning about each other. I was beginning to really like that guy, Davey.

It's been a tough year for me, and I think I still might not make it. I think the principal flute player here—a guy named Jacques Smithson—doesn't like me. He is a super flute player. Concertos are written for him. But the flute section is his—and I get the impression that I don't really fit in or come up to his standards and expectations. I was not included in the Asian tour last Fall, but I did get to go with the orchestra to Carnegie Hall this spring. But still, these next few months will be critical for me.

That means improving my playing technique for the upcoming concerts at the Blossom Festival. I really could use a guardian angel and sponsor to look over me like Milos, as the principal assistant conductor, was for Cammy. Davey tells me not to worry. He says that the current music director here only cashes in older players who have become sloppy and careless. But I can't afford to take time off from scheduled concerts—that's for sure. As it was, I think I asked long enough in advance for leave for the weekend concerts that occurred on the 27th and 28th of May when I went to Cammy's wedding, so that I didn't do myself too much damage. I was able to play the Thursday concert that weekend, where Smithson premiered a new concerto written specifically for him. Even though he was out front, as a soloist, he did tell me that I had done a really good job playing the background flute in the section. That was the nicest thing he has ever said to me yet in a year and a half of playing next to him.

Anyway, all this meant that I was committed to going to the Blossom Festival that summer. Unlike Tanglewood, it was near Cleveland and it is not too difficult to continue living in Cleveland and commuting to the concerts out at the Festival grounds in Cuyahoga Falls. Being in Cleveland made it possible for me to accept Davey's invitations—he had also decided to reside in Cleveland and commute out to the Festival grounds when needed—to join him in his favorite pastime, namely sailing. The first time, in late June, I was petrified by the wind and the waves on the lake—and not just any old lake—but the gigantic Lake Erie. But after that first time out on the water, I saw that he confidently handled the boat. And even though I was wet through and through by the time we finished and the wind was chilling me to the bone—I really liked it. Sailing I mean. Sailing with Davey. But it's best on really warm days. The second and third times were really hot days, and not so windy and I liked sailing even more.

Facetime

5 July 2011

"Hey Maddie, I have the best news for you. You wouldn't believe it. I have to tell you."

"Yeah, Cammy. What is it?" [Cammy looked flush with excitement.] "Where are you by the way?"

"Well, that's part of the news. I'm pregnant! I took one of those pregnancy tests from the kit today, and it showed positive. I'm in Boston just now. I had to come back to play in the Pops Fireworks concert last night. And this morning I was feeling funny—uncomfortable, sick to my stomach. So tried the test. And it showed positive. That means the sickness I was feeling last night and this morning was morning sickness. I'm pregnant. I'm going to have Milosh's baby." [She was hooting and giggling at the same time. I recognized their house in the background.]

"That's great news". You've told Milos already, haven't you?"

"Yeah, I called him on his iPhone out at Tanglewood as soon as I got a second positive test. The first few times he didn't answer. Must've been off. But he called me back about an hour ago. He's really happy with the news too. I really love that man."

"You know what that means, don't you, Cammy?"

"Yeah, I think I know what you're going to say."

"You're going to have a baby—and that is your third life goal."

"Yeah." [And she squealed through the phone, so loud I had to turn down the volume on my end the speakers distorted it.]

"But we agreed that I need to get an appointment with an OB and confirm the test. And also get a CT. Milosh reasonably thinks we need to monitor the fetus carefully, because he said the fetuses of older parents are the ones most likely to have deformities. He's right. So I'm setting up an appointment now to check on all of those things. It's so wonderful. I could squeal."

"You already have. A couple times."

"I need to go out and buy some folic acid. That's always needed. Ah, there's so much I need to do for this first baby. The OB was recommended by a friend of my sister. She's here in Boston and her reviews highly recommend her."

"So that probably means that you conceived before your wedding."

"Yes, that's what I've been thinking. But I'll find out more and let you know as soon as I do. I'll go back out to Tanglewood after my appointment with the OB."

"Well, if you have morning sickness, the fetus is probably already a few months old. That means you were working hard with Milos well before the wedding then. I'm really glad to hear this news, Cammy. I'm only sorry I can't be nearby."

"Oh, that's alright. We can hang-out through FaceTime."

"Maybe, but it makes it harder to skip and hop around you in delight."

"Yes. That's true. I've gotta run."

"Yes, I understand. Be careful driving back to Tanglewood. I love you, Cammy. I think this is the best news I've heard since your wedding party."

"Yeah, bye."

This was the first time in a long time where I actually felt excited and happy after hearing Cammy's good news. I am not envious of her happiness and her good news. I am elated and the good feeling lasted for me through the rest of that day and through the night and into the next day.

A few days later I got another message from Cammy.

**8 July 2011**

**CammyFB**

Hi Maddie. What a week this has been!!

I had my appointment with the OB yesterday. And after doing a number of scans she told me that I am about three months pregnant and that the fetus looks good, normal. No malformations that she could see. I even was able to watch while she was running the Ultrasound scan. Couldn't make out much, but it was still thrilling to see this living creature inside of me, in real time. And she laid out for me a schedule and routines I need to follow. No more rugby, she joked. We talked about my diet in the coming months, and made all kinds of recommendations. And she gave me a primer on the activities I can do and shouldn't do. Sex is alright. I can stop drinking alcohol though. And yes she put me on folic acid. And she set up our future appointments.

I'm so excited. I'm going to be a mother. Can you imagine? It's just now starting to hit me just what a life changing event this is. She didn't tell me the likely sex of the fetus. She said she could tell with certainty a little later.

I'm leaving shortly to go back to Tanglewood. I'm
dying to see Milos. He's conducting tonight. I'm
playing but I haven't rehearsed tonight's concert. He
sounds so happy over the phone. I'll drive carefully.
I'll take my time. Three hours instead of 2 ½. BFN

Davey and I had altered our schedules so we could be together in our
spare time. And that meant getting together on the weekdays, Monday
through Wednesday. Thursdays through Sunday were days for rehearsals,
mostly, and concerts. And as it was summer and hot weather, our
get togethers were to go to Hamilton Beach to the west of Cleveland
where Davey kept his small sailboat and to go sailing. And swimming
afterwards if it was still hot enough. We had already done this in late
June and in early July. After Cammy's last happy messages, about her
imminent motherhood, we went again that week. It was torridly hot
so the sailing was quite refreshing, except that the winds were maybe
too light. So we ended up after an hour and a half of difficult sailing,
coming back in and going to the beach, changing into our swimsuits
and splashing in the warm waters of the Lake. I don't remember that
the sea waters around Boston ever got so warm and comfortable for
swimming, which is why I never liked beaching there. We went all three
weekdays of that week of the 11th. And on Wednesday, wearing only
our swimsuits, we ended the afternoon lying on the sand caressing and
kissing and stroking each other like real lovers. We went back to his
apartment and continued to arouse each other until—well you know
what happens next when all of this public foreplay occurs.

A strange thing has occurred to me with regards to Davey. When we
first met at our blind date at the Fountain in downtown Cleveland a
few months ago I didn't find him handsome or attractive. Not merely
because he is Chinese. I've learned that there are too many Chinese
types to be able to say whether or not they are good or bad looking
people. Not that Davey is ugly. I just didn't find him very attractive or

good looking. But the strange thing is that after spending a lot of time with him over the past three months, I began to think he was good looking. I had grown accustomed to his looks. And he had shown me a greater range of facial expressions than he had when we first really met.

We went again that next Monday and went sailing. For nearly two hours. It was a great day and we took turns controlling the tiller or the sails. I was beginning to be pretty good at handling Davey's boat. Now I even know that it is called a Sunfish dinghie. When I got back to the docks and took my things out of the locker, I saw that there was a text message waiting for me from Cammy.

*DISASTER. MILOS HAS DIED. Heart attack. Will try to write later. I'm devastated. Can hardly see straight or stand for all the crying.*

I nearly dropped my phone. It would have fallen into the shallow water next to the pier if I had dropped it. She had written it about forty minutes earlier. Shortly before one pm. Davey could see at once that I was upset because I gasped and put both my hands with the phone up to my face. He knew of Cammy—I had spoken a lot of her and of course had gone to her wedding not long before when we were still in dating mode. Itold Davey the message I had gotten from Cammy.

I wrote her back a text message. *Just got your message. When can we FT?*

Davey continued putting away all the sail rigging and equipment without me.

"This is awful. I think Cammy's destroyed." I said out loud half to myself, half to Davey.

"So what do you think happened?"

"Heart attack of course. All I know is what she wrote. I might have to go to Boston to help her." Only then did I notice that I was pretty badly sunburned in several places. I'd forgotten to put on sunscreen before we went out that morning. It hurt on my neck and upper back, and especially badly on my thighs.

"Let's go get some lunch." said Davey.

"I need to get to my computer so we can talk on FaceTime. Maybe we can pick up some take-away and go to my apartment. And I have to stop off to buy some aloe vera."

And that's what we did. By the time we got to my place, I still hadn't gotten an answer back from Cammy. We ate take-away Chinese food from our favorite Chinese restaurant which serves even in midafternoon and waited. I wasn't interested in doing anything. Finally Davey got frustrated and left.

"Call me when you know what's happening. Remember we have two concerts this weekend. That means rehearsals on Thursday and Friday out at Blossom."

"I won't miss them. I can't afford to miss anything. Certainly not on short notice."

Finally around eight o'clock I got a text message from Cammy.

*"I'm destroyed. My world's fallen apart. Milos dead, in a hospital morgue. Can't talk now. tomorrow. I'll write first."*

I wrote: *"Where are you now?"*

*"Back at Tanglewood. Have to go back to Pittsfield tomorrow. Crying too much to talk."*

*"Hold on, Babe. Don't do anything crazy. Have you spoken to your parents yet?"*

*"No. But that's a good idea. I'll try now. Thx"*

The rest of that evening I was thinking of what I could do for Cammy. I looked at airline schedules (and prices for tix) to fly to Boston. I checked the weather forecast for the next six days, through the weekend. Only Wednesday was forecast to be hot and clear. Tomorrow was going to be stormy so no sailing. And maybe thunderstorms on Saturday. But usually storms were in the afternoon and didn't wash out our evening concerts. I thought about how I could console Cammy. Nothing I thought of then seemed like it would be much help to Cammy. Have to avoid saying things like, "At least you will have his baby." I must not offer bromides, best just to listen and let Cammy talk out her misery.

Facetime

19 July 2011

"Maddie, the last forty-eight hours have been the worst hours in my entire life. A horrible nightmare. And now I have so many awful things I have to do which I had not thought I would have to do anytime soon. You'll have to excuse me if I start crying again. I couldn't sleep at all the last two nights." {I could see through the screen that her eyes were red and swollen, and her skin color was off, and her hair disheveled. I don't think I've ever looked so bad.]

"That's understandable. Can you tell me what happened?"

"Sunday it was hot and humid. Unbelievably hot, with a burning sun. We went down to the Bowl to swim. When he got in the water with me—the water was intensely cold—and he started to have trouble right away. He asked me to help him get him out. I did. He collapsed on the grass, moaning and complaining of the pain, the sharp aches everywhere. Especially In his chest. I ran up across the field still in my wet bikini and I stopped a person and asked him to call for an ambulance down at the Bowl at the bottom of the Gould Meadow. And then I ran back. I thought he was having a heart attack. He was rolling and thrashing around on the ground and moaning that the pain was unreal. His eyes were mostly closed and he was frothing at the mouth. People had gathered around."

"It took the ambulance an hour and twenty minutes to get there. The paramedics took him up and said he had had a heart attack. I asked if I could go with them, but they said no. Milos told me 'Ahoj, Camille'. And they started off, but first I stopped them and asked where they were taking him. They had already given him a shot for pain, and put oxygen on his mouth. They said the emergency room of the Berkshire Medical Center. I saw on the ambulance that that was in Pittsfield. They left and I took Milos's clothes and our towels and ran back to our room to change and get the car keys and my wallet. And then I drove up to the hospital which is about ten miles away. I ran in and asked where Milos was—that he came in with what I thought was a heart attack on an ambulance. They challenged me, wanting to know who I was. I told them, his wife. They checked the emergency room admission records, but of course did not have anything. Because he was without ID and only had swim shorts on when they took him away. And they told me I couldn't go there. But I went and asked someone who came out if they were working on an older man with a heart attack. The man in blue said yes, but that he had been stabilized already and moved to the intensive care unit. So it took me another half hour to find him. He was in a ward covered with tubes and the oxygen mask and a doctor and a few nurses were standing around him. He looked already dead, but the man in white was a heart surgeon said "he's not dead yet." But he was clearly not conscious and he was no longer moaning with pain. He was completely ashen in color. It was awful to see."

[And then Cammy began to cry.]

"Excuse me. I can't go on." [And she disconnected.]

She called back in the late afternoon, just before sunset.

Facetime

19 July 2011

"Sorry about that. I'm alternating between an overwhelming sadness, and a bit of inexplicable anger. And then feeling totally helpless and eh bereft."

"What do you mean anger, Cammy?"

"Oh there were things I could have done, we should have done, but didn't. Since he proposed to me and the time when I moved in with him and began living our conjugal life together, he didn't go for a complete medical check-up. And in fact, I found out after our wedding, he confessed to me that he hadn't had a medical checkup, heart health, you know the kinds of checks, for years and years. And he was stressed, and had been stressed for the past year from the heavy work load and the drive to complete it. You may have noticed–I did but said nothing–that his hair suddenly went gray at the beginning of this year. I'm told now that is a sure sign of stress."

"And we played a game of tennis last month out here, he demonstrated signs of a mild heart attack afterwards with sharp pains in his arms, especially the left arm which lasted about three days. I didn't notice or ask him to look into it. But I should've." "Anyway, I left him in the hospital on Sunday night. He was sleeping but heavily sedated and filled with strong pain killers, under masks. Being closely monitored. The doctor had told me that he had had a massive heart attack, but that he could see that he had had several minor ones before. But he had taken no notice. And we took no notice after that tennis game. When I came back the next morning, he had already passed away. The doctor told me that during the night he had cardiac arrest and the staff monitoring him could not restore him. They brought the defibrillator too late to restore his heart and bring him back to life. But he said the night shift was not to blame. That there was too much damage already done to his heart. He didn't recover consciousness from the time he arrived in the emergency room. I didn't see him off and didn't say goodnight. They had already moved his body to the morgue."

[Cammy started to cry again. And again, she switched off.]

She called back again about twenty minutes later.

Facetime

19 July 2011

"Sorry about that."

"That's okay, Cammy. You don't have to tell me everything. Right now." "And you know these past few days, he was looking so happy. He had finished the first draft of his opera. The one about Janacek and his lover. He had even written a long letter to Jiri outlining what he was going to do the rest of the summer, after he took some time off to relax and enjoy his new wife. He wrote that." [Cammy again began to bawl. She left the FT line open and grabbed a Kleenex. She stepped away from the video camera and all I could see was the room. After a few minutes she came back.]

"I told my father today. They are shocked. I think I am shocked—it's just I have never known what that actually meant—to be shocked by something. Dumbfounded. Speechless. Numb. I still can't believe that he's gone. Forever: gone. I'll never see or talk to him again. He won't ever see our baby. The one he wanted to fill his house with noise." {She began to sob.]

"Anyway, he's going to hire a funeral home, there in Salem. My pa that is. Here I have to get a certificate of cause of death, and then the funeral home there will take over and do the rest. Transport the body, or get it embalmed so it can be transported. I don't quite understand how things work with this death business. But they will do everything to arrange a funeral and burial—that means also getting a gravesite in St. Mary's cemetery in Salem."

"Are you going to cremate his body, or do you want to bury it?"

"Actually, he once mentioned to me that he would prefer not to be cremated. His Catholic childhood, and his resistance to the Communists who required cremation."

"And what about costs?"

"That won't be a problem. He had bought a funeral policy for himself just before our wedding. I don't think he thought it would be needed so soon after." [And Cammy began to sob again.]

"Why did he have to leave me? Why now? {she moaned.] We were going to live together still for many years. How can there be a god who is so cruel and capricious? So indifferent to our suffering?" [A long pause. Cammy was not looking into the video camera, but off in some indefinite distance.]

"Maddie, you can't believe how much pain he was suffering after I pulled him out of the lake. I mean he was moaning and howling. His eyes were rolling. His head was jerking back and forth. And he did this for the hour it took the ambulance to get here. The shot made an immediate difference. It must've been a very strong pain reliever. He sighed and his eyes began to focus again."

"When they picked him up on the stretcher, he was able to say goodbye to me. "Ahoj, Camille." he said. He knew it was me. Those were the last words I heard him say." [Cammy again began to cry. Through the tears and sobs, she tried to say:] "Ahoj. Did I tell you that that means goodbye in Czech? He taught me just a few words. He promised he would teach me more."

She cut the line and did not call back again that evening. I could just imagine her crying and sobbing on the red divan on the second floor of their house. But then I remembered she was still in Tanglewood—all alone. That was worse for her. Alone in a stranger's room. I worried about all kinds of things that could happen to her in her grief and misery.

20 July 2011

**CammyFB**
Sorry Maddie didn't call back yesterday. It was just too much to bear.
Today I have finished all the arrangements I can do here. I notified the Festival manager and said I would take off two weeks. And I had to tell them that Milos has died. Of course they were surprised and saddened. The funeral manager said he would set the date for a last viewing and remembrance service followed by a burial on next Tuesday, the 26th. Do you think you could come? They're going to put up a website announcement today. They also informed the Globe for an obituary

I'm going to take the car and head back to Boston in
a couple hours. So maybe we can FT this evening.
Is that alright for you?
I hurt everywhere. I think it's from the crying and
moaning. Terrible headache.
I'll be careful on the road. BFN. Cammy

MADDIE

> Do you know how to contact Dr. Spann? He could
> help with the obit.

She wrote back in the late afternoon saying that that was a good idea. She'd look for his contact address. She was already back home in Boston. She asked if we could FT at around seven. As it turned out I missed her that evening. I had already told Davey that morning that I couldn't go sailing that day because I needed to stay close to my communication devices. And I told him that I would fly next Tuesday morning to Boston. He understood and said he would see me tomorrow at rehearsal. It was a shame, of course: the weather on that Wednesday was just what they forecast– beautiful and not too hot. I don't know what I was doing that evening to miss Cammy, but she wrote a short note to ask if we could FT the next morning, Thursday.

Facetime

21 July 2011

"Sorry Cammy, I missed you last night. I can't explain it."

"That's alright. I wasn't feeling very good yesterday by the end of the day. I don't know what I'm going to do. It's hard to live in this house without Milos."

"You miss his presence?"

"Yes, of course. But it's more than that—his presence is everywhere. I can smell him in the sheets on our bed. There are the wedding portraits in the bedroom and the main room in sight of the dining area. I don't hear him faintly through the walls practicing or playing music as he composes, but there are concert programs laying around in almost every room. His clothes are hanging in the closet and his winter coat is hanging in the front entry foyer."

"But you can wash the sheets and put the clothes and portraits away for a little while. Can't you?"

"Still it's his home. His presence permeates the air here—even though he's not here. And won't be ever again. I'm going to go up to Salem tomorrow and spend the weekend with my parents just to escape this house. I also have to take one of Mili's suites to the funeral home. They need it to dress and lay out his body. He's already embalmed and lying in a refrigerator. I guess that the viewing service will be the last time I see him."

"Don't move back to your Somerville place—don't do anything rash."

"All these things I have to do to arrange his funeral, they seem endless, and they're so dehumanizing and bureaucratic. I had to file the death certificate with the civil registry in Berkshire County, there in Pittsfield. Why? I don't know. Because he died in the county. But I also had to notify some registry office here in Boston of his death too, in Suffolk County. I had to find his last will. And you know what? He wanted me to be the executor of his estate, even though I am the only beneficiary. Soon I will have to notify his banks and his investment managers. And I have to find his title deed on this house and find out if he has any outstanding debts. But a lot of that I can take care of after the funeral. It all makes me even sadder."

"But you don't have to do all that before the funeral, do you?"

"No, I can start a lot of these things after the funeral. But you know what I found out in reading the will? Milos is a rich man. He owns this house, outright—no mortgage. And its market value is probably around one and a half million. But he has almost two million in investment and retirement accounts."

"Wow! I would never have guessed just from looking at him in his day to day comportment."

"Nor I. He was always very generous, especially to me. But he also lived very—how do you say?—frugally, except when he was celebrating something. And he's left everything to me. Except he left one hundred thousand dollars to his niece in Czechia, for her to finish her studies and get on her feet. You know she's rather orphaned after her mother died earlier this year. We met her this last time in Prague. She's a wonderful girl. About twenty-two, twenty-three years old."

"Well, it was always clear to me from the very beginning that Milos was very generous. Especially to you. He gave you such nice, expensive gifts."

"And he dedicated several of his compositions to me."

"But when he wrote the will, he probably didn't know that you were pregnant. Isn't that right?"

"I think that's right. I think I will set up a trust fund for him out of these funds. For his eighteenth. A memorial trust fund." [And then Cammy began to cry. Just blubbering.]

"Excuse me, Maddie. I can't go on... I'll try calling another time."

So Cammy thought, or maybe she knew, that her fetus was a male. I wondered. And again, I wondered if Milos knew that also.

I was sorry that I skipped out sailing on Wednesday. I kind of missed him. But that day after rehearsal we went back to his apartment and jumped into bed together and made the bed hot and sweaty until hunger—for food—finally drove us out to find some take-away. I spoke to him about Cammy and her loss of her new husband. He said that grief was a very complex thing, that it included lots of different reactions. He saw that with his mother, after his father died. And he said it took a long time to get over. I told him that I thought maybe grief was another aspect of love, just like affection, lust, pride, yearning, or possessiveness. To mention just a few. He made a face. "Maybe. But if it is then it is an aspect of non-presence, like yearning or missing a person you love. While those others are aspects of presence."

I then told him as we were finishing up the spring rolls, that I was flying to Boston for a few days from next Tuesday for the funeral. Starting next Tuesday. And I would probably stay a few days but would be back in time for the Saturday concert.

I didn't really have the clothes to wear to a funeral. So Friday morning I went out to find a somber, preferably black suit dress with a white blouse. I found just the thing, it cost a lot, out at Neiman Marcus. It wasn't suitable for our concert nights, but I suppose a necessary part of every woman's wardrobe. I had just enough time to get out to Cuyahoga Falls for rehearsal. And it was then that I was overcome with feelings of sadness. I suppose empathy for Cammy. But sad for the whole situation that had shaped up over the past week. I could barely get through the rehearsal. Even Smithson, the principal flute, noticed I was off. But no one mentioned anything. Afterwards when Davey approached me, he couldn't figure out what was wrong. What could I say? I love Cammy. I loved Milos, because he loved Cammy and he was so good for her. And now I was far away from both of them—I suppose as far as you can possibly be from Milos as he had left this earthly realm and was unable to do anything about Cammy's misery or Milos's final departure. I felt like crying, but couldn't figure it out. Davey was standing in front of me questioning if there was anything he could do for me, and whether we could go out, get dinner or hang out together. "How can I cheer you up, Maddie?" And I couldn't answer him. I dragged and moped around for half an hour, and asked him if he could just wait for me to get over it. Whatever it was. There was a bit of feeling sorry for myself as well. A single girl, unmarried and alone in the world, more than thirty years old and without any prospects or love—how could I tell Davey that?—and my dear friend had already completed an entire life and already lost it. It was strange. I told Davey to wait for me down by the concession stand. And after about forty minutes I went and found him. We didn't make love that night, nor on Saturday or Sunday. And I didn't explain to him what had come over me. That evening after eating we took a long walk—without speak around the beautiful grounds of the Blossom Festival and I went to my room by myself. After our weekend concerts, I told Davey I was feeling better and that—and this was true—I didn't really know what had come over me. He asked me if the weather was nice on Monday if I would like to go sailing with him again. I agreed. And it was when I got ready to push the boat out that I noticed that all the places where I had gotten sunburned early the previous week the skin was badly peeling.

When I got to Milos's house in the South End, I hesitated a little. I didn't know how to behave. I didn't know what to expect from Cammy. She came down and greeted me at the front door. But it wasn't the usual smiley, beaming Cammy that had been my best friend and companion for the past fifteen years. She looked much older. A little wan in the face, with noticeable dark shadows under her eyes which it was obvious make-up had been unable to hide. And her smile was weak and begrudgingly given. She directed me upstairs.

"Do you want anything to eat, to drink? I don't have much to offer, but we can find something. Maybe a coffee?" We sat at the kitchen table and drank some coffee and she brought out butter cookies. She was unable to look me in the eyes. We did not say much.

"I found the draft score of Mili's opera." She said as if just out of nowhere. "Apparently he had printed it out before we went out to Tanglewood. And he left it in his studio in a place where I would not fail to see it. I've only just cast a glance at it. The oboe plays the motivs for Kamille, and the English horn plays the motivs for Leos. I'm going to have to learn how to get into his computer application for composing to find everything that might be there. I hope it's not all locked up behind passwords."

"I suppose you'll have to find all the publishers who have already published his past scores. And claim the inheritor's right to the copyright royalties."

"Yes, a headache. I know he had some. But we're not talking about a lot of income from those royalties. I wonder if I'll need a lawyer to claim them? But I will also need to check his correspondence and his letters to his publishers. I don't know where they all might be. Some I know are printed out. And he has an archive of past-pre-computer printout-letters. But I'd rather not think about it now. I did get a nice reply from Dr. Spann. He offered me some help in finding all of Milos's published scores."

"Do you think the opera is good?"

"I haven't looked at it enough. And the libretto—Milos wrote it himself—is in Czech, so I don't know at all how to judge it. Maybe it will get performed in our lifetime. I don't know."

"You could ask Milos's friend, Jiri. Maybe he would be able to get it performed there."

"Yes, Maddie. That's a good idea. He's been so helpful to Milos in these past few years. A good friend. Maybe he would help. I need to write to him and tell him the sad news."

"Yes, of course."

And then it was time to put on cosmetics and get dressed. And shortly thereafter we left in Milos's old Volvo. Cammy drove first to her parents' house—it was a large yellow colonial house on a wooded lot. Cammy did not say much or shed her stony expression the whole way. We visited a few minutes with her parents and then went in their big SUV to the funeral home which was located in north Salem in the part of town where there were several cemeteries. I asked if there was someplace where I could buy some flowers and we stopped at a florist shop which was only a few hundred meters from the funeral home and a few hundred meters more from the entrance to the cemetery.

We arrived a little early and greeted the guests as they came later. The coffin was set in a somber room, but was closed when we arrived. But when the service started an attendant in a black frack coat opened it, and all the mourners took turns laying flowers and viewing the preserved body of Milos. Cammy remained standing at his head trying to soak in all the last views. She was sobbing for much of the time. A man was asked to make some comments. It turned out it was a Professor from the Conservatory who had acted as Milos's best man at their wedding. The BSO had sent a large wreath in honor of the years of service Milos had given as an assistant conductor and at Tanglewood and it stood guard on one side of the coffin, while an only slightly smaller wreath from the Conservatory stood guard on the other side. Most of the service seemed to me to consist of mumblings. It was sad, oppressively sad, not helped by the dim lugubrious air of the chamber where all this took place.

An organist was playing tunes, in broad andante maestoso modes. They all sounded like dirges. It was hard to know how long we stayed there.

Then the director gave a final spiel about what a great man Milos was and how much we would miss him. Cammy's father by this point was supporting her on his arm. And the director instructed us to proceed to the cemetery in about an hour to C section, row 18, rank B4, and that there would be signs up to direct us. Then the service was over.

Outside, contrary to all the stereotypical depiction of funeral weather—in literature and in films—it was warm with bright sun and a few jolly looking white clouds floating in the sky. At the burial service the coffin remained closed, and the priest appeared in his appropriate raiment to give the final eulogy and bid Milos farewell. Cammy had told me that it was the same priest who had given them instructions several months before and then had wed them. Then some men lowered the coffin in the grave—the earth was the color of milk chocolate I thought but it was full of small flinty stones that sometimes glinted in the sunlight. The priest invited Cammy to throw the first handful of soil onto the coffin, which she did with a steady hand. And then the men began shoveling in the mounds of soil back over the coffin which they accomplished in very little time. And then mourners laid their flowers and bouquets on the pile and men from the funeral house put out the two large wreaths, which were of fir boughs and were called the "Evergreen" models and the whole funeral was over. People—maybe there were fifteen people there in attendance—filed by and said a few quiet words of banal consolation to Cammy, who was still being held up by her father, and then headed back slowly back to their cars. For a moment I thought everything seemed strange, and then I realized that it was strange that unlike all the film depictions of funerals: no one was wearing a dark coat or raincoat, some were wearing only street clothes, and not everyone was wearing black. One man I did not recognize was wearing brown and brown shoes—looked like a tweey professor just between classes. It was by then positively hot outside and the cemetery looked lushly green. And the maple leaves in a light breeze—large as they are—all seemed to be clapping at the whole performance.

We had decided to spend the night at the Salem house. Cammy's mother had arranged a light funeral repast to be catered. Only Cammy's family—her parents, and her sister (who had a small baby with her along with her two other kids) and Cammy's brother-in-law-and me were in attendance. But the repast was a grimly quiet affair. Cammy's sister had to constantly excuse herself to attend to the immediate needs of her baby or the toddler who was only a little bit older. Cammy herself didn't say anything and she ate little. Her face showed a hollow anguish. I drank a little wine and even with that lubricant could not think of anything to say. In fact, I was feeling like my head was stuffed full of cotton wadding. I told Cammy that I had an open ticket and could stay as long as she needed me to be with her, but that I did have a concert on Saturday evening that I would like to go to. (I didn't say that I desperately needed to attend. That would have been too cruelly honest and show that I wanted to run away.) She said she appreciated that and just having me near helped her a lot, even if she couldn't say anything.

The next day–it was a Wednesday–we drove back to the house in the South End. We didn't do much. Cammy puttered around the house re-arranging things. She realized that she did not have any portrait of Milos, and that caused her to cry again. "I need some black ribbon. To put on our wedding portraits." But she couldn't do that right away. She didn't want to eat all day. We drank several cups of coffee. Finally in the afternoon, I suggested that we go out to the local food market and buy some basics and some grazing food to put in the fridge. Toward the end of the afternoon she agreed and we walked to the store. On the way back she said, "Maddie, there can be nothing worse than losing your loved one. The pain of torture even cannot be worse." And later that evening as the house began to echo back to us the sounds of our moving about, she said further, "How can I live in this empty house, without Milos by my side?"

In maybe the smartest thing I said all week, I said: "Yes, can you imagine how Milos all those years lived in this house by himself? And maybe the emptiness of this house made his love for you even more intense, until you finally agreed to join him."

"Yes, I guess that possibly happened."

"And maybe we often keep ourselves busy with things just to avoid acknowledging that we don't have any love in our lives."

"I need to be busy now, but it's going to be hard."

As the day wore down, she was increasingly trying to hide her sobbing from me. She would go to another room and cry for ten or fifteen minutes. After night fell, we ate a light meal of tuna salad. We watched some TV, a documentary. But it was clear that Cammy was not focusing or paying close attention. Finally she said she was ready to go to bed. I wasn't ready so I said goodnight to her and she went to her room. Is it appropriate to say, "Sweet dreams" to someone who is in grief?

About ten-thirty, my phone beeped along with that obnoxious vibration. It was a text message from Davey.

*Maddie, Forecast for Saturday, warm and sunny with light breezes. Late rehearsal before the concert. Would you like to join me sailing in the morning?*

I wrote back: *Yes, I'll come. Gladly. I'll fly back early Saturday morning.*